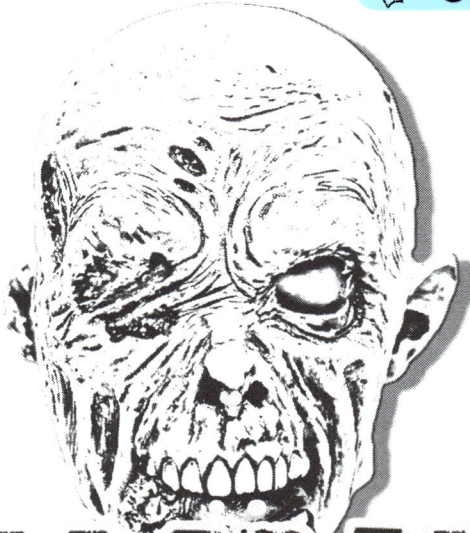

HELLSPAWN
ODYSSEY
BOOK TWO IN THE HELLSPAWN SERIES

RICKY FLEET

HELLSPAWN: ODYSSEY – Book Two in the Hellspawn Series
©2016 Ricky Fleet
First Edition
Edited by Christina Hargis Smith
Cover art by Jeffrey Kosh Graphics
Published by Optimus Maximus Publishing, LLC

ISBN-10: 1-944732-05-5
ISBN-13: 978-1-944732-05-9

DEDICATED TO

To my beautiful wife, who has been my rock through life. Your constant smiles in the face of your illness shows me how lucky I am to have someone that brave behind me.

To my kids who hawk my wares to teachers, friends, and random strangers, I love you with all my heart. I know you will be successful and do great things in this world.

To my friends across the planet, you are the driving force that keeps me going. Every review, every message that says "can't wait for the next book" motivates me to aim higher and come up with even more twisted ideas to horrify you with.

Acknowledgements

The journey to indie published author has been a rollercoaster of niggling doubt and dizzying highs. I couldn't have been more grateful for the support and help I have received from the good folks on social media.

My family, as always, have been totally supportive of my efforts, showing patience where I would sit for hours tapping away on the keyboard.

My publisher and editor, Christina Hargis Smith, from Optimus Maximus Publishing who has been pushing me to write the best story I possibly can.

Jeffrey Kosh who continues to create disturbing covers for my work.

My amazing beta readers who give me advice and tips on the novel before it hits the shelf. Denise Kinsella Keef, Stephanie Lunsford, Jodi Ussery, you are true superstars for giving up your time to help me, it won't be forgotten.

And to all my new friends who I have been privileged enough to meet on social media, I know we may never meet in person but I value each and every one of you. Thank you for making me what I am, because without your support and reviews I couldn't achieve my goals in life.

HELLSPAWN

ODYSSEY

BOOK TWO IN THE HELLSPAWN SERIES

A Novel by
Ricky Fleet

PROLOGUE

The disparate survivors had borne witness to the final days of man. On television and social media, the beacons of life across the globe had been extinguished, prey for the new apex predator; the undead. Utterly without feeling, remorse or the ability to reason, the walking corpses had swept through the world like a decaying pestilence. Loved ones fell victim to loved ones, strangers to strangers, and the fallen quickly joined the legions of the damned to continue the onslaught.

Within days, over ninety percent of the world's population was dead, or a blasphemous imitation of the state of being. Slowly decomposing as they wander, always searching for the flesh of the living to devour. The few remaining areas of humanity would face a winter like no other, battling both the elements and the relentless husks who besieged them on all sides. Food would be scarce and the need to scavenge the ruins of their old lives could only increase the danger.

The Taylor family had fought back using whatever was available to them, inflicting casualties in the hundreds, truly dead bodies littering their surroundings in festering heaps. In the scheme of things this is a single grain of sand on a beach, the countless millions that remain await them on the next leg of their journey.

CHAPTER ONE

"How are you feeling today, mate?" Kurt asked, leaning over Braiden and filling his water glass.

"Not too bad, I can speak more easily now. The pain is nearly gone when I breathe too," Braiden answered, his voice still husky from the smoke inhalation following the arson attack five days ago.

"You really had us worried there, damn you." Sarah sat down and hugged him where he sat on the bed, propped up on pillows. Braiden returned the contact without the previous reluctance, finally feeling like a part of a real family.

Braiden had 'died' in the true sense of the word. His heart had stopped and he was gone for nearly two minutes before Paige had inexplicably brought him back, her words of love working where common resuscitation had failed. They still spoke of the event and tried to apply logic, but it always went round in circles until they decided once again, that it was a miracle. Gloria had been quiet during the discussions, her faith had been stretched to breaking point by the inhumanity they had endured, yet the resurrection of the young boy had given her strength. If they had asked her why some had been saved but not others, why they had been given another chance when millions had been ripped apart, she would have been stumped. The old adage 'God moves in mysterious ways' was never truer than during this apocalypse. It could, however, just be coincidence and his youth and desire for life had been the catalyst, not a miracle at all. She smiled to herself while sitting in the corner and watched her 'children'. They were not blood related, yet shared a bond that was stronger by far; they had fought for each other, been prepared to die for one another. They had even killed men; fellow humans only in name, the evil nature of the beasts made them worse than the walking dead. They took sadistic pleasure in the suffering and deaths of a family who had been unlucky enough to fall prey to the group. God's fiery wrath had been merciless, delivered by Sam and Kurt in response to provocation and attempted murder.

"You ok, love? You were miles away," John asked, sitting down beside the old teacher.

"Sorry, I was just thinking about the past few days and how lucky I am to have joined Kurt when he left the school," Gloria responded.

"It was the least we could do after you saved Sam," Kurt said from across the room, overhearing the conversation.

"We saved each other, he and Braiden were superheroes," Gloria complimented the boys and Sam smiled at her and then returned to checking the area outside.

It was still nearly clear, the zombies numbered about twenty and none of those had a clue about the survivors. Earlier lessons had been learned and they kept a very low profile now, staying to the shadows even in daylight. They resisted the temptation to light the fire in the bedroom of their new, temporary home. It was only used for food preparation and then left to die. John had been wise in suggesting they try and acclimatise to the approaching winter while they were still secure. Windows had been opened to lower the temperature further and after a couple of very uncomfortable days, they had gradually become accustomed to it. Their clothing was tried and tested to see which gave the best warmth at the lightest weight to ensure they could stay quick on their feet. Trudging around in heavy clothing would have been lovely if they had been going skiing or on a nice hike, but in this new world it would just be a game of zombie pass the parcel, stripping layer after layer of the garments to reach the tender, juicy prize within. The exception was the several pairs of socks they each used to protect their feet from the biting cold.

"It looks like a day or two and we will be moving out then." John nodded to Braiden, "Do you think you will be ready?"

"Yeah, I want to get moving too. I know each day I rest means it is more dangerous for us," Braiden explained.

5

"Not at all. You being fully healed is more important and safe for us, we need you fighting fit for the journey," Paige said and Honey wagged her tail from her position next to Braiden.

"Dad, have we decided to try for the Land Rover too? It gives us a backup," Kurt asked.

"There is not much fuel left; it was lower than a quarter of a tank. I agree that it would be better to have more than one option. The only thing I don't like is that it has been sat for so long, we aren't even sure it will start," John said.

"I hate to be the one to bring this up but what are the chances we will be able to get far in the vehicles anyway? I have seen the movies and you always see the roads blocked with hundreds and thousands of cars. How many roads are there out of Emsworth?" Paige added and they knew she was right.

"Four out, one each north, south, east and west from when it was an old market town, all single lane roads. Also there is only one road onto the Barracks which leads to the bridge and the guardhouse," Kurt said. Any blockage to the main roads could be ignored and another route taken, but the single track for the army base would be a real problem if there was any traffic at a standstill. They would have to walk the rest of the way and abandon the relative safety of the van and Land Rover, if they decided to take it.

"On the other hand, do we have a choice?" Sarah finished the discussion. They had set their course of action and if they could clear even a mile of the two-mile distance it would be worth it. The potential safety of the soldiers stationed there was too good to pass up; despite not being military they could fulfil other roles to help the group.

"I have an idea that might help us, but don't laugh at me," Sam said.

"Let's have it, Sam," John replied.

"Well, we have been using the water from the old copper water tank. Dad, do you remember when we used to cut them up for the scrap man?" Sam asked and Kurt nodded. "Why don't we cut pieces of the thin metal down and secure it around our arms with that duct tape? It will stop them biting us there if we get caught."

They had found some useful items in the house, but a lot of their best equipment had been lost to the fire. By cutting the tank apart they could probably cover half of the group, to do more they would need to break in next door and get a second cylinder.

"I think that's a great idea, it's light and strong. What made you think of that?" Kurt asked, complimenting his son.

"I saw how a lot of the zombies had bite marks on their arms, legs, and face. We can't wrap it round our legs because it could slow us down, nor our face because we need to see, but I thought if we could take away some of the danger it would be worth it." Sam shrugged. The group agreed it was well worth the effort and they would all benefit from some bite armour in the event they were on the run.

"I am not so sure about the legs, why can't we cut short sections for below our knees? It won't affect movement if we tape it well and keep it away from the joints," John said, taking the idea further.

"We would need at least one more water tank for that to work," Kurt stated, reaching down and looking at his lower leg, wiggling the ankle that he had sprained after the initial outbreak. "I think it's a great plan, we just need to get through to the other houses without going outside and with no drills."

"We could just do what I did," Sam said sheepishly, thinking back to the devastation he had been part of nearly a week ago. "Take out the tiles and hop over the roofline."

Sarah glowered at him; she was still furious at his actions, how he had endangered his life to even the score with the vile murderers.

"We will have to wait for nightfall to be sure. I see no reason why we can't get them tonight and cut them up tomorrow. The day after that we can make our break for it."

"Do we still try and get to the other home?" Gloria asked, knowing they had been betrayed by their naiveté with the previous attempt at making contact with other survivors.

"I think we should try, we can see who is in there and if we don't feel right we can just drive off," Kurt said. They were still hopeful to find the good in the midst of all the horror, if they could save others it would be a vindication of their previous failures. It would also give them more protection, safety in numbers was a very apt phrase in these times.

The night fell and the temperature dropped again. Sam, Kurt, and John retrieved the cylinders without incident, breaking through the roofs, piercing the metal and letting the water flood through the ceiling and then passing the tanks from house to house.

In the morning they cut the water cylinder apart and started to fabricate personal forearm and lower leg guards. Each piece was cut and taped around the edges to prevent the sharp metal from cutting the person it was meant to protect. Sam was first to be fitted but when his arms had been done he noticed a mistake.

"We have to put all our clothes on that we will be wearing when we go, or they won't fit when we leave." Sam pointed out the obvious.

"What a stupid thing to do," John commented, shaking his head. John cut the tape so that Sam could put his coat on which added more girth to the arm, he was right, it wouldn't have fitted properly. "There you go." He resealed it and Sam flexed his arm, moving it around and checking that he still had free movement.

"That's good, Grandad, its light enough to not matter," Sam said

"I'm a bit dubious," Kurt told them, "Four pieces of thin metal is not a lot but on the road it may get heavy very quick, sapping our strength. Perhaps we should only wear it when we are exposed."

"I have to admit I am also worried. I am no spring chicken and if we are forced to abandon the vehicle I think I may just slow you down," Gloria added. They could understand the fear, but as long as they were careful they should be able to avoid danger.

"Don't you even worry about that, I will carry you if I need to," John replied chivalrously and Gloria laughed.

"I will hold you to that. You shall piggy back me across the country," Gloria answered and hugged him. John turned and bent at the knees, inviting her to hop on and when she duly leaped up he caught her legs and commenced walking around the room, causing the group to laugh.

"*Ow!* My back!" John dropped her and lay on the floor, clutching his spine and gritting his teeth with the pain.

"John, I am so sorry. Are you ok?" She knelt beside him, trying to offer him some comfort as he lay in agony. He was holding a hand to his face but her concern turned to anger when he sniggered and then burst out laughing.

"I'm sorry love, I had to get you," John said grinning.

"You beast!" Gloria slapped at his chest, "I thought I had hurt you. Don't ever do that to me again."

The rest of the group had been taken in by the ruse. Seeing all was well, they sat back down, relieved that their plans had not been ruined by a slipped disc or torn muscle. Gloria continued to slap his arms as he tried to defend himself against the assault, laughing the whole time. He sat up and cuddled her tight, stopping the attack.

"Sorry, I was just being stupid. I know how serious the next couple of days are. I just wanted to lighten the mood," John explained, still holding on to Gloria for dear life in case she resumed her slapping.

"Well you nearly lightened my heart right out of my chest," she answered.

The family carried on with the task of fitting their armour, a cheap imitation of the knights of yore, thin copper in place of majestic suits of the finest steel. They would not be dodging swords or spears, but decaying teeth and their virulent bites. Kurt suggested they wear the plates for the next day until they were ready to make a break for the army base. It would be a good indicator of how much fatigue they would experience out in the big wide world.

9

CHAPTER TWO

A cold breakfast of tinned meatballs was eaten in sullen silence. The group had turned in early to maximise their sleep and build their energy. It had been less than successful. Each had lain there in the dark, fearful of the coming day and the abandoning of their new home in search of possible salvation. Their chances were unknown, though they all knew that the winter would be impossible to survive in their current situation. Their food and water was dwindling, and temperatures were moving into the single digits and even lower when the darkness fell. It was not a pleasant choice to make, a slow painful death from thirst or starvation, or the bites of the dead rending their flesh?

"Ok, everyone has their gloves, dust mask, and safety glasses?" Kurt asked the group as they prepared to leave the house and gathered their last belongings. "I don't know if you need to be bitten or if their blood and gore can infect us. If we have to fight I want to be prepared for every possibility."

They checked their pockets for the glasses and masks, the gloves already worn for the insulation against the chill.

"Sam, can you pick off the two that are hovering by the van please?" John asked and Sam moved into position, cupping a bearing within the slingshot pouch.

The previous night had been the first time the temperatures had gotten near freezing. The two shuffling zombies had small icicles hanging from their chins from the gradual release of black drool. They were fresher members of the dead. The group was simply calling them either new or old. The newer ones were the bitten, the torn or the shredded, partly or nearly completely eaten before suffering the change. The older ones had been interred and rose as they had been buried, rotting and covered with bursting pustules of ichor.

Their radio had been saved but still gave no explanation about what had occurred on that fateful day in September when a pulse was released that ignited the fire in the engines of the dead. The last transmission they had listened to had hinted that the scientists were close to a breakthrough, though at this stage what did it matter? Everyone was already gone and mankind was nearing extinction.

The first bearing to be shot impacted at the rear of the female cadaver's skull, between patches of partly eaten scalp. The bone imploded and a huge chunk of face was torn free upon exit, splashing the lawn and resulting in the undamaged nose lying to the side of the body. Sam was morbidly fascinated at the sight until the second zombie saw him at the window and did the 'old raise and moan', the guaranteed response of a mindless eater when seeing a meal. Paige had noticed the behaviour and coined the phrase, and at least the subtle groan of the walking meat sacks gave them some warning. The exceptions were those that had their throats ripped out or eaten. They were either silent, or 'whistlers', another Paige term for those whose attempts at moaning resulted in strange tones from the torn flesh of the neck.

Sam saw that it was Perry, one of the children from the estate. He had been badly mauled, was missing one arm and could only do a poor attempt at a Nazi salute instead of the usual zombie wave. He felt an inner chill at the sight, the realisation hit him that they would likely see a lot more of the people they once knew before escaping the area. He didn't draw the slingshot back as far as before and the bearing didn't rupture clean through his head, instead shattering the bridge of the nose and settling within the brain, still killing the boy. Gloria had witnessed the hesitation, the haunted look in Sam's eyes, and gave him a reassuring hug, knowing there were no words to convey her sorrow that he didn't already feel.

"All clear. The rest of them are far enough away that we can ignore them as long as the van starts," said Sam, pocketing his weapon and picking up the bag of blankets and assorted clothing they may have use for in the future. They gathered by the back door of their friend's home,

11

said their final farewells to the dwelling, and looked out into the morning light.

"Wait here, I am going to try the engine. I doubt there will be an issue but it's always better to be safe than sorry," Kurt told them and ran for the driver's door, jumping in and turning the key. The van turned over immediately, it was a reliable work horse and may prove their saviour. "Let's go!"

Honey leaped in and skidded on the metal floor. They all bundled into the rear of the vehicle and shut the doors, using the suitcases as temporary seats for comfort. John climbed through the bulkhead and sat in the passenger seat, looking out on the encroaching danger. They had been spotted and were going to be quickly surrounded if they remained parked by the house. Kurt looked over and put the van into gear. Honey climbed through and put her paws on the main console, surveying the scene and growling quietly.

"Easy girl," Kurt soothed and scratched behind her ear.

"Let's go and get those people," Sarah said to the family and Kurt drove out onto the main road.

"Swing by the Land Rover, I want to see if it starts," John told him and Kurt swung left, passing the pendulum blade and the scorched piles of corpses it had wrought. The heat had caused the clothing of the dead to ignite and the charred mounds were surrounded by blackened liquid, most likely the boiled blood and fats that had run from the bodies while the buildings had burned to the ground.

The walking Hellspawn were converging on them slowly as the van approached the abandoned Land Rover. Kurt stopped by the old fence and John climbed out closely followed by Sam with the slingshot and Gloria with the shotgun. They had time to spare but Sam wanted to try something and dropped to the ground looking for a suitable stone. They had several hundred bearings left although the larger ones were now in the minority. Finding a rounded pebble with a couple of sharp edges, he cradled it in the leather cup and aimed at the festering head that was closest. The stone struck the creature in the forehead, only managing to tear the skin and fracture the bone underneath.

"I don't think its heavy enough," Sam said dejectedly.

"Try this one. It's a bit sharper around the edges. Does it feel heavier?" Gloria passed a small flint to him and he aimed again. The stone ripped through the skull and came to a stop in the brain, causing the ghoul to tumble backwards, dead.

"*Yes!*" Sam punched the air. "It was about the same weight but maybe the sharp edges helped. Or maybe they just need to be closer for it to work?" he questioned and looked at Gloria.

"I don't know, you are the slingshot expert." She smiled at him.

"I'm going to try again, test the range," Sam explained and moved off with a fresh stone. Sarah looked nervous but Gloria winked and snapped the gun shut before releasing the safety and following him closely.

John had got the Land Rover started and stood by the door. "What do you all think about having a backup car?" John called to them.

"Why not just use our car, it has more space," Sarah suggested, taking her eyes from Sam when it was clear Gloria had him covered.

"Because if we need to go off road, the Rover will handle the terrain better," he answered.

"Ok, follow us closely. Dad, I was going to draw the zombies away and try and circle the estate, see if we can get close enough to the house to make a judgement," Kurt said.

"No, I will draw the dead away on my own. If the people need to jump from a window, the van is the safer bet," John explained and climbed back in the Land Rover. He drove forward slowly and reached the wooden fence. Revving the engine more, he pushed through and the old posts split and fell, allowing him to pull up to the side of the others.

Sam had destroyed two more of the reanimated and had judged that distance was a factor. He could get a kill shot from about double the range with a bearing over a pebble, but at least he could conserve the important ammunition where possible now. They all mounted up and followed John as he headed down the road. Driving around the zombies in their way, they pulled up at the corner of Dymoke Street and surveyed the home that sat about forty yards from the turning. The amount of agitation in the crowd was testimony to the fact that survivors were inside. They could see in the daylight that the front door was open,

13

which meant they would have to jump to the roof of the vehicle regardless.

Sam looked to the right, and saw the burned pile of rubble that he had caused while seeking justice and retribution. The gas pipes were still burning fiercely. Filtering through the bricks and mortar, the flames fluttered and undulated like a row of Bunsen burners on a school science desk. Piles of incinerated Hellspawn lay here and there, overcome by the need to feed on the trapped murderer, but lacking the cognizance to flee the spreading heat. Guilt hit Sam; the anonymity of the darkness was gone in the morning light. He had caused people to die here. Deserving though they were, it still affected him. He wanted to talk to Braiden about it, the way he had killed HP didn't seem to be affecting him at all, but so far they hadn't been alone long enough to broach the subject. The blaring horn of his grandad in the Land Rover caused him to flinch, and he ducked down with the rest of the group in the van. The aim was to have the focus of the shambling dead on John at all times. Heads turned at the sound and the crowd started to advance down the road, passing between cars, and leaving gardens, eager to feed. John started to crawl down the street in the Land Rover, drawing the dead in procession like a crazed version of the Pied Piper. Trails of leaking viscera and scraps of flesh were left in their wake. The distraction was working, the area was clear of all but three corpses who had caught sight of a man, who craned his neck while trying to see what was happening from the upper window of the house. He was young, in his late twenties or early thirties, with brown hair in a short, side parted style. They could see him leaning back and communicating with someone in the room, who then pushed passed and put her head out to look. She was of a similar age, black hair tied back tightly, giving her features a sharp, pinched look.

"Let's go, we won't get a better opportunity," Kurt said with resolve and turned down the road.

"Ram them, Dad, run those buggers over," Sam shouted and gained a disapproving look from Sarah.

"Can't do that mate, if I hit one too hard and damage the radiator we will be sitting ducks as the engine will overheat," Kurt explained.

"Really?" Sam was unconvinced. He had watched plenty of movies where the cars had crashed and still been fine, what was a few zombies against the large metal body of the work van?

"It's not like the movies," Kurt said over his shoulder, reading his mind. "I can do this though." He coasted forward at the zombies by the house, whose attention was rapt on the leaning form from the window. The van struck the dead at less than ten miles an hour and the impact caused them to simply fall over and under the wheels. Bumping and crunching sounds echoed up through the floor as they were crushed. Kurt looked in the side mirror and the broken bodies were flopping around, immune to the pain and only wanting to eat yet unable to make any concerted movement. Their arm and leg bones were visible, the skin broken from the sharp fractures. They were no danger anymore, unless someone would be foolish enough to go near the intact heads which could still bite.

"Are you both ok? I'm Kurt," he called out to the people in the house, waiting to reposition the vehicle until he had made a judgement on them.

"I'm Peter," replied the man after he pushed past the glowering female who seemed unable, or unwilling to answer. "That was Debbie."

"Don't push me, I can answer for myself," Debbie reprimanded Peter from the shadows. "Who are these people?"

"It's nice to meet you, Peter," Kurt said, trying to ignore her complaints in the background. The man smiled and it was a warm, genuine gesture.

"You too, but why are you out there with those things?" Peter asked, nervously looking up and down the street.

"I suppose you must have heard the explosion and seen the fires. That was our home. We are going to try for Thorney Barracks for safety before winter sets in fully," Kurt explained. He could see the understanding on Peter's face, they had watched the glowing sky and felt the vibrations of the blast.

"We wondered if you needed any help, or wanted to come with us?" Sarah asked, leaning out of the passenger window.

"We don't have much food left, I suppose we-" Peter started to reply, but was cut short.

15

"Shut up, we don't know those people, they could be dangerous," Debbie sneered and Peter lowered his head.

"If you really are short of food it would be suicide to try and make it through the winter," Kurt tried to reason with her and Debbie leaned out of the window.

"Do you think we are stupid? We know that no food will mean we die," she called down.

"Don't speak to them like that." Peter tried to assert himself.

"Shut up, you will get us killed," she rebuked him once again and Kurt was trying to maintain his cool.

"He didn't mean it like that, we know you are not stupid, you couldn't have survived this long if you were." Sarah tried to talk woman to woman.

"Don't patronise me, I am not a child," Debbie answered, narrowing her eyes.

"Why do you always get like this?" Peter asked from the background. "All they want to do is help."

"I told you to shut your mouth!" she screeched at him.

Kurt sighed and she turned her ire back to the strangers.

"Don't you sigh at me!" Debbie shouted down at Kurt.

"Would you keep your voice down! They are attracted by the noise," Kurt hissed back, but it was pointless.

"Who do you think you are, trying to tell me what to do?" Debbie carried on the tirade, oblivious to the danger she was drawing down upon them.

Kurt felt pity for Peter. It was bad enough to be trapped in this hellish world. However, it must have been even worse being cooped up with someone like that. Kurt knew the type; overbearing and abusive, never satisfied with whatever her henpecked partner provided. John had circled the block and was driving slowly towards them, closely followed by his pus filled entourage. They were out of time and Kurt could see no point in continuing the conversation. Debbie was still raving and he could see Peter trying to placate her.

"Good luck," Kurt said to the pair and pulled a U turn, facing back to the estate entrance and ready to move out as soon as John reached them. The shrill voice was now ignored, as much for the awful attitude as for the danger she would pose if she went on a rant in the open. John pulled alongside, having sped up after seeing the strangers were not going to be joining them.

"What happened?" John asked.

"Can't you hear?" Kurt said and John looked confused. Debbie had stopped shouting and had gone back into the room. "Never mind, let's go." Kurt started to drive forward and John prepared to follow but John tooted his horn once and they stopped. Peter was lowering himself from the window after throwing a bag down onto the lawn. Debbie was grabbing at him and attempting to stop him leaving.

"You bastard!" she screamed as she watched Peter make good his escape and drop to the ground, grabbing his bag and running toward the waiting vehicle.

Kurt was tempted to speed off and leave him there. Despite the attitude of his partner, Peter was leaving a defenceless woman to the dead or at least a slow lingering death by starvation. His foot hovered by the accelerator, ready to press it. He hesitated and the back door swung open. Instead of Peter climbing in to escape, he just threw his bag in.

"Can someone help me? We can't stay here and she knows it, she is just stubborn." Peter looked at them beseechingly

"Stubborn? That's an understatement," Kurt replied. "Peter, she has to quiet down or we will leave you both behind, I won't have my family put at risk. Sarah, jump in the driver's seat, we will be right back."

"Are you sure we have time, they are coming!" Sarah shouted the urgency. The large group of shamblers were only a minute away at most.

"I don't know, but I can't leave her to die," Kurt yelled as he and Peter rushed back to the house.

"Debs, please come with us, we can't stay here," Peter pleaded with her, but she had crossed her arms in a gesture of defiance.

"You didn't care about me when you jumped out of the window a minute ago, why start now?" she said, sounding like a sulking child.

"I came back for you, didn't I?" He knew their time was up, the corpses were nearly on them and Kurt had run out of patience.

"Get your fucking ass out of that window or stay here! My family are waiting and if you think I will risk them getting hurt for a pompous, jumped up bitch like you, then you are mistaken!" Kurt started to walk away. Peter grabbed him by the shoulder.

"Please wait, look," he said to Kurt. Debbie was coming, carefully sitting on the windowsill and preparing to jump. They didn't have time to get her turned around so that she could lower herself before leaping, at that height she would break a leg.

"*Wait!*" Kurt shouted and ran forward with Peter, holding their arms out to try and break her fall. "Ok, now!" Debbie landed with less than athletic grace and her skirt rode up on their arms which drew a glare of disapproval. The putrid monstrosities that reached for them focused her attention and they ran to the waiting vehicles, climbing through the open doors. Sarah pulled away and picked up speed, driving out of the estate that had been their home for thirteen years. Honey jumped down from the passenger seat to give them a warm welcome, licking all three.

"Get away from me you disgusting animal!" Debbie pushed her away forcefully.

"Don't you touch her, don't you hurt her." Paige had grabbed Debbie and screamed in her face.

"Get off you psycho! Peter, aren't you going to help me?" She was cowering at the verbal assault, unused to being the victim. Peter was making a fuss of the dog who appreciated the friendly contact and it was Gloria that gently pulled Paige back.

"It's ok sweetheart, no harm was done, look." Gloria indicated Honey who was frantically licking the laughing face of their new companion.

"Oh my God, she is crazy! She attacked me!" Debbie was babbling.

"She thought you hurt her dog, that's all," Gloria tried to explain but Debbie was now furious with Peter, who was still fussing over the yellow furred licking machine.

"Peter, are you going to let her do that? What a poor excuse for a man," Debbie belittled him.

"He's kept you alive, I'd say Peter was a hero," Kurt tried to support him.

"You shouldn't have touched her dog, she was only trying to say hello," Peter said, not even looking at her which made her even angrier, but one glare from Kurt was enough. He would happily stop and drop her out of the van. Her volatile attitude was bound to be a problem and he leaned in close to whisper his threat.

"If you don't be quiet, you will be left by the side of the road, do you understand me?" Kurt met her poisonous gaze and she broke contact first. Satisfied he had made his point, he held out his hand to Peter who shook it and smiled warmly.

"Nice to meet you mate, I'm Kurt. That's Paige, Sam, Gloria, Braiden, and Sarah, my wife." Peter nodded to each of them. "And of course you have met Honey." The dog barked at her new name and laid down, putting a paw onto Peters legs.

"Pleased to meet you all, I'm Peter. That's Debbie, we are engaged," Peter explained. Kurt thought at least the zombie apocalypse had stopped the wedding. Debbie merely looked at them all with disdain. Kurt was having none of it.

"Pleased to meet you too, Debbie." He smiled sardonically and held out his hand once more, but she didn't take it. He looked at Peter who gave an embarrassed shrug.

"So how did you two end up at home together when it happened?" Gloria asked, trying to defuse some of the animosity that had fallen on the group. Debbie was still ignoring them so Peter took his cue.

"Can you believe we had taken the day off to plan the wedding?" he laughed then quickly fell quiet when Debbie shot him a withering glare. It was plain to the group that the end of the world had not brought them closer together.

"Well I think that's romantic. Young love," Gloria continued, sensing the atmosphere and trying her best to brighten the group.

Sarah was concentrating on the route. They would soon be at the bend in the road that led through Emsworth, passing underneath a motorway and railway bridge before turning left at the roundabout that would take them directly towards the Barracks.

"Shit!" she muttered upon turning the corner. Kurt came up to look through the windscreen and why she had cursed was obvious; hundreds had gathered under the concrete overpass, the road was thick with the dead. The group was lucky, the slow approach of Sarah had only revealed the front of the van to the horde and only a small handful broke away and began a leisurely stroll over for their meal.

"So, what do we do now?" Sarah asked and looked at Kurt. John had pulled up and joined them at the driver's door.

"We try through Warblington or Southbourne. Warblington will be the fastest and the train gates are already broken." John had heard the tale of their school escape.

"Ok, we go through Warblington," Kurt agreed and swapped seats with Sarah. John meanwhile returned to the Land Rover and turned around in the road. The small group had now grown into a tide of putrescence; the whole swarm was converging on the van, more appearing from the shadows of the dual bridges as they watched. Kurt wasted no more time and swung in a wide arc, mounting the pavement before dropping back onto the road to continue the journey.

"Jesus, there were hundreds of them. Why were they all under the bridge?" Braiden asked. He still had a hard time speaking without coughing but it was getting better each day.

"I don't know, shelter maybe? I can't see why they would need to, they're dead." Kurt was at a loss. They looked like the huddled penguins he had watched on the Discovery Channel, sharing heat from their bodies.

Conversations ceased and Kurt concentrated on the task, the roads were clear apart from the occasional body or abandoned car. On small semi-rural villages like this it wasn't a surprise. The real test would be if they needed to take a main road or motorway. Kurt prayed this wouldn't be necessary, that the Army would provide sanctuary. The train station was ahead and the pile of electrocuted bodies had been churned up and strewn down the line from a passing train. They tried to avoid looking at the recognisable pieces, staring at the passenger platform instead, which had a lot of zombies on either side, waiting for a train that would never come. They passed the school and it was even more sinister than they remembered; the dark, empty classrooms and echoing corridors haunted Kurt's waking thoughts, probably as a result of what he had witnessed inside. The family felt for each other, Sarah squeezed Kurt's arm, Gloria did the same to both Sam and Braiden, unconsciously seeking reassurance from the horror of that day.

As they reached the westward entrance to the village, the concentration of zombies increased and necessitated some careful driving to avoid the thronging masses. They passed no other signs of life, no homes were besieged and no undead were grouped like those under the bridges. They reached the roundabout and it was blocked with cars, some were burned out shells, others had flailing dead inside, safely buckled in against the crash that was now inevitable.

"Hold on tight, I've got to punch through the cars!" Kurt yelled and they all braced themselves. He picked out the rear side of a Volvo that had smashed windows and moving occupants, the sound of the roaring engine was a magnet to their reaching arms. He prayed the engine would survive the impact and was thrown painfully at his air bag when metal met metal in a rending shriek. The Volvo was sent spinning and the dead were spared any serious injury by their vehicle's top notch safety. The van shuddered and stalled. No smoke issued from the bonnet, but there could be oil pouring from a split gasket which he didn't dare risk checking. Turning the key, the engine cranked but refused to fire.

"Fantastic, you've just got us killed!" Debbie shouted at Peter, still seeking to make him feel useless. Kurt had to begrudgingly agree with her. They had entrusted him with their lives and he had failed. The dead were filtering through the available gaps in the traffic, seeking the warm pulsing meat of the stranded survivors.

"Sorry." Was all he could say, the doomed expedition would soon be at a horrific end. The sound of a blaring horn made Kurt look at the wing mirror. John was frantically trying to get his attention.

"...bloody window down!" John was yelling as Kurt complied. "I will push you. Keep the handbrake off, when you hit the downward slope try bump starting it!"

Kurt raised his hand in agreement and John revved the engine and drove at the bumper. The group felt the contact and John increased the power. Inch by inch the van rolled forward, only the displaced Volvo gave them a slim chance of survival. If there had been any other obstacles they would have ground to a halt. The undead reached the rolling convoy and started to hammer at the glass and side panels, John was totally exposed and if any of the panes on the Rover gave way they would all die screaming. The proximity of the faces and the slime of decomposition they smeared against the clean glass made Kurt gag. He was spending far too much time worrying about the spectators and missed the zombie that stepped out in front of them, a crack of head on windscreen brought him back to his senses. They had still only reached about five miles an hour and even a soft body under the wheels could stop them dead, literally. Fortunately it was rolled and broken by the undercarriage and then, subsequently crushed again by John who couldn't see the source of the snapping and thumping. Kurt passed a hideous sight, a body stripped clean of skin, flesh and clothing, only a red muscled mess like the images from a medical journal remained. It passed by and left a bloody handprint on the glass before reaching John in the Land Rover. It drew its head back and lurched forward, connecting bare skull to the window and Kurt watched in horror as the glass imploded, covering his father. The zombie's momentum plunged it headfirst through the opening and only the copper arm guards saved John from the virulent bite that would have meant certain undeath.

"*No!*" Kurt screamed and almost put his foot on the brake which would have undone all the speed John had built up. They were so close to the decline in the road he could taste it. The blood sack was now waist deep into the vehicle and John was leaning over to the side, still accelerating and keeping them safe. Their eyes met through the mirror and it was as if time slowed down, all of the grief and arguments of the past few years melting away in an instant. John gave a smile and barely perceptible nod, the downward slope was reached, he had done all he could to give his family a fighting chance.

"Dad, no!" Kurt pleaded, but John's attention had shifted skyward. He twisted in the seat and got his knees against the chest of the horror, pushing it away as far as possible. Twin blasts of a shotgun punched a gaping hole in the windscreen and the skinless monstrosity's head was blown apart, the scatter of buckshot had been only inches from John's legs. Kurt looked back and saw that Peter and Paige had held the ladder to the roof opening for Gloria to climb, where she had then taken her shot.

"Thank you, Gloria, oh God thank you!" Kurt shouted up at her but only able to see her legs from the angle of the driver's seat.

The decapitated creature fell from the window and John straightened in the seat, covered in all manner of vile fragments and liquids, yet alive. Kurt waited to get clear enough to risk a bump start on the engine. He put the van in second, turned the ignition and released the clutch which threw them all forward. The engine refused to fire.

Rolling the window down Kurt called back, "One more try, then we abandon it!"

"Ok, I'll get you rolling faster again, hold on." John replied, wiping his face of brains and other foul globules.

The Land Rover hit them once again and coupled with gravity they hit ten miles an hour rapidly. Kurt repeated the process and the engine coughed into life, roaring with the depressed accelerator and lurching forward, leaving the gathered swarm in their wake. John met their speed and leaned out of the broken window to see, the cobwebbed windscreen more dangerous than the air that whipped his face, causing his eyes to water. How dogs enjoyed this he couldn't fathom. They reached the turn for the Barracks and drove into the tree lined avenue, fields lay on either side with a deep drainage ditch between them and the road. They were safe for now and pulled up next to one another with engines idling and spoke through the windows.

"Are you ok?" Kurt's heart was racing. They had come close so many times.

"Yeah, Sam's idea saved my life, look at that." John held his arm out to them and they could see the indentations of teeth on the copper band. Sam stuck his head through from the back and smiled, overwhelmed that he had inadvertently saved his grandfather. "You are a star, mate." He winked at his grandson. Sam blushed and sat down in the back once more.

"So we are just going to drive right up to the gate if we can, the army should have been able to hold them off with their hardware," Kurt assumed logically.

"And if they haven't?" John left the question in the air, Kurt didn't want to countenance the possibility they would have to stay on the road and try and reach Chichester.

"Are we just going to sit here all day? We nearly died once already!" Debbie complained and Kurt just ignored her.

"Shh, we are nearly safe. It's just down this road," Peter said.

"Don't you shush me, I-" she started to lay into Peter again.

"Thanks, Pete. Sorry for the near miss back there," Kurt cut her off mid-sentence and glared at her in the rear view mirror. "Let's go."

They moved off and John fell in behind again, driving carefully, though it wasn't necessary. Any zombies they passed were trapped in the boggy ditch, sunk to the waist and gradually melting with the flowing water. They managed to get within half a mile of the guarded front gate before the abandoned cars choked the road solid and proved impassable. Kurt opened the door and stood on the step to get a better vantage point. He didn't have the words, he simply froze and stared.

"What can you see?" Sarah asked, concerned at the look on his face.

"I'm afraid it's not good," Gloria said after looking out through the top of the van.

"Well that's just great!" Debbie huffed and crossed her arms, sulking again.

"What is it, Kurt?" Peter tried to get him to speak. Gloria just looked down at the group with fear in her eyes.

"We can't get through," Kurt said quietly.

"That's ok, we can just take our stuff and walk around the cars," Peter replied with a grin, not understanding what Kurt was trying to convey.

In the distance the cars gave way to an open area that ran alongside a deep river that filled and emptied with the tides of the Solent. The guardhouse was situated on this side with a bridge that then crossed the river to the Army complex. The gates were broken and hanging from the hinges, the bridge was filled with the dead, as was the whole area surrounding it. Tens of thousands of the zombies were trying to reach the small island, but were prevented by four Viking armoured personnel carriers parked at the other side of the bridge, side by side. Soldiers stationed on the heavily armed vehicles were carefully patrolling, keeping a close eye on the masses of cadavers but not engaging, their rifles slung on their shoulders. Two more sat within the rotating turrets, cradling mounted Browning heavy machine guns. Large holes were littered around the entrance area where the initial attack had been met with lethal resistance and Kurt could see arms reaching from the artillery craters, forever trapped in their unfilled graves.

"Impossible, there are thousands of them," Kurt explained and Peter looked crestfallen.

"Oh, ok," he answered, seeing the all too familiar look of scorn from his fiancée.

"Options?" John had joined them and was wiping the gore off himself with the baby wipes that Gloria had passed to him.

"We head to Chichester I guess," Sarah offered.

"No, why don't we head to the marina and see if we can get a boat?" Kurt suggested, "We could get to the island from Emsworth Harbour."

"I don't like boats, they make me sick," Debbie added.

"I'm sure being torn apart would make you feel worse," Braiden rasped at her, which was enough to still her tongue.

"Does anyone know how to sail?" John asked but the group came up short, blank faces stared back at him.

"So we need a boat with an engine. Let's go and take a look." Kurt pulled a three point turn in the road and John did likewise after climbing back in the Land Rover, trying to ignore the dampness of the bloodied seat he was forced to drive from.

CHAPTER THREE

They followed the road back towards the main village and turned into the yacht club that was normally the preserve of local sailors and posers, those that loved the status that came with expensive yacht ownership. Rows of boats of varying sizes and ages were stowed on large dry dock storage racks but they lacked the machinery to get them down to use. The family stopped at the main entrance; looking left they could see the main clubhouse where people went for a drink and a meal after a day on the open sea. Zombies were stood around it in large numbers, which could be a sign of life within the building. At this point they could do nothing about it. There was no way to coax the dead and draw them away without blocking the main entrance, so they ignored it with regret. On the right were rows of stilted houses that had been rebuilt after a particularly bad flood had washed the previous homes away. They were quiet, only a few of the lingering dead stood in the area. None had noticed the new members who coasted their vehicles without noise towards the dock area.

"This is as far as we go. We need to fight our way to the moored boats." Kurt pointed. There were ten or more between the survivors and the possibility of salvation which rocked and bobbed with the lapping waves.

"I will do no such thing, Peter. We will stay here while they clear the way," Debbie stated. Peter ignored her and picked up a length of steel pipe that had been saved in the escape from the fire. "Peter! What the hell do you think you are doing?" her eyes blazed at him.

"I'm helping to save our lives," he answered without looking at her.

"You can follow closely behind us, ok? I don't want to leave you in here." Kurt tried to reason with her, a tantrum now would bring a hundred more down on them from the surrounding area. Thankfully she stood, still angry but quiet for now, self-preservation more important than her temper. Peter looked at Kurt and nodded gratefully.

"Gloria, don't fire unless we have no other choice," John instructed. She knew what was at stake; only if one of her loved ones was in mortal danger would she risk the noise.

"Do we take our bug out bags and suitcases?" Sam asked as he and Braiden moved them to the rear doors.

"No, leave them. Grab your weapons, put your safety gear on and let's get going. Sam, can you pick a few off as they get closer? We will cover you." Kurt stood aside as Sam readied himself, Honey stood next to him, teeth bared, growling low in her throat. They formed a circle and held their weapons, a mix of hammers, crowbars, and steel pipes plus Gloria with the loaded shotgun. The zombies were voicing their inhuman cravings; the living flesh they desired was so close they could practically taste it. Sam picked off the first with ease, but the advance of the larger group was causing him to shake with fear and adrenaline. His second shot missed, ripping a portion of the cheek away.

"Sorry," he said shakily and reloaded.

"You got this, bro," Braiden said into his ear, wielding his trademark, long shanked screwdriver.

Sam aimed carefully and took his shot, shattering the brain on the corpse with no cheek. The rest of the group readied themselves, raising their weapons as they were slowly surrounded. Debbie was preparing to scream, Kurt could see it in her eyes. He would have no choice but to knock her unconscious or kill her too, the fate of his family was too important. She saw the look, realised what he was about to do, and held her hand to her mouth, stifling the urge to cry out.

Sam had the chance of one more kill and then the remaining dead were on them. Paige missed the attention of one of the zombies while she swung her steel pipe at a second. Honey leaped and hit it in the chest, barrelling it to the ground which allowed Gloria to step forward and crush the skull with the wooden gun stock. Kurt was wrestling with another and they fell in a tangle to the gravel, sharp blackened teeth trying to close on his hammer hand. Braiden leaped on the back of the monster and rammed the sharpened point through the skull and all motion ceased as it fell dead on top of Kurt. John was being set upon by two of the creatures which held his arms and were trying to reach the softer parts of his upper biceps. Peter rushed forward and stabbed the steel bar at the faces which knocked one to the ground, giving John the chance to jam the point of his crowbar through the other's eye. Peter stepped forward and crushed the skull of the fallen cadaver, covering the gravel with stinking blood and brain. The gore was swiftly coated by Peter's bile and scant breakfast of dry Weetabix. He was out of the battle for now. The others formed back up to protect Debbie and Peter. They were now in the majority as the final horrid abominations came at them. Kurt had watched Honey's heroics and tried the same tactic for the slow moving threat, swinging his boot and kicking the nearest zombie in the midriff. It collapsed to the ground and one swing from the hammer finished it. The last fell in sprays of green tinged plasma and the group surveyed the carnage. It looked like a horrific child cartoon of the sun, the group the blazing centre and the splayed out zombies the rays, red and green in the place of golden yellow.

The whole episode had lasted a minute at most but they were all breathing as if they had sprinted uphill. It was a mixture of the exertions and the foes they had faced, otherworldly fiends whose bite would predicate a quick demise and resurrection. Honey moved between the fallen bodies and sniffed, satisfied the threat was now gone. The area was clear and the sound of the scuffle had been shielded by the racks of clean hulled vessels.

"Is everyone ok?" Kurt asked and they all checked each other over and apart from some light bruising they were all unharmed.

"It was close," John stated and they all agreed, they could not go recklessly into combat like that again, they would not get lucky every time.

"Follow me," Kurt said and walked to the docks, looking for any vessels that were suitable. Most were small, personal fishing boats for taking out with friends and some beer. None had the outboard motor fixed in place as they were taken off to deter thieves. The larger ones would all be started by key and a spare set was often kept in the clubhouse safe, but gaining entry was out of the question with the crowd of rot surrounding it. If they could even fight through the horde they lacked the requisite safe cracking experience, and nobody had the skills to hotwire one either. Their only choice was two less than sturdy looking row boats which had the oars laid within.

"Well it isn't like we are used to luxury anymore," Gloria told them and climbed carefully into the boat, switching weight from leg to leg with the gentle rock before seating herself. The others split themselves and settled in, only Debbie remained on the dock, a resolute look on her face.

"You won't get me on something like that. Look at it, it's going to sink," she complained despite the fact they were both holding several people with no signs of leakage.

"Please just get on, Debs, it's safe, I promise," Peter pleaded with his fiancée.

"How many boats have you ever been on, you fool?" she questioned with a taunt.

"Bye," Kurt said and started to row away, leaving her blustering on the jetty. He looked at Peter who was torn between the choices and winked, trying to communicate that it was just a scare tactic. John made to push off and she came running, stepping down into the curved bottom and slumping onto the wooden seat. Kurt was twenty yards away and decided to clear the air with Peter.

"Sorry, I had to do that, every second counts," Kurt told their new member.

"I know, it's ok," Peter replied, embarrassed at the whole situation.

"Has she always been like this?" Kurt had to know, "How the hell could you put up with it?"

"She was never this bad, you know, before it all happened. She didn't hit me as much before." He lowered his head and watched the water as it splashed against the wooden side. The oars left a sudsy wake on the surface from the dirty sea. The harbour was not pristine by any stretch of the imagination, debris and rubbish washed in with the tides.

"She shouldn't hit you at all," Paige added and the rest agreed.

"It's not like that. She would only ever do it if I made her angry." Peter tried to defend her, but he heard how pathetic it sounded as he was uttering the words. Paige gave his arm a squeeze and Honey jumped up and licked his face, showing her canine love.

Kurt reached the harbour wall first, rounded the concrete marker, and the long island which housed the army divisions came into view. Houses, workshops, industrial storage units for the real hardware, and the evenly spread, manned watchtowers were surrounded by high fences and razor wire.

"Watch out!" came a shout from the other boat and Kurt looked around, unsure of what the problem was as they were a good distance from any land or obstacle. Then he saw it, a bloated, wet, decomposing zombie was floating along like a piece of driftwood, carried on the current that was heading out with the tide. Kurt backstroked and stopped the vessel just in time. Its arms reached and were within inches of finding purchase. Who knew if it would have the ability to pull itself on board, but with the weight of the passengers, the rim of the hull was only eight inches clear of the water's surface. It cleared the craft and carried on the long journey out to sea. This new revelation, that even the open water was dangerous, filled them with a deeper dread. The planet was a death trap, every inch now held mortal threats to the remaining humans.

"Thanks for the heads up," said Kurt to those in the other boat which was now alongside. They looked as the zombie floated away, carried past the massed thousands that were blocked by the troop carriers on the bridge. They were surprised to see the crowd was unwilling to go into the river to reach the meal on the island. Any dead that fell were pushed or jostled into the water, where they would bob around for a bit before following the same path out to the Solent as their receding bloated friend.

The group rowed the remaining distance and ran the vessels up the pebble beach. The fence was eight feet high, and from what they could see, it ran the complete perimeter of the island. Corpses were scattered here and there as far as the eye could see, some still clinging to the chain link fence. They had all been shot in the head at close range, open skulls and gaping wounds the work of the rifles and pistols carried by the soldiers.

"I told you we would make it!" Peter told Debbie triumphantly, but she was still unhappy.

"Let's walk and see if we can get the attention of one of the guard towers," Sam suggested. They didn't need to as soldiers were running towards the group, guns raised.

"Halt, don't move!" screamed one of the men as he dropped to one knee and sighted the group with his assault rifle.

"Drop the gun!" shouted another to Gloria who quickly lowered the shotgun and placed it on the stony beach.

"Wait, we aren't infected, we need your help," Kurt pleaded and moved to talk to the pair.

"Don't fucking move I said!" bellowed the man. Honey ran to the fence, barking ferociously with her hackles raised. The soldier aimed the gun at the dog and Paige rushed forward, shielding her.

"Please, we just want to talk." Kurt had raised his arms and spoke to the larger of the two men who had two arrows on the arm of his uniform shirt which indicated to Kurt he was the most senior.

"Call it in," said the steely eyed man, not lowering his gun.

"HQ, this is Mills, come in, over," the junior soldier spoke into the radio with a crackle of static.

"This is HQ, go ahead, over," was the tinny response.

"We have civilians in the western quadrant, request course of action, over."

Seconds passed that felt like minutes facing the barrels of the guns.

"Sit tight, Mills, Lieutenant Baxter is on his way. Keep them covered, over."

"Copy, over."

Kurt tried to speak to the men, but they refused to be drawn into a conversation. The guns never wavered and the group understood that they would be shot if they pressed the issue. Despite the fall of mankind, the army was still maintaining strict discipline and security where possible.

"I knew we should have stayed in our house," Debbie exclaimed, totally forgetting the fact that their food would have disappeared within a week or two and they would have had to run the gauntlet through the gathered dead, probably fatally.

"Will you just shut up!" Braiden croaked at her.

31

"How dare you speak to me like that, you horrible little shit!" Debbie spat back venomously and Braiden stepped towards her.

"I said don't move," yelled the soldier, aiming the pistol directly at the youngster who paused mid stride.

Debbie and Braiden stared with hatred at each other and Kurt was bitterly regretting his decision to stop at their house. Peter was proving to be one of the good guys, but Debbie was as far removed from him as it was possible to be. How they ever ended up dating he didn't know. He would make a point of asking at some point if they survived this episode.

"Braiden, this isn't the time, mate," Kurt whispered, trying to calm the teenager before he did something drastic. Braiden relaxed but refused to break eye contact with the awful woman.

In the distance three more men were approaching, casually and in no rush. They knew the fence and the firearms would ensure cooperation in the group that had reached their base. The lieutenant stepped forward and appraised the survivors, looking at each. He was well turned out, his uniform crisp and ironed, six-foot-tall and with misty blue eyes that were unsettling when they met your gaze. It was as if he was looking at their souls, judging them for their deeds past and present.

"What can we do for you folks?" he finally talked and his voice was warm and friendly, but the eyes still exuded ice despite the smile.

"I'm Kurt, this is my family and that's Debbie and Peter," Kurt started.

"Pleased to meet you all, I'm Lieutenant Baxter, 42nd Artillery Regiment," he replied and nodded at the group.

"We need your help. We have been through hell to get here," Kurt said and the massed groans from the thousands of moving corpses half a mile away was testament to the fact.

"I'm sorry but we are under strict orders to not take any refugees, our facility is small and we simply cannot house civilians," Baxter answered, still smiling.

"But you have to! We can't go back out there, look at those things!" Kurt shouted at the senior soldier and the smile disappeared in an instant. "I'm sorry, but going back means death, please?" Kurt implored.

"I know what is out there. I have lost men to them before we barricaded the bridge with the vehicles," Baxter said, reliving the first hours of the outbreak and remembering the brave men and women that had been on guard duty, who had died rather than abandon their posts.

"I'm so sorry to hear that. We can help you. We can pull our weight and earn our keep." John took over, seeing the look of frustration that was boiling below the surface of his son.

"It's just not possible, I'm truly sorry, believe me. We have had to turn others away, some forcibly." The lieutenant emphasised the final word, telling the group that they would be shot if they tried to break in.

"Who is the commander here? Can we speak to him and plead our case? There must be a way," John pressed on, ignoring the threat because the tearing teeth were far more terrifying to them.

"You are talking to me," he stated, all warmth now gone, only the icy stare remaining. "And I am telling you that you must leave the island or you will be treated as a threat and be fired upon."

The other soldiers cocked their weapons but didn't aim, the message was loud and clear. Only one of the troops had a look of sympathy, the rest were as resolute and committed to their orders as their commander.

The family huddled up. All hope was lost now, their spirits crushed. They had all secretly known that the army would take them in, house them, feed them and protect them. The truth was; they had risked the journey for nothing.

"I'm sorry everyone. I don't know what to do," Kurt said, lost and forlorn.

"We keep moving!" Braiden whispered, which allowed him to talk with no pain.

"That's a great idea, let's just go and say hello to the creatures over there!" Debbie rounded on Braiden who was still furious at her. Before he could act she defiantly stormed over to the fence. "Now you listen here, I pay my taxes, which pays your wages. So technically you work for me, now I am demanding you *let us in*!" her voice rose to a shriek at the end.

The lieutenant took out his sidearm and fired a shot directly over her shoulder and she could hear the hiss of the passing slug as it tugged at her hair.

"Jesus! Don't shoot!" Peter shouted and grabbed at Debbie who was staring in shock at the man, before falling onto her rump as she was yanked away from the fence.

"You have five minutes to leave, after that, shoot them," Baxter told his men who looked ready to carry out the order. Only the young private looked uneasy at the prospect of firing on some of the last remaining humans on Earth. With this he walked away and the four subordinates took up positions to cover the group, their rifles and pistols were raised though not aimed any more. The single shot had been a suitable deterrent.

The family made their way back to the small boats, slump shouldered and quiet. They exchanged looks, lacking the words to convey the sense of desolation they all felt. Even Debbie was mercifully silent for once, though the shock would not last, they were sure of that.

"Hey, wait!" shouted the young soldier and the family looked back to see him approach the fence. The three others were not happy that he was trying to talk to them and disobeying orders, but they didn't interfere. "There was a FOB set up at St Richard's Hospital at the start of this." Kurt just shrugged, unsure what the man was trying to tell them.

"Sorry, forward operating base. Some of our guys were dispatched to secure the medicines, equipment, and medical staff to help fight the outbreak. They may still be there," he explained, desperately wanting to help them.

"You know how many of those things are between us and the hospital?" Kurt asked and the look on the young man's face told them he did.

"It's a chance," he replied, knowing how weakly it came across.

"Have they been successful?" John asked, seizing this small sliver of hope.

"We haven't had contact for a while," replied the soldier and the conversation was over.

John and Kurt looked at one another and climbed in after the others, picking up the oars and pushing off from the stony beach. The silence that marked their return to the jetty was only interrupted by the occasional sound of water splashing as another zombie was displaced and fell into the water, ready to begin their unceasing flow with the changing tides.

They reached the barnacled moorings and tied the boats off before climbing back onto the wooden dock. They stood there for long minutes, holding one another silently, only Peter and Debbie standing to one side, estranged more so than ever. Paige reached out and pulled him in and Gloria tried to do the same with his cold fiancée but she just stepped back and ignored the gesture, while shooting hateful looks at Peter.

"So what do we do now?" Sam asked and Honey looked from face to face as if she waited for an answer too.

"It will be dark soon. I think we should reverse the vehicles to block the dock, then bed down in one of these larger vessels," John suggested.

"Why don't we try for one of the houses? The ones on stilts that we passed," Debbie added, joining in for the first time. It was likely because she wanted more luxury than the hard floor of the boats. It would be a lot warmer and no one raised any objections.

"We will need to clear the area to be safe. I only saw three or four by the homes. We will need to be careful of the large group by the clubhouse. Do we risk moving the vehicles and the noise or shall we try and go on foot?" Kurt asked.

"I would be happier being closer to the vehicles. If we need to escape quickly I would prefer it if we don't have to cross the marina to reach our transportation," John answered and Kurt had to agree. Following the main roads and pathways it would only be about five hundred feet and on foot through the storage racks probably half the distance. In a world of walking horror, it could mean certain death.

They drove slowly back into the rows of stored boats, small and large laid out on racks ready for their owners who would never again take them out on the open sea. Kurt glimpsed the square community of twenty homes and came to a stop.

"Shit!" he muttered.

"What's the matter, sweetheart?" Sarah asked, leaning forward. Kurt's pointing finger indicated the much larger numbers who were now wandering around aimlessly by the stilted sanctuaries. Around twelve were immediately visible with more probably hidden by the environment, far too many to risk fighting for a good night's sleep. Kurt

35

opened the window and pointed for John to survey too, he could see the look of disappointment register on his father's face. John thumbed backwards, trying to say 'Boats?' and Kurt gave him the thumbs up, slowly reversing, careful not to rev the engine and bring attention to themselves. They parked blocking the access ramp. The only way in would be to break through the van and climb out through the back doors.

They took all of the bed sheets and duvets they had salvaged to use as covers for the coming night. It was going to be long and bitterly cold, sleep would be difficult. The rhythmic motion of the boat and their fatigue would aid them. They picked a small for-hire fishing boat that had a sizeable canopy which would be a lifesaver if the grey sky shed the rain that was massing in the clouds overhead. Without mattresses they tried to use some of the thick duvets for comfort, but it left them with little to lay across their bodies when the temperature dropped.

"Shit!" Kurt muttered, sitting down on the edge of the boat in frustration.

"It's ok, Dad, me and Braiden will go and see what we can find on the other boats," Sam said and the boys set off to forage for anything that could help.

"Don't panic, Kurt, worst case scenario is that we sleep on the deck and get bad backs. We will be warm enough." Peter smiled, still cheerful in spite of their situation. Kurt nodded, appreciating the sentiment.

Honey chuffed quietly in agreement and licked his hand, Peter stroked her and she lay down, exposing her belly which he gently scratched causing her hind leg to kick involuntarily.

"Thanks, Peter. You are right, we will get through this," Gloria said and smiled at their new friend.

"Great, a freezing floor and sharing blankets with strangers. Count me out. I am sleeping in the van." Debbie huffed and picked up a duvet. Kurt grabbed it and pulled it from her hands aggressively, putting it back on the pile and meeting her furious expression.

"You sleep in the van and you do it without our blankets. Understand?" Kurt spoke quietly. He was seething and she knew it, he would either hit her or throw her into the dirty water.

"Fine, fuck you all!" She stormed off and Peter was tempted to go after her but he knew it was what she expected. Kurt sighed with disgust and passed a duvet to Peter.

"You should go to her, we will be ok." Kurt was tired in body and soul. Fighting the Hellspawn was one thing, but his faith in human nature was being tested to the limit by the prevalence of malevolence and selfishness in those he encountered. What was the saying, the meek will inherit the Earth? Bullshit, Kurt thought to himself.

"No, she can sit there and get cold. She will come back in time," Peter said and put the cover down, "Shit, where are the keys?"

"Here, don't worry." Kurt pulled them out of his pocket. "Do you really think she would have driven off?"

"No, well I don't think so, but I'm glad you have the key anyway," Peter told him. In truth, he wouldn't have put it past her to leave them all stranded.

"Peter, how the hell did you end up with that?" Kurt asked, pointing at the van, meaning Debbie.

"Kurt!" Sarah admonished him. "Don't be so rude."

"No it's ok. We met at university and have been together about six years, she was doing Sociology and I was in Business. We met at a student night in Portsmouth. We were only friends to start with. She didn't want to be tied down to just one guy," Peter explained and they tried to be understanding.

"When did she become... difficult?" Gloria tried to be diplomatic and Peter laughed.

"She has always been a bit of a bitch," he replied and cast an anxious look down the jetty, fearing she would hear him.

"Then why did you stay with her?" Paige asked, genuinely interested in their dysfunctional relationship.

"I guess I was scared to leave. I tried to at the beginning, then she would attack me and threaten to kill herself. I caught her taking a bottle of painkillers once and I just decided to stay and see if she would change if I loved her enough." Once again, Peter could hear how preposterous he sounded and was grateful his new friends didn't mock him. Paige stood up and hugged him, pity and sadness for this poor soul pouring forth. Metal clanged as the back doors were slammed shut and they all grimaced and watched for renewed movement on the horizon. Luckily the quick bang wasn't sufficient for the walking dead to pinpoint the location of the sound and none came to investigate.

"Oh God, she must have seen you hug me," Peter said with real fear in his voice, he would be made to pay for this.

"Don't worry. She won't be touching you again," Kurt vowed and meant it. He would gladly leave her to fend for herself if she tried anything.

"She just gets angry sometimes," Peter repeated the same excuse again, the same one that domestic violence victims the world over have used to justify their ill treatment.

"Never. Ok?" Kurt clasped his shoulder and their eyes met. Peter grinned and Kurt smiled back, his mood lightening a bit.

"Dad, we have some stuff!" Sam declared, passing over armfuls of cheap, but spongy life preservers.

"Pillows," Braiden whispered, pointing at the bright orange padded jackets. He wafted his hand in front of his face to indicate they were not the most pleasantly fragranced headrests they could hope for.

"We also found loads of these." Sam passed bait and tackle boxes over the side.

"Ok... what do we need these for?" Sarah asked him.

"Mum!" Sam exclaimed as if she was dim witted. "We can use them like bricks and block the opening to keep the wind out and heat in under the roof."

Braiden started stacking them and spread his arms like a magician's assistant at the climax, Ta Da! They would probably have enough to close the opening, or at least block it most of the way which would make a real difference in the frigid darkness.

"Great idea, boys," John told them, patting them on the back and jumping from the boat to help with the collection.

"You know, I think we could use these as body armour," Kurt mused, holding a life jacket at arm's length and turning it around. "We have our arms and legs protected but the thick foam pads would protect our backs and chests too."

"That's a great idea, we will stink of sea and fish, but at least we can carry our new pillows with us too." Sarah smiled, happy that Kurt was coming out of his funk and thinking again.

"I think we could all do with something to eat, I shall go and fetch it from the van," Gloria told them and laid the shotgun on the steering console at the bow of the boat.

"I will come with you," Kurt said, rising.

"No, I will be fine. I think I need to have a word with our new guest," Gloria replied and the look on her face made it clear that she wasn't going to be easy on Debbie. She carefully stepped over the side of the vessel and passed Sam and Braiden who had found more building materials, John shot her a puzzled look.

"Food," she told him.

"Ah, ok," he replied and carried on to their temporary home.

Reaching the door to the van, Gloria opened it and found Debbie rummaging through the bags and suitcases. Clothing, food and other belongings were scattered over the floor of the vehicle and Debbie was half finished with stuffing a chocolate bar into her mouth. The expression of being caught started as shock, then fear, then scorn, then anger, a multitude of facial changes in a couple of seconds. She slowly chewed, savouring the melting delicacy and challenging Gloria who ignored the spiteful woman and, instead, leaned in and retrieved a selection of food and a large bottle of clean water for the group.

"Not going to say anything?" sneered Debbie at the old woman, chocolate smeared all over her thin, cruel lips.

Gloria ignored her and took a couple of the thick wool jumpers that had been thrown around in Debbie's temper tantrum at seeing Peter embraced by Paige. The ex-teacher was used to challenging individuals, differing social backgrounds and personalities were part and parcel of the job role. Debbie was on another level, bordering on sociopathic. Her erratic behaviour and lack of empathy was a dangerous combination in a normal world. In this apocalyptic netherworld it would be catastrophic.

"Don't you fucking ignore me, you shrivelled old hag!" Debbie was nearly shouting as she leaned forward to deliver the insult.

Gloria reached out and slapped her hard across the face causing chocolate spittle to hit the side of the van and run down in brown streamers. Debbie was momentarily shocked and then looked as if she would launch herself at Gloria.

"Try it!" Gloria hissed and the anger in those words gave Debbie pause, she was unused to being challenged in this way.

"You have an hour, no more, to tidy this mess. If you touch any more of our food while I am gone, if you take a sip of our water, if you touch any of our clothing or supplies I will shoot you dead and throw you in the water for the fish to eat. The next time you touch Peter, or have an outburst that threatens my loved ones, I will feed you to the zombies. Do you understand me?" Gloria threatened and she could see Debbie's inner turmoil as she weighed the options, finally settling for a glare of hostility and silence. Gloria could deal with filthy looks; she was used to them from wayward pupils.

Satisfied that the point was made, she picked up the items and closed the door. She said finally, "Sixty minutes, tick tock." The metal latch engaged, sealing Debbie in her metal bubble of poison.

Dinner was cold meat and crackers, nothing extravagant. It filled a hole and provided much needed energy. The sky was beginning to darken, the onset of winter assured that night would draw in earlier and dawn would come later in the days. The cold would sap their will and slow them down. If it was part of God's plan to make survival as difficult as possible, then he had made a good job of it, Gloria though to herself.

"I should go and check on her," Peter said, hoping a meal would entice her from the vehicle and into the group.

"I will go, pass me the food," Gloria offered and could see the look of relief on Peter's face. Taking the gun which drew a couple of quizzical looks, she made her way to the vehicle, fully expecting for Debbie to be sat on a pile of damaged items and discarded food, or absent altogether, running away from the group in her twisted mental state. Gloria was not going to shoot the girl; it would be far too noisy and messy in their transport. Standing back in case Debbie made to leap from the van and tackle the gun from her, Gloria reached out and in a quick, fluid motion, opened the door and took aim. The back of the vehicle was immaculate, all of the scattered goods had been put away and the cases and bags stacked neatly. Debbie was perched on one, her expression still angry and hateful but it was as nothing to Gloria who simply put the food down and closed the doors once again.

"Did she say anything?" Peter inquired when she returned to their boat.

"No, I am afraid not. She is still sulking at the moment. A drop in temperature will straighten her out," Gloria informed him with a comforting smile.

"We have laid out the blankets as best we can, we will be sharing body heat tonight. Sorry, everyone," Kurt stated with embarrassment. He had such a romantic notion in his mind of the soldiers greeting them, taking them in and training them up so they could fight back for humanity. The cold indifference to their plight was haunting him and he was regretting not staying put on the estate, foraging for food where possible. It wasn't a great existence but it would be better than what they now faced.

"That's ok, you have got us this far. You will get us to safety," Sarah encouraged and the group spoke their agreement.

"But I don't know how we are going to make it to the hospital," Kurt told them, feeling lost. "There are so many of those things in our way."

"Don't worry, we will stick to the back roads and take the fields on foot if necessary. You kept me safe like that remember?" John said, recalling the advice Kurt had conveyed. "The hospital is to the north of the city and may still be secure if the dead remain in the most heavily populated areas." John meant where there was the most human food.

"Don't forget we can also take the old smuggler tunnels," Sam added and they all looked at him. Preparing for another lesson he sat down on the floor and wrapped a duvet around himself, which prompted the rest of the group to do the same. It was like a child's sleepover but without the popcorn and movies, just the faint cries of the walking abominations carrying on the chill wind.

"During the eighteen hundreds, smugglers used to bring spirits and other contraband through all of the local ports: Pagham, Selsey and Hayling Island. They would set up a torch in a boat and float it to the beach and when the local police would investigate, the illegal stuff would be unloaded elsewhere. The old pubs in Chichester were notorious for having hidden tunnels that spread out like a spider web to other establishments, meaning they could move the goods without being seen. A lot of them still exist and people have been searching for them because of the reported valuables hidden in the darkness," Sam explained with excitement. He had always loved the thoughts of pirates and their treasure, he had hoped to find the tunnels himself when he grew up and find some gold bullion or jewels. Reality asserted itself once and he stopped smiling, his dreams and ambitions were gone. Water and food were far more valuable than some gaudy trinkets of old.

"Sam, can you remember the names of some of the pubs? Are any of them near the western side of Chichester?" John asked and Sam furrowed his brow in concentration, trying to remember the work sheet he had been given in school.

"Yes! The Beachwood Pub is the closest. It was supposed to be the end of the line before they would load onto horse and cart to distribute to the rest of the country." Sam clapped his hands together.

"What about to the north?" John continued.

"Umm... sorry, I can't remember, Grandad. There must be some though," Sam offered hopefully.

There were several older pubs on the road to Lavant, all with age blackened timbers and thatched roofs, John thought to himself. One of these, the Owl's Nest, was situated on Spitalfield Road, only two minutes walk from the hospital. It was a long shot, but if they could find a route to it underground, they could make it to the soldiers who had set up at the medical facility.

"Do we use the torches tonight, or one of the lanterns?" Sam asked naively.

"We don't use anything, mate, it's a waste of our light," Kurt told him and hugged his son who looked scared at the thought of spending the night in both freezing cold and pitch black darkness. "Don't worry, buddy." Kurt smiled in the fading twilight.

"Look." Paige pointed to the sky. The clouds were breaking and the crescent moon was glowing coldly, it would give them some small comfort in the coming hours.

The family hunkered down and as the temperature dropped, their initial reluctance to move closer to one another disappeared. Intimacy issues had to be put aside for the greater good, old phobias and insecurities were falling away and they quickly appreciated the warmth and proximity of living beings. Gloria was a light sleeper at the best of times and as they fell asleep one by one, she allowed herself to drift with them. The sound of footsteps on wood roused her from her slumber and she raised the gun, ready to fire, but it was only Debbie. The moon gave her cold features an even more spectral quality and Gloria shivered, seeing no love or emotion in the eyes that regarded her.

"Can I sleep here?" Debbie asked without apology.

"Ok." Gloria was too tired to argue or refuse. Perhaps the girl would come around in time. Debbie laid down and covered herself with more huffing and puffing than was necessary for the task. Within five minutes she was snoring softly. Gloria unloaded the shotgun, placed the shells in her pocket and closed her eyes. Sleep took her and she was reunited with Albert, but it wasn't a happy dream. He was one of the shambling corpses, but was able to talk, accusing Gloria of betrayal and infidelity which caused her to shift and whimper in the boat, until John placed a protective arm around her. Snuggling closer, the dream faded and sleep took hold, taking her to a safer place.

CHAPTER FOUR

"What the fuck did you do?" Kurt shouted at Debbie, grabbing her and pulling her from the boat.

"Huh, what?" she was ripped from her sleep and looked at the group who stood there accusingly. Confusion took hold as Kurt pulled her unceremoniously down the jetty, the rest followed silently.

"Get your fucking hands off me!" she yelled, finally waking up and pulling free of Kurt's grip. Gloria had the gun aimed directly at her and this just increased her bafflement. She hated the feeling of being the centre of such hostility, preferring to be the one ridiculing and bullying those around her.

"You have killed us, you fucking bitch, but you can be damned sure you will die first," Kurt made to throw a punch at the evil woman and she cowered away.

"Wait, what are you talking about?" she cried out, sobbing into her hands.

"Slashing the tyres," Peter said, joining in with the inquisition, face cold and expressionless.

"What?" Debbie blustered, looking at the vehicles which were lower to the ground than they had been, each tyre was flat and a large gash had been torn in the rubber side walls. "Wait, I didn't do this!" she pleaded.

"Then who did? Who else could possibly be lurking around wanting to hurt us?" John questioned and they all waited for an answer.

"I promise it wasn't me. Why would I risk hurting you when it would mean I would die too?" Debbie argued, tears running freely down her cheeks.

"Your tantrums yesterday could have got us killed, why wouldn't you slash them in one of your rages?" Peter asked and she rose to hit him, the mask of fear replaced by the mask of hatred they were all too used to. Braiden blocked her and threw her back to the hard dock and Peter just looked on, pity on his face.

"How could you let him do that to me?" she demanded, totally ignoring the fact that she would have struck her fiancé if she had been able, her mind was twisted and warped beyond redemption.

"So if not you, then who?" Gloria asked, surveying the surroundings, feeling eyes everywhere but seeing nothing.

"I don't know, but it wasn't me, please don't kill me." She shied away again, adopting a pose to solicit pity, but the group was too shocked and afraid to play her pathetic games. They had no transportation and seven miles to cover of hostile territory. It was a near impossible task. The thought even occurred to Kurt to travel back to the barracks and have the army make a quick, clean end of it.

"We can try and see how far we get on the flats?" Sarah suggested, "And then swap to another car we find on the way."

"It's our only chance. We can't reach the cars by the stilt houses even if we wanted to," John agreed.

They left Debbie on the wooden dock, no one going to her aid to help her stand. She cursed them under her breath and stood up, waiting while the rest of the group collected their belongings and loaded them into the crippled vehicle.

"We have to take it slow, preserve the rubber for as long as possible, keep your eyes open for a suitable replacement," John told them as they started the Rover and van. Kurt nodded in understanding.

They drove out of the marina, past the raised homes and the clubhouse that was surrounded by the zombies. One final glance at the possible hiding place and they were gone, turning awkwardly onto the main Thorney Road. The rumbling of the flattened rubber was a constant companion as they cruised at ten miles an hour back towards Emsworth with heavy hearts. No one spoke while they all scoured the driveways and side roads for a large enough means of transportation. None were suitable; they would have to leave far too many provisions behind.

45

"Dad, look!" Sam said and pointed at the cars they were looking at, all of them had flat tyres, slash marks were visible in the morning light.

"What the hell is going on?" Kurt asked himself. The sudden braking of the Land Rover caught his attention and he stopped before climbing out. John was stood in the road, looking at the junction they would need to drive through, yet it was clear this wasn't going to be possible. Since the previous day, a barricade of cars had been set up, two deep and blocking the whole exit. Several dead were trying to get through to the group, only the metal vehicle bodies were stopping them getting past. Fury surged through Kurt and he made to run and destroy them, to destroy anything that would lessen the throbbing hatred he felt in his mind and heart. John caught him by the arm, recognising the look.

"Together, calmly, ok?" John said quietly, talking out the crowbar and waiting a few seconds while the fire dimmed in Kurt's eyes a little.

They climbed over the first row of cars as the zombies were stretching out in desperation to reach their breakfast. Swift blows shattered the skulls and the cadavers lay fully dead, spreading pools of green ichor running from the cars shiny paintwork onto the black tarmac.

"Looks like we go on foot," Kurt said and ducked instinctively as a large rock seemed to loom out of nowhere and go arcing over his head, smashing through a windscreen by his side. Before they had time to get a bead on the location of the thrower, the mad wailing of the car alarm sounded, ripping through the silent morning.

"Who the hell threw that?" John called over the din.

"Fuck knows; I think it came from over there. Shit!" Kurt pointed, looking around and seeing the walking corpses as they streamed from gardens, roads and pavements towards them.

"Grab the bug out bags, leave the rest!" John shouted at the rest of the survivors who were looking around in terror, momentarily scared stiff, which Kurt always thought was an exaggeration. Sprinting back, he shouted again and they finally came round, shouldering the rucksacks he proffered from the rear doors.

"What about the suitcases?" Braiden shouted, croaky voice breaking.

"Too heavy, no time!" Kurt answered bitterly, they were leaving so much behind but life was paramount. Honey was barking and howling in tune with the alarm and the only reason they hadn't been overrun was the temporary roadblock. Dozens were banging on the vehicle bodywork, with even more joining them by the second.

"Ok, this way!" John shouted to be heard and they moved off between two houses. John kicked the gate open, crowbar raised in case of attack although the way was clear. They followed his lead and Kurt pulled up the rear, closing the gate and standing two heavy plant pots in front of it to buy them some time.

The garden was surrounded by brick walls six feet high, the trees were shedding their leaves in beautiful yellows, oranges, and browns, ready for the coming winter. A barbecue was exposed and set up near a set of garden furniture, food was rotting on the cold grill and glasses of fresh poured wine had long been washed clean by falling rain. A party had been interrupted and the group looked around, expecting to see the hosts emerge, ready to eat a fresher meal. The sound of banging on the gate brought them out of their morbid thoughts and they looked around for the best means of escape. Kurt rushed to the back wall and jumped, looked over and saw open fields beyond which would lead to the next village.

"Come on, we need to get over." Kurt pulled himself and sat with one leg either side of the wall, assisting the others as they clambered over before landing on the muddy ground of the field. John boosted Gloria and Kurt held her as the two boys lowered her gently.

"Thank you, gentlemen," she said and Kurt hopped down after her.

"Let's move. That noise may work in our favour, clearing some of the roads we will need to take," John explained and they set off at a brisk pace, stepping carefully over the recently turned soil which was ready for the next crop to be planted.

Honey was enjoying every minute, the local bird fowl were feasting on the worms and assorted insects that were just below the surface. She would rush over, chasing them away, before coming back to them panting and tail wagging.

"Stupid dog," Debbie muttered.

"Just because your life is empty, don't take it out on her," Braiden argued back, sick of the woman and hoping she would fall prey to the stumbling multitude. Peter sniggered and stroked their canine companion, Kurt's promise giving him some much needed confidence, however when he saw the look Debbie gave him the bravery evaporated.

"Don't even think about it," Gloria warned which stilled the volatile creature.

They reached the demarcation of the next field and dropped low, watching the events unfolding.

"Would you look at that?" Sarah whispered in awe.

The hedgerow shielded them from view and they stared through the gaps. A crowd of zombies, numbering fifty or more were walking back and forth over a compressed patch of earth. The seagulls and other species of birds were herding them, taking off in a blur of feathered wings before settling to the ground again.

"Why are they doing that?" Paige questioned. No one was sure until Peter spoke up in explanation.

"Look, they are feeding." He pointed at the rapidly pecking heads as they cleared the mud, before watching the approach of the festering dead and then taking flight, circling over their heads and landing once more in the space they vacated.

"It's the maggots," Debbie said, trying to still her churning stomach, the nausea giving the group temporary respite from her bitchiness.

"You're right; they are using the dead as a food source," Kurt said with respect. It amazed him how other creatures were making the best of the situation and he felt jealousy of their wings, the way they could escape and hide in the heights. It was completely irrational but he couldn't shake it.

"There is a break in the hedge over here," John informed them after having a quick scout. "When they head south, we make a run for it, keeping close to the hedgerow. Hopefully their attention will be on the flying food."

Some birds left, full and content, ready to feed their young. They were replaced by more and the opportunity was there, the ghouls stumbled slowly towards the wildfowl.

"Go, go, go!" John encouraged and they ran as one, much like the birds they had been observing.

They kept low as suggested and only one or two of the dead saw them and gave chase; however they were too far away to be a threat.

Ducking into the small patch of woodland that separated the main road into Southbourne, they took great care as the tree trunks provided perfect cover for hiding assailants. They came across two that were reaching up and trying to get at a cat that had climbed a tree, it prowled to and fro, spitting and hissing at the dead. Kurt approached carefully and slammed the steel head of his hammer through the brains, killing them and allowing Honey to do what dogs have done since the dawn of time; chase poor cats. The frightened feline blazed down from its perch of safety in the tree and ran off in a ball of fur. Honey only ran a few feet in pursuit before returning obediently to Kurt's side. She somehow knew that the old games were no longer played and looked up at him, waiting for their next move.

"Let's get closer to the road and see what is going on," Kurt said. The group navigated the small forest and stood under cover of the trees, shaded from view of the groups of zombies who were shuffling towards the faint siren song of the alarm. The alarm would have normally fallen silent but the dead must be hitting it, searching for sustenance and triggering it in a cycle that would cease with the dying battery. Watching patiently, the last of the corpses were gone from sight and the street was mostly clear. Those remaining had seen the cat go running past into a small cottage and pounded on the door.

"We go slowly. Stick to the middle of the road, away from the gardens. Try every car that we see," Kurt instructed.

The attempted murder had worked in their favour, clearing the way for them to make it to the other side of the village. Kurt knew for a fact that if the zombies had not been drawn away they would have faced hundreds instead of a handful. They couldn't possibly have fought them all and lived. Gloria kept a wary eye on their rear, watching for any movement or sign, either human or once human.

"Dad, what about that one?" Sam had spotted a Mitsubishi L200, a large pickup truck with rear seats and a flatbed to the rear. "It will carry us all. I can jump in the back with Braiden and the bags," Sam suggested, thinking how cool it would be to sit there, the breeze running through his hair as the scenery passed in a blur.

"Go take a look," Kurt told him and the boys ran off as the rest of the group kept them covered after seeing the trails of blood that led from the vehicle. Sam returned with a set of keys, smiling broadly and jangling them at the group. He frowned when he saw the look on their faces, why were they not happy? Then he caught sight of the keychain and the picture that hung from it, a smiling family; mother, father, and two beautiful blonde girls seated before a fake background in a professional photography studio.

"Oh, sorry," Sam said, lowering them and feeling rotten.

"Don't be, mate, it's how things are now," John answered.

Kurt gave him a quick hug before taking the keys and stepping around the congealed mess. There must have been a hell of a spillage for it to not have washed away in the weather they had been experiencing. They unclipped the rear shelf that acted as a protective cover for the flatbed and placed it to the ground, trying to keep quiet. They climbed in, thoughts of the family that had been dragged from the metal tomb fresh in their minds. Sam, Braiden, and Honey jumped into the back and covered themselves with a couple of the blankets they had taken before fleeing.

"What route shall we take, the motorway or back roads?" Kurt asked, knowing that neither would be an easy option.

"Head to the overpass, we can see what it looks like before committing to one or the other," Peter suggested.

"Good idea, buckle up." Kurt started the engine and drove slowly; slaloming between cars and mounting the pavement where he needed to pass a crash scene or multiple vehicles.

The abundance of mindless flesh eaters increased as they got further from the alarm, they daren't stop or they would be quickly surrounded and the fate of the key chain family played through Kurt's mind again. He slowed while passing the local One-Stop grocery store, though they had become the sole focus of far too many zombies to do a quick stop. Honey was leaning out and Kurt watched in the side mirror as her tongue lolled and she squinted from the air that blew in her eyes.

"I would love a gin and tonic," commented Gloria as the shop passed and they all chuckled, even Debbie, but as soon as she saw them looking the expression vanished.

"Here we are," Kurt told them and slowed to a stop. The bridge was clear and the nearest zombie was minutes away, so they climbed out to witness the true scale of the sight that met them.

The motorway lanes were totally blocked; there were hundreds of vehicles as far as the eye could see in both directions. Many more thousands of monsters were milling among the cars, wandering aimlessly without a source of food to pursue. It was an awful thing to behold. The terror that must have gripped the people as the roads ground to a halt, seeing that neither side would be able to escape the coming death, then watching from the mirrors as a tsunami of rotting flesh washed away all life in its path, adding to the overall power of the torrent. Below there came the mass groans of another group who had gathered in the shelter of the overpass, a strange behavioural anomaly for creatures without fear.

"I guess it's the back roads then," John said, climbing into the pickup.

No one spoke any more, there was nothing that could be said that would allow the horror to be unseen. They just put it to the back of their minds to process later, when they were alone and all was dark and quiet. They drove in silence, heading through Ashling Village, a beautiful hamlet of century's old cottages, farmhouses, stables, and water mills that ran along the river, once grinding wheat for the local bakers. The small pond that Kurt had taken Sam to feed ducks when he was younger was now awash with zombies. They must have fallen in trying to reach the nests that were built in the middle of the water, the ducks hadn't waited around but flew away to safer places. The small wall that surrounded it was now a barrier to the damned, meaning they walked around, waist deep in quickly festering water. He was so fixated on the sight that he nearly missed the cars in the road. Slamming the brakes on, the truck skidded and came to rest with the front end perilously close to the water's edge and the eager dead who would welcome them.

"Sorry, that was stupid," Kurt apologised and he looked back to see Honey pick herself up and shake off, the sudden stop had propelled her into Sam and Braiden. Sam was holding his face, blood running down and dripping from his chin. Kurt's heart leaped in fear, he had hurt his own son.

"Sam, are you ok? I'm so sorry, mate." Kurt ran to him and hugged him over the side of the pickup.

"I'b ok, Dad, it's just by dose," Sam said, the bruised nose causing him to speak awkwardly. Honey was whining, upset at the distress of the young boy and trying to paw at him.

"I'm really sorry," Kurt repeated, nearly crying. Sam tried to smile to reassure his dad, yet his bloodied teeth and crimson chest from the broken blood vessels only served to make him feel worse. Honey licked them both, trying the same approach.

The family had climbed out and the dead in the pond were splashing around like excited children in a swimming pool. The small local cemetery had given up its deceased, the varying state of decay was evidence of recent burial as well as those long in slumber. Some had rotted down to barely skeletons, loose tatters of flesh and skin remaining but little else. Others were from the local population, fresher, but missing limbs and flesh from the grisly end they met at the bony hands of the previous generations.

"What is the time?" Paige asked.

"Three twenty," Peter said, looking at his watch.

"Thanks Pete." She smiled at him warmly. "Do you think we should find somewhere safe for the night?"

"This is as good a place as any, low population and most of those are having a dip." Kurt indicated over his shoulder.

"Let's find a place set back from this road, we can set out fresh in the morning and try to move those cars. I don't relish being on foot after dark," John advised and they loaded up the bags, looking down driveways for a suitable abode.

CHAPTER FIVE

They settled on Whyke Farm, which was a farm in name only. The increase of automation and technology had necessitated far fewer farmsteads in each area. The old building had been made into a family home long ago and sold for a premium price; people loved the nostalgia and architecture of the age. Low ceilings held aloft by thick, dark timbers, inglenook fireplaces that were once used for cooking and heating, though most now stood empty, replaced by modern electrical appliances. The cobbled driveway was immaculately tended with tidy hedges at each side and seasonal flowers in bloom in the beds at their base, holding on for the final drop in temperature that would herald their demise until the warmth of the spring returned. Gloria scanned the area, Sam helping with a bearing at the ready. Honey sniffed the air and they watched her intently, satisfied when she wagged her tail that the immediate area was safe.

They circled the thatched farmhouse, checking windows for signs of movement and life, or death. All was still within and the lack of cars outside hinted at the owners being gone. Reaching the rear door which was set back in a small alcove, they tried the latch and it was open. People in this type of area were more neighbourly and trusting than those in the larger cities or population centres. The iron banded door creaked on aged hinges and the smell that escaped was musty but not unpleasant, a mixture of wood, smoke, and flowery fragrances.

"Hold back, I will check it out," Kurt said while wielding the hammer and stepping through into the shadowed kitchen area. Honey followed swiftly but showed no fear, she just started sniffing in the corners at the new scents, fascinated at one spot but Kurt could see nothing out of the ordinary there and the dog just regarded him with a look that said, 'well you're not a dog are you?' before sniffing again.

He opened the lounge door and the smell of stale smoke and wood grew, the source was an original Aga solid fuel oven that had been installed in the inglenook fireplace. The inset bread oven was still complete with the iron door, and old hooks were bedded into the cement to hang cooking pots from over the old coals. The floors of the room were hand carved stone laid in small mosaic pieces with soft sofas and armchairs facing the widescreen television. The wooden smell was from the large scuttle of logs and kindling that sat to one side of the Aga, combined with the warped and twisted timbers of the ceiling. Kurt paused, listening intently and Honey did the same, her ears pricking up for any sounds. The silence was total.

"It's safe, come on in," Kurt shouted and he heard the shuffle of many footsteps on the flagstone floor of the kitchen.

"Sam, can you get those candles lit?" John asked as he stepped into the lounge.

"Ahhh," Debbie sighed happily, slumping into the sofa and putting her feet up.

"We have stuff to do before we get comfortable," Gloria informed her.

"I am having a rest if you don't mind," she replied dismissively and looked away.

"Fine, when we have secured the house, you sleep outside with the doors locked," Kurt said with no animosity, he was done with her and would drag her by the hair, kicking and screaming if necessary into the cold night.

"You wouldn't dare!" Debbie hissed but the look in his eyes told her not to push the point.

"We will see I guess." Kurt smiled. "Ok, Dad, take Sam and Braiden and check upstairs. Paige, please shut all the curtains and move the candles away from the windows, we don't want to be a beacon. Gloria, would you mind getting the fire lit? Peter, could you get some pans ready and see if there is anything worthwhile in the pantry to eat? I'd rather save our provisions."

"What about you and Sarah? I suppose you get to sit around doing nothing, just barking orders," Debbie asked, looking for support from the rest of the group and getting none.

"I am going to go and check that old barn out the back. I saw a chopping block and a solid looking axe, maybe they have some good equipment we can use," Kurt explained to them, ignoring Debbie. "Sarah, would you mind checking for water in the taps and tanks?"

"Not at all," she replied, staring at Debbie then hurrying off to the task.

"Go fuck yourselves! You have always been against me. Peter, come on we are leaving," Debbie shouted, picking up one of the bug out bags. Peter walked over and she mistakenly thought he was offering to take the bag for her, she passed it over smiling, but he gave it to Kurt and her face reddened with fury.

"I'm not going anywhere," Peter stated defiantly. It looked like she would explode but she just turned around and walked into the kitchen and out into the afternoon light.

The rest of the family breathed a sigh of relief. It was exhausting trying to accommodate someone like that, always unsure of their mood swings and instability. Kurt looked at John and they each knew what the other was thinking, she had to go.

"Sorry," Peter said quietly, understanding the mood of the group.

"It's ok, don't worry." Paige smiled and took his hand. "She will calm down and be back soon."

"We have plenty of water, the tanks are full," Sarah informed them as she entered the room.

"Kurt, take this with you for protection." Gloria passed the gun, locked and loaded, safety off. "Just point and shoot. Sarah, I found this by the side of the fire," Gloria said as she handed over a wickedly sharp short bladed machete.

"Why would they have this?" Sarah asked, turning it over in her hands and feeling the sharpness.

"It's for splitting kindling wood, but it will split skulls just as well I should think. It's light too, so your arm won't get as tired as it does with that spear," Gloria said.

Sarah put the metal spear down. She would miss the range but it wasn't a viable long term zombie killer. Swishing the small blade through the air a couple of times it felt good, light and powerful. They all got to work. Sarah and Kurt left the house and saw Debbie sulking on a metal bench in the back garden.

"I will talk to her after, woman to woman," Sarah suggested.

"No, she is what she is. We will find somewhere safe and she stays there," Kurt told her and reluctantly she agreed, the new world was dangerous enough without loose cannons to complicate matters. Debbie watched them pass with barely disguised contempt. Kurt was getting sick of it, the gun in his hands was tempting him, one crack and it would be at an end. Reason won out, he wasn't an executioner, he would kill if forced to but this was not the time.

The chopping block had a large axe for log splitting and a smaller hatchet, these too were sharp and well maintained. The linseed oil was still fresh on the polished blades, covered by the small lean to that protected the huge log pile from the elements.

"Those may come in handy." Kurt signalled to the weapons and carried on around the side of the barn, gun raised. Quick footsteps caused Kurt to spin, nearly pulling the trigger until he saw it was just Honey joining them. She found a small patch of grass; bending her hind legs she relieved herself before resuming the search.

The barn was still used for storage; massive bales of hay were stacked twenty feet high reaching the underside of the hayloft. The sweet smell got into their nostrils and made them sneeze, the air was thick with swirling eddies of hay dust. To the right was a small workbench and more tools. Some old farming implements were hung from hooks and they had not been used in many years, scythes, hoes, an old wooden rake, they were tools of a bygone era.

"Look at that." Kurt pointed at a hay fork, thin pointed tines that would be great at piercing brains.

"What about these?" Sarah held up two brand new bill hooks, similar to machetes but with sickled ends and used for lopping vegetation.

"They are deadly, this was a great find, someone must be watching over us," Kurt said and raised his hand to the sky in mock thanks.

A sudden scream brought them running from the barn and they saw Debbie being attacked by two zombies, more were coming through the wide wooden gate which led to the public bridleway for horses. They hesitated a fraction longer than they would have for any other member of the group but quickly shucked off the inaction and ran to her aid. Kurt raised the gun, aimed at the head of a third zombie who was nearly on top of the woman and pulled the trigger. The loud crack of the shot echoed and the head burst apart, flinging the decapitated creature into the path of its friends. Sarah raised the machete and swung it sideways at one of the pair who were on Debbie, taking the top of the head clean off. It toppled sideways and the remaining pulpy brain spilled out like a tipped cup of vile paste. The second zombie was biting at her chest, only the padding of the life jacket saved her life. It sat up triumphantly, mouth full, and Kurt used the second shot, blasting it in the back and lifting it clear of the miserable harpy. It groaned, surprised at why its food was spongy and unfulfilling, then stood and attacked again. The head snapped sideways and Kurt could see the glimmer of the bearing as it punctured the skull, killing it.

"Here!" Sarah passed out the bill hooks to Peter and Braiden who had run outside to investigate the scream. Braiden looked at his sharpened screwdriver, looked at the new blade, the screwdriver once more and slid it into his belt, happier with the chopper.

Kurt passed the gun to Gloria who reloaded, but cautioned her about using any more shells. The noise was deafening and who knew how many more it would bring down on them. They lined up, facing the rows of the dead as they bore down. Fifteen were now in the garden, spread out and hungry for screaming, bloody meat and sinew. Sam shot one but missed the head, tearing the neck instead, causing the head to flop to the side on the remaining cartilage and tendons. Kurt stepped forward, rammed the fork at the head, punched through the skull and destroyed the brain.

"Stay behind me, if I miss any with this, take them out." Kurt used the fork like a spear, jabbing at the horrors and withdrawing instantly, like infantry soldiers of the middle ages. Four dropped, small leaking punctures in eyes and foreheads before it got wedged in a skull and threatened to pull Kurt to the ground. He let it drop and the others got ready to cover him as he retrieved the small hatchet he had put in his belt, his hammer sat on the lounge coffee table where he had put it after taking the gun.

"Where's Debbie?" Peter shouted. Looking around, they couldn't see her.

"She must have run," John said with disgust.

The next wave got within grabbing distance and the survivors were ready. They covered each other, raining down blows and severing heads, shattering skulls, and crushing brains. Some of their fear started to dissipate. They could win against small numbers as long as they were careful. The overriding need to feed made the flesh dripping abominations predictable; they would not flinch or try and avoid the killing blows. The dead were falling, only four remained standing, the rest were laid at the feet of the family.

"Let me try something, make some noise for me," John instructed and the group waved their arms and blew raspberries while he circled, taking advantage of the distraction. None turned to follow him; they were intent on the raucous sight in front of them. One by one he caved their skulls with his crowbar, swatting them like flies. The final cadaver was a small toddler, no more than four years old when she was turned. One of her thin arms had been gnawed clean like a chicken wing; the small amount of meat would have amounted to nothing. John was still, unable to raise his arm to kill the creature as it made small steps towards the group. They had seen zombie children before, though none quite so young. It was heart-breaking and they quietly mourned as the girl fumbled at the piled corpses, unable to get over the obstacle.

"Just do it already," Debbie mocked, stepping forward and slamming the claw hammer into the small skull. The body dropped, joining the heap of dead flesh and Debbie threw the hammer at Kurt's feet before smiling and walking back into the house.

"Poor baby," Paige gasped, kneeling and stroking the filthy, bloodied hair of the child creature.

"Give me the gun." Kurt held his hands out to Gloria who stepped back a pace.

"Kurt, no! It had to be done, you know that." John stopped him. He hated the loathsome cow as much as the rest, but she was right to destroy the girl. She didn't need to enjoy it with such relish though.

"Let's just get inside. Peter, you keep that whore away from me, if I see her face I will kill her," Kurt said and it was no idle threat, at this point in time he would live with it.

"Ok, I'll take care of it." Peter rushed off into the cottage, seeking his fiancée.

***

The Aga was roaring when they entered, Debbie and Peter were nowhere in sight. They could be heard moving around on the upper floor, shuffling and stomping. Warmth enveloped them, and they all sat down, sinking into the soft cushions of the sofas and chairs. Honey was content to curl up on the rug at the foot of the expensive cooker, blissfully ignorant of the small burned patches she laid upon. If any of the logs popped in the fire she would be singed too. No one felt like eating but Gloria prepared a meal anyway. The sustenance would fuel them for the next day's hike towards the Beachwood Pub which would, hopefully, give them access close to the hospital grounds. Peter came down the stairs and joined them in the cosy lounge, still apologising for the actions of his companion.

"She will stay upstairs, she isn't happy about it though," Peter explained and Kurt stood up.

"I don't give a fuck if she is unhappy, she can leave anytime she wants!" Kurt shouted and banged on the ceiling. An answering stamp on the floor from above nearly set Kurt running up the stairs. Sarah stopped him, making him sit down to eat the steaming vegetables that Gloria had cooked.

"She has to go, I'm sorry, Peter," Kurt continued, speaking through boiled broccoli. "I am sorry that I ever took you away from the safety of your home the other day."

"I'm not, she was intolerable. We were nearly out of food and she wanted me to go and get some more while she stayed put," Peter explained. If truth be told he was close to making a run for it anyway, no

59

matter the outcome. Gloria handed him the dinner plate and he tucked in with relish, but the mood soured when the banging resumed from upstairs.

"Peter, get up here!" came Debbie's yell and he put his plate down.

"You take her food, then come straight back down. If she makes any more noise I will throw her from the upstairs window," Kurt ordered.

They listened as Peter crossed the floor above, timbers creaking and groaning. Voices started to be raised and they heard the plate smash as it was thrown against a wall. Kurt ground his teeth, wanting her gone. Only Sarah's calming touch prevented him rushing upstairs and making good on his threat. The floor protested again and Peter came back down, bits of food on his clothing and face. Paige rushed over and started to clean him, picking the larger pieces off and giving them to Honey who was happy for the extra treats. Peter welled up and started sobbing, falling into the space on the sofa where he had been sitting.

"I tried, I really tried with her," he said through the tears and Paige held him close.

"We know you did, of course you did," she crooned.

The awkwardness of public emotion was gone, they all accepted the psychological fragility of each other and how this wouldn't be the last time they broke down. One by one they gave Peter a hug or supportive pat on the shoulder.

"Sorry about that, what a pussy I am," Peter said when he had finally calmed down.

"Not at all, mate, this world is fucked up. I'd be more worried if you didn't cry," Kurt commiserated.

"What is the plan for tomorrow?" John asked.

"We try and cover the last three miles, on foot if necessary, over the fields like you did," Kurt laid it out. "The Winspit Stone Mine is close, that's a shortcut that will save us half a mile."

"Winspit Stone Mine?" Braiden asked.

"It's where they mine the stone to repair the local churches and castles. It's been there for hundreds of years," Kurt explained.

"Won't that be a bit dangerous?" Paige asked, but quickly dismissed the question with a wave of her hand. Everywhere was dangerous.

"We can vote on it, but I think the time we save will make up for it. Then we make a beeline straight between Chichester Road and the Motorway, steering clear of the homes if possible," Kurt offered. "A show of hands for the mine?"

They looked at each other, no one had the faintest idea what was the best course of action so the shortest journey won the day, hands shot in the air.

"Ok, we go through the mine." Kurt nodded.

"Shall we try the radio?" Gloria suggested.

"Good grief, I had nearly forgotten we had that," John said incredulously, rummaging through the bags until he found it. "Here it is." He wound the charging lever for a couple of minutes and re-tuned it to the previous channel as it had been knocked around in the bag. The familiar female voice came through, the signal still poor but it was comforting, like hearing from an old friend.

"To anyone that is still out there, keep holding on, keep fighting the good fight. Our power seems secure, we have had a couple of interruptions but we are still on the air. It can only mean that the Government, in however small a capacity, is still in their bunker and keeping the juice flowing. We have yet to make contact with them, I'm afraid. The concentration of the dead is diminishing. More leave the area every day which we can only assume is in search of new food sources." She paused and they could just imagine the presenter giving an involuntary shudder.

"I pray that wherever you are that you are safe and secure, winter is coming and all Met Office advice before the end hinted at a harsh one. The gulf streams were pulling a cold front from the Arctic that would ensure a lower temperature range than normal."

"Well isn't that bloody marvellous?" Sarah said, shaking her head. "As if we need another reason to suffer."

"We shall be ok, as long as we make it to somewhere secure before it drops below zero," Kurt answered and gave her leg a gentle rub.

"And if we don't find somewhere?" Peter asked, meaning no disrespect. He wanted to have an idea of what lay ahead.

"We will," Kurt stated, certain of their goal.

"We had a brief transmission from the 3rd Division of the British Army, they have formed a safe zone on the Porton Down facility and remnants of the Army and Air Force have been rendezvousing to defend the site and their research, which is still ongoing. They have asked that for the time being, survivors stay away as they are under sustained heavy assault from the surrounding cities and towns. Numbering in the thousands, the zombies have been relentless but have not yet breached the wall."

"That's what you get when you mess with the army!" Sam yelled with excitement, the images of battle and victory playing over in his mind.

"You can always count on our boys and girls in a fight," John said with pride, "Though not to help people it seems."

"They must have had their reasons, you could see they weren't all happy about it," Gloria added and John just shook his head, unable to comprehend the decision to send them away.

"I'm hungry!" came whining down the stairs, souring the mood instantly.

"You had your dinner, eat it off the floor," Kurt replied and waited for the sarcastic reply.

"Prick," Debbie muttered quietly from the stairway, but loud enough that Kurt would hear. She didn't push the issue further, retreating into the bedroom and slamming the door like a petulant child.

"We have also been informed that the Daresford Institute is in close contact with Porton Down, the subterranean structure ensuring their safety for the time being. Virologists and biologists from the PD site have been working on isolating the source of the brain aberration from test subjects, with no success thus far. They are working closely with the DI who have almost decoded the pulse of energy and this, they hope, will give some clue as to the nature of the outbreak. All they will theorise is that it has possibly triggered some dormant region in the brains of the deceased; synapses have been observed firing despite no signs of life. How this anomaly is then transmitted, they simply do not have an explanation as yet. We will bring you updates as soon as we receive them,"

Braiden tapped his head, wondering what part of his brain could cause rotting immortality.

"I am totally baffled, what the hell is a synapse?" John asked.

"They connect nerve cells together in the brain and can cause a chemical reaction," Sam answered and they looked at him, dumbstruck. "Biology class," he offered, blushing.

"You are such a clever boy," Paige complimented him and his cheeks darkened further.

"Someone has a crush," whispered Kurt to Sarah and she smiled.

"We need to discuss what happened earlier, who the hell is risking their life to kill us?" John posed to the group.

"The logical guess would be Archie, Phil, and Eddie, but we... took care of that problem," Kurt responded, his mood darkening with thoughts of fire and murder, and more to come he feared.

"Debbie?" Braiden questioned.

"She didn't have time to sneak off and move those cars, and the stone came from the other direction," Gloria replied.

"So we are back to square one, maybe we just ran into another group of assholes?" Paige said and it was possibly true, though it would be terrible luck and they would need to be on their guard constantly.

"What we do know is that they moved around freely between the dead, got to our vehicles and then ensured we were trapped on that road. If we see anyone suspicious, we take no chances," Kurt vowed.

"Do you mean kill them?" Peter looked worried, but he would do what was necessary if the situation called for it.

"If we have to, yes. I would like to find out more before we do that, if we can take them alive that would be good," Kurt said, hoping that he would get the chance to question them personally. They had threatened the lives of his loved ones and they would pay in blood. He tried to reconcile the change in himself, the willingness to commit heinous acts and bloodshed. He had always tried to avoid conflict in life, both physical and emotional. Whenever he had been witness to an argument or physical altercation, his mouth would go dry and his stomach would cramp with anxiety. Weeks spent in the zombie apocalypse had caused a rapid metamorphosis and he was not sure he would like what he was becoming.

"Are we going to sleep upstairs?" Gloria asked, changing the subject and interrupting his reflections.

"No, this house is too vulnerable, I want us together," Kurt replied, ignoring their black sheep who was probably settling into a comfortable bed as they spoke.

They blew out the candles, relying on the slight glow from the damped down fire in the Aga cooker. It would not penetrate the thick curtains and the home would appear abandoned to anyone passing who meant them harm. The sofas were cosy and sleep came quickly after nightfall. Kurt was pleased to see Paige lay her head on Peter's shoulder before closing her eyes, he responded by stroking the hair from her face and over her ear. They were a much better match, but the complications it would cause with Debbie would have to be dealt with in due course. He waited for them all to drift into their dreams, carefully lifted Sarah's head from his lap and laid her in the seat he vacated. He stalked from window to window, looking out into the night, clenching and unclenching his fist around the handle of the new machete. He wanted the mysterious attackers badly.

CHAPTER SIX

"How clear is it?" John asked the family who were all checking for threats in the grounds of the farmhouse. The pile of zombies was the only thing that they could see and they no longer posed any danger.

"I think we are good, let's go. We take the bridleway onto Kinsen Road, and then go round the lake that was carved out to provide water for the steam pumps at the mine," Kurt instructed and they left the quaint farmhouse in single file, several more blankets and duvets wrapped and bound to their backpacks. They would need to try and find some sleeping bags soon, the thick covers were too bulky to carry for extended periods of time, but for now they would aid in keeping warm.

The small child zombie was still laid on the top of the pile, like a bloody decoration on a cake from the deepest corner of hell. They each paid their respects, some with a small nod, only Debbie was whistling cheerfully.

"Shut your mouth, we don't want to draw attention to ourselves," Kurt growled and she glared in her accustomed manner.

Honey ran on, trying to pick up a fresh scent.

"Do you think she is scouting for us?" Sam asked Kurt.

"I don't know, mate, she may just have picked up a fox or rabbit smell," Kurt replied. It would be a boon if she could act as an early warning system.

The short journey to the lake was uneventful; no milling zombies were in the area. The road was clear of cars at the end of the horse track and they looked in all directions, making sure they weren't being followed by anything, or more importantly, anyone. They trekked the short distance down the country road, passing fields and small stables in which horses were once kept. The stable doors were open but there was a lack of blood, a couple of the walking dead were laid on the concrete ground.

"Look at that!" Peter said, pointing. The zombies had been knocked down and then trampled, curved hoof marks imprinted their rotten flesh and their mashed skulls leaked clotted gore.

"They fought back, what magnificent creatures." Kurt was filled with awe. He could see the shattered locks on the timber door frames. The horses must have kicked their way out and then slain the source of their terror.

"And here's where they got out," Sarah said, a small patch of fence had been broken down and the splintered timber had a clump of horse hair swaying in the wind.

"I love horses. I used to have two when I was a little girl," Paige said happily, she was overjoyed to see that they were free, hopefully roaming the countryside and staying a safe distance from any zombies.

"I once ate horse in France," Debbie added callously.

"I love horses too. I've always wanted to own one," Peter started walking by Paige's side.

"Since when you idiot? You have never mentioned it to me," Debbie carried on trying to provoke an argument.

"I can show you how to ride one day, if you want," Paige offered Peter, blanking her.

"Over my dead body. Peter, get away from her," Debbie hissed, furious at the snub.

"No, I want to talk to her. The reason I never mentioned wanting a horse is because everything was always about you, what you wanted, when you wanted it, I barely even registered. I'm not having it anymore," Peter answered defiantly.

Debbie shrieked and launched herself at Peter, pulling his hair and trying to kick him. Peter tried to push her away and Kurt rushed back to help.

"You leave him alone!" Paige screamed and Kurt grimaced, looking around for what the ruckus would bring down on them.

"Debbie, get off me, you've gone crazy!" Peter shouted through the assault. Paige grabbed Debbie's black hair and punched her in the face, catching her in the eye. She fell to the ground, clutching her rapidly swelling eye socket.

"You fucking bitch, you hit me," Debbie ranted through the tears, she had never been subject to her own harsh treatment.

"You're gone," Kurt snarled at Debbie, before picking up her backpack. "Leave her there."

"You can't do that, you bastard!" she sobbed.

The group moved away, no longer feeling any empathy or pity for the awful creature as she cursed and wailed on the cold road. They reached the entrance for the lake, a high wooden arch made from local lumber and carved by expert carpenters to feature birds and other woodland animals. It was a picture of serenity, the surface of the lake was still, granting a beautiful mirror of the sun pierced clouds, surrounding trees, and rolling hills. They could almost believe they had imagined the whole apocalypse; majestic swans swam on the surface, craning their necks at the newcomers. Where once they would have approached, seeking a meal of bread or grain, now they paddled away. They had learned a new fear and respect for the dangers of these upright walking, food throwing oddities.

"Over there, see that wire fence?" Kurt indicated the boundary of the mine, "That's where we get in. Otherwise we need to walk around to the main entrance which is another half mile."

The swans watched the group warily, circling and hissing from the safety of the lake. It was only a walk of minutes; the lake was not natural and only contained enough water to fuel the long dismantled steam pumps and machinery. The rusted pipes still projected from the bank of the lake near the fence, but had long ago ceased to draw water. It had become a dog walking site and a hugely popular picnic area. During the summer months it was usually packed with families frolicking at the water's edge.

"That's the old pump house. I have taken a tour of it when Ken worked here." Kurt crouched and pointed to the brick building just inside the fence line. "It's now the main offices for the operation. When we are over the fence, we hug the wall and see what we see."

He pulled at the bottom of the chain link; it was already deformed from the antics of youngsters. They would break in to explore the shafts and cave systems for dares, or to take their young ladies into the darkness for more carnal desires. Kurt smiled to himself; he had used this very spot many years ago before he met Sarah. They climbed under and ran to the wall; the building was about sixty feet long with high set windows and one rear door. It blocked the view of the main site completely, they would need to be cautious to see what threats existed. Honey was still but silent, waiting for them to move. The metallic rustle of the fence caused them to look round and Debbie was struggling to shuffle underneath, the chains catching in the back of her clothing.

"Un-fucking-believable!" Kurt groaned and hurried over as her desperate struggles to free herself caused more noise than was safe. He clutched her jumper and ripped the chain free, leaving large gaping holes in it. She stood up and faced him, surly but no longer glaring, the closed right eye had been a painful lesson in humility. Peter would not meet her gaze; he had made his decision to move on.

"Stay behind me," Kurt directed and they moved to the corner.

He looked out across the crushed gravel covered trucking area where the stone blocks were loaded before making its way to the required structure. The churches, cathedrals, and southern English castles had been supplied by this mine for nearly a thousand years. The loading area was the size of a football field, giving good access to the roads that spread out like arteries from the heart of the operation. The mine was originally known as Skull Rock, so named because of the projecting stone that looked like the top of a human cranium, smooth and white, surrounded by the lush emerald colouring of foliage and trees.

Land had been cleared to almost a square kilometre and the excavations had grown, the layered stone veins cut and loaded onto waiting boats for delivery by the River Lavant to Chichester Cathedral and Arundel Castle. The rock faces rose into the sky, deep caverns had been cut into the base bed and the dark openings looked like the missing teeth of the buried skull. The closest excavations were the originals, carried out by masons who had used simple tools and sweat to create square blocks that formed the walls of the most formidable fortifications known to man. The hard cap, a solid layer of rock, was held aloft by pillars of stone that had been left in strategic places, supporting the massive weight above. Kurt held out hope that the efforts of those ancient ancestors would provide a sanctuary, if they could reach the soldiers at the hospital and convince them of the safety of the high walls and towering crenulations that Arundel Castle would give.

"What do you see?" John asked from behind Kurt.

"There are only a few of the creatures. If we can make it to that road." Kurt pointed and John leaned around to see. "We will end up near the bridge that crosses the river. Then it's a quick run to the Beachwood Pub through Winspit Woods."

"Good, let's take care of those first," John replied.

They left the cover of the brick office building and rushed as quietly as possible towards the dead. The loose stone was crunching with each step and the zombies turned as one, sensing fresh meat. Cleavers cut the air and the noises were akin to a butcher's chopping block, severed muscle and splintered bone spreading over the ground. The contrast between the off white gravel and the putrid, dark blood was stark, a mad artist's canvas of spattered corpse paint.

"Right, we head down that pathway, it leads us around the spiral road that follows the deeper mines, one of the branches from it takes us to the emergency entrance, in case there was ever a collapse and this way was blocked," Kurt advised and they walked on, carefully stepping over the drenched ground.

"Come on, Honey, this way girl," Paige encouraged the faithful hound who was stood perfectly still, staring at the pitch black opening of the nearest cavern. Suddenly she crouched low and bared her teeth, growling deeply.

"Oh my God!" Sarah shouted at the unfolding horror.

The cave mouth issued a flood of death, spewing forth like a tide of vomit from a rancid mouth. First ten, then a hundred, more and more flowed towards them.

"*Run!*" Kurt yelled and turned on his heels, only to be confronted by a large group that had followed them from the rear of the office. Debbie was screaming, hopping from foot to foot in her terror, knowing they were trapped between the closing jaws of eternal damnation.

"Dad, in there!" Sam shouted, making a break for the main door of the building. It was constructed of thick metal, designed to keep thieves from breaking in and stealing the expensive machinery of the mining operation. Three steel roller shuttered doors were set alongside the main entrance, behind which would be assorted tools and mechanic areas for servicing and repairs. If the door was locked they would be doomed, their last stand would be short but they would go down fighting to their last breath. Kurt grabbed the handle and pushed but it was locked tight, totally immovable.

"Oh God, I'm so sorry, I love you all," Kurt wept. The swarm was closing fast, greedy for food that screamed. He held the short hatchet at his side, ready to hack at the approaching zombies, even though it was futile.

"Dad! Sorry, Mr T. Look!" Braiden had pulled the door wide open. In his haste Kurt hadn't even tried both directions. He ushered the rest through the opening and felt the first grasp on the back of his life jacket. Bellowing his hatred, Kurt twisted so hard and fast it ripped the arm from the socket of the cadaver who wanted to feast, his axe cleaved the forehead and bridge of the nose before bursting forth through the upper teeth. The attacker fell and Kurt seized the chance to duck through the door, pulling it shut with an ear splitting crash in the small reception area. He slipped the deadbolt into the holes at the top and bottom. It was unlikely the Hellspawn would have the ability to open the door with the weight of putrescent flesh pressing against the other side, but Kurt wouldn't take any chances. The frame was sturdy, solid steel and would hold for a while, if not indefinitely.

"That's disgusting," Debbie gasped, stepping away from Kurt. The arm was still holding him tightly, hanging from his jacket.

"Come here." John stepped forward and pried the fingers loose, before throwing the severed limb to the ground.

They all stood in the main foyer of the mine reception, looking around and trying to calm their racing hearts. The curved desk was made of cheap melamine panel, the useless phone and computer gathered dust on the desk top and the company logo was embossed on the wall to the rear. A water chiller sat in the corner alongside a coffee machine for waiting guests. The bottle was nearly empty, but they would be able to

70

retrieve a few litres of life giving fluid before it ran dry. Steps led up to the main offices above, a sign saying 'Authorised Personnel Only' was fixed to the door at the top. To the right was the entrance to some more offices and they could see the open garage area beyond through glass partitions, they surmised that these offices housed the mechanic staff and administration team.

"Where the hell did they all come from?" John asked and everyone just shrugged. It was as if they had been waiting for them.

"It doesn't matter right now; we need to clear the building. I can't hear anything over that ruckus outside so we will need to be careful, we won't hear them coming," Kurt spoke loudly, the combined hammering and moaning from a thousand cadavers was a tumultuous din that frayed their already stretched nerves.

"Stay behind me. Gloria, are you loaded?" John moved towards the stairs and she nodded, raising the gun to keep the barrels clear of the others.

"Ok, we check up there first." Kurt ascended slowly, trying to hear any sounds from inside that were being masked, but it was useless. The clatter of the metal being struck sounded like heavy rainfall on a tin roof, the roller doors must have been under assault now too. He prayed that they would hold against the surge of zombies. He put his ear to the 'Authorised Personnel Only' door but it was still fruitless, he longed to scream and tell the corpses to shut the hell up, though they were unlikely to comply.

"Ready?" Kurt asked and the group prepared itself for the unknown, only Debbie remained at the bottom of the staircase, watching yet refusing to help. Gloria saw the look and rolled her eyes at Kurt, sympathising with his frustration.

The door was pushed open inch by inch, revealing the open floor plan. Cheap office partition walls separated the desks of the employees into groups of four. To the rear, about forty feet away, were the more important offices; individual spaces where the executives would sit to carry out their business. Kurt put his finger to his lips, instructing silence in the group. If the slamming door had summoned any mouldering bodies, they would have been waiting. He looked behind the door, it was clear. He walked between the desks, ignoring the signs of the lives of the

71

staff; a personalised mug, a small calendar with cats in various humorous poses, a spilled handbag with assorted female accessories strewn across the carpeted floor. The disturbance grew the deeper they got into the office, chairs toppled over; paper had been thrown around by the passage of escaping people desperate to reach their loved ones. They checked office by office, the plush finishes belying the money that was in this lucrative business. The meeting room was likewise empty, the mugs of never finished coffee had grey mould festering within and the papers of the third quartile targets and profits felt like the obituary of the company, the worship of money was as dead as their besiegers.

John pushed open the double doors that led to the office of the director. The desk was marble topped, ridiculously expensive but loyal to the mining history of the company. A leather sofa suite surrounded a glass table that was once used for casual talks and schmoozing of potential clients by the head honcho. The potted plants were in a state of decay, brown leaves littering the floor from the lack of water.

"This is a dead place," Sam whispered.

"Every where's a dead place, mate. You are just spooked," Kurt answered quietly. They were safe, nothing rotting haunted this floor.

They went back into the meeting room and seated themselves, pushing the cups away in disgust but appreciating the quality of the high backed chairs.

"What the hell do we do now?" Kurt asked, angry at himself but taking it out on his family.

"We don't panic for starters," John scolded him. Kurt sunk into the seat, a look of defeat passing over his face.

"How many bullets do we have?" Paige asked, looking at Gloria.

"About one hundred and ninety. Nowhere close to enough," she answered.

"Can we just wait them out and see if they wander back into the caves?" Braiden suggested.

"I don't think we can risk it, we can stay here tonight but our water will only last a couple more days, and our food will be gone in a week at most. Every day we spend here is less chance we can make it to the hospital," Kurt explained.

"So we make a run for it," Peter said, dreading the idea and hoping someone would come up with a solution.

"About the only one who would make it is Honey." Kurt smiled, rubbing the yellow head. "We aren't all as light on our feet."

"Can we get some ammunition and I can shoot them, it will take a while but it could work," Sam offered, holding out the slingshot.

"That won't work Sam; the rubber is already showing signs of wear, look." Gloria pointed out the drying elastic and the hairline splits that were appearing.

"But I have a small roll of spare rubber; I could replace it when it breaks." Sam tried to convince them of the plan.

"We don't have any way to actually shoot them though, the windows are set high and don't open far enough so that people can't fall out, they are there for light and ventilation solely. The only way we get out is through the front or rear door, or the roller doors," John said, proud of how Sam was trying to help. The sheer number made it impossible, there must be over a thousand in the vicinity. The logistics of even killing one a minute would mean an unceasing barrage for nearly twenty hours. A mournful siren sounded from outside, wailing into the morning over the surrounding fields and hills, causing them all to jump.

"What was that?" cried Paige.

John checked his watch and the straightforward explanation came to him, "It's the change of shift alarm, so that people deeper in the tunnels have a chance of hearing. That's what drew them all here and with no food they just headed into the caverns."

They all sat, trying to calm their frayed nerves from the sudden noise. Kurt was holding his head in his hands and the group thought he was giving up, but in fact he was planning. Looking up at them he had a look of resolve, his eyes blazed once more.

"Let's clear downstairs, and then we can come up with a plan. We aren't going to die in a fucking office," he growled and stood, the group taking some comfort from his determination.

They descended back to the main reception where Debbie was holding her water bottle under the dispenser, gurgling bubbles rising as the displaced water flowed.

"Thanks," Kurt said, snatching the bottle and spilling some of the precious liquid.

"What the fuck do you think you are doing?" Debbie shrieked at him, clawing at the bottle which he held out of her reach.

"You don't help, you go thirsty and hungry. *Got it?*" he screamed back at her, pushing her in the chest and feeling both guilt and satisfaction when she stumbled over one of their bags. The commotion brought a more frenzied assault on the door and John pulled the 'what did I tell you' look at Kurt, he wasn't helping the situation by bringing more attention to themselves. Debbie was picking herself up and Peter went to help her, but she slapped his hand away.

"Go to your whore, you pathetic bastard, she's the one you really care about." Debbie glared at Paige who smiled; a challenge and an insult.

"Do you want another black eye?" Paige asked, stepping forward. The hatred she felt for this woman was all-consuming. Her attitude, and the way she had taken joy in killing the toddler zombie, was eating at Paige.

"Get away from me you psycho!" Debbie shouted and fled up the stairs, taking refuge in the upper floor they had just cleared.

"Paige, would you mind staying and keeping her away from the food and water?" Kurt asked.

"Not at all." She smiled, brandishing the curved, razor sharp bill hook. She sat at the reception desk, and even with the grime of their recent travels she was extremely beautiful. She was a secretary once more, only heavily armed with a lethally sharp weapon.

"This way." Kurt motioned and pushed through the doors into the smaller office downstairs. The space was clear too. More disturbances were evident but no movement caught their eye. The massive garage and machinery area was full of dark corners and hiding places so they chose to sweep the other rooms first. The first two were small utility rooms, brooms, mops and various cleaning implements were stacked up, bottles of bleach and pine disinfectant stood in neat rows. The last door led to a small canteen area with two vending machines, one had sold chocolate and the other potato crisps. Both glass frontages were smashed, the contents looted and eaten. The debris of the feast was all over the tables in the recreation area, wrappers and crumbs scattered everywhere.

"Wait, look." John held them back, pointing at a vast pool of congealed blood. Bare patches of carpet showed where the gore had settled around three objects; the shape was round, two small circles close together. The blood was then spread around and footsteps marked the passage of three people from the pool.

"It's their bottoms. They sat against that wall and died." Peter knew it was true, the marks were indicative of someone, or ones, trying to stand, the hand prints now obvious.

Noise at the kitchenette door drew their attention from the vile carpet and the first zombie walked through, still covered in the dried blood that had drained from its torn wrists. Another followed and then one more, the trio of people that had slowly starved in this room, before cutting their wrists when the hunger pains became too much. They moved between the tables, grey fleshed from their blood loss, arms raised showing the clumsy incisions that had severed the arteries.

"Dad, those poor people," Sam said, pitying the creatures that would kill them if they were given a chance. He raised the slingshot and at such short range the bearing ripped through one side and out of the other, before punching through the thin plasterboard wall of the kitchenette and smashing some crockery or other china. Kurt took his hammer and held one at bay by the chest. She was dressed in a business suit and would have been fifty when she had died. He wondered who she had been thinking about as the blood flowed, her body starting to feel the chill of the grave as her temperature dropped. Two blows crushed her skull in and Braiden finished the other zombie, the small machete separating the head from the shoulders. It bounced off the top of a plastic table and came to rest on some Walkers crisp wrappers on the floor. The discarded packets crunched and rustled as the snapping mouth tried to bite at them, still alive. Kurt raised his boot and the bone cracked, again and again he stamped until it was just a pulpy mess.

"Baby, enough," Sarah pulled him away, worried at the bright red face and sweat that was pouring down his forehead.

"Sorry," he apologised, finally understanding the fear and rage that the two men had displayed outside the Hare and Hound as they kicked the zombie to death on the first day the dead had risen. "Peter, can you go back with Paige, there may be more around and I want us all to be in groups. Shout if you see anything."

Surprisingly, no one volunteered to go and keep Debbie company. To be safe, Kurt popped his head in the small kitchen alcove, but it had only been the three of them. The room contained a small metal sink, a white plastic kettle, and a microwave. It was enough for people to make a drink and warm some lunch, nothing more. Sam's bearing had blown a cupboard door open and several cups were broken in pieces on the floor. Retrieving the steel ball, he passed it back to his son and they left the reception area for the final check on the workshop.

The door swung open and they were greeted by the familiar smell of garages across the world, oil, diesel, grease, and metal. The tool chests contained every type of socket wrench, screwdriver, and tool that any mechanic would ever need. The group checked the inspection pits, the store rooms, and every hiding place. It was deserted and they felt safe for the first time in hours.

"Whoa, look at that!" Sam gasped in awe, at present there was a large JCB digger and a JCB bulldozer stored in the garage. He rushed over and climbed into the cab of the bulldozer, ogling the levers and controls. Sarah laughed and Kurt smiled, happy to see their son enjoying himself again, for however short a time. Braiden took control of the other vehicle and they looked across at each other with real joy. The adults and the pet left them to their games. The steel roller doors were holding firm, the fists and heads of the zombies were not even denting the strong panels.

CHAPTER SEVEN

"I'm really sorry about Debbie, I shouldn't have hit her," Paige apologised to Peter.

"It's ok, really. She always gets like that when she doesn't get her own way, I'm glad you hit her," Peter replied, looking at the stairs just in case.

"I just didn't want to see you get hurt," she explained and he blushed.

"No one has ever looked out for me like that. I don't have any friends now, she wouldn't allow it," Peter said, a dark cloud passing over his face at the memory, how she had alienated him from all of his family too. God, what a waste.

"You have us now though," Paige said cheerfully, and the painful memory faded in his mind.

"Yes I do, we would have died if you hadn't rescued us. Thank you," Peter said with sincerity. He was so grateful to have found kind people who had stuck up for him more in the past few days than his, now ex, fiancée had done in years.

"You are more than welcome. Kurt and his family looked after me for a while after I was attacked," she conveyed with her own dark memories coursing through her head.

"Oh dear, what happened?" he asked with genuine concern, putting a hand on hers.

Paige froze, the scene playing through her mind once again. *The terrified escape from the tearing, biting horrors. The hiding beside a stranger's car, praying the monsters would not find her. The noise of her daughter crying in the back seat and the heart stopping realisation that she had forgotten her own child in her panic. The guilt eating away like an acid in her veins, yet unable to stand and go to her aid. The shrill, mortal cry of her child as it was ripped from this world. The appearance of the kind stranger who had helped her to her feet, and then... nothing.*

Tears burst from her eyes, and she vomited on the carpet, splashing some on Peter's legs. He didn't flinch or shy away, instead he held her hair in a bunch away from the expelled bile. He stroked her back, supporting her through the retching.

"Are you ok?" he asked, thinking she was physically ill, but it was an emotional sickness, a blemish on her soul that would never be cleansed.

"I can never be ok," she cried, "You should keep away from me." A small dam had broken inside, the acceptance of the loss of her child was about to begin.

"Why would I want to stay away from you? You are the prettiest, kindest person I have ever met." Peter was welling up now, he wanted to comfort this special lady, wanted to take all her pain away.

"You don't understand, I abandoned my baby to them, she died while I cowered behind a car," she bawled, only managing a word at a time between gasping sobs. Peter stood her up and held her tight, feeling the reluctance to be soothed, the need to punish herself for her cowardice.

"I am so sorry. No one can blame you for being afraid." He stroked her hair, talking and calming her through the breakdown. Her arms slowly rose and returned the cuddle, and he was far too aware of her warmth and loving nature.

"I blame myself every minute of every day. Her name was Lilly. She died while I lived." Finally having voiced the name of her lost daughter, the healing could begin. Paige pulled away and looked at Peter, sensing the purity and honesty of their new friend. *Why hadn't they met before this, why couldn't he have been the father to her child? If he had been with them, Lilly might still be alive.* It was impossible for her to articulate these feelings to him, the words were held back by the belief that she deserved no happiness, only suffering to atone for her sins. The others entered the reception, seeing the contact they smiled until they caught her red eyes, her wet face and chest from the flood of tears.

"Oh, sweetheart." Gloria guessed the reason for the tears, passed the gun to John and went to her. Paige broke down once more and flew into her motherly arms, the tears seemingly endless.

They stood in mourning, never knowing the child, yet feeling the deep loss as if she had been one of their own. Paige eventually settled with Gloria, the reassuring embrace helping to calm the grief. Gloria looked at them over her shoulder, happy that her concern over Paige's mental state was unjustified. The long recovery could now begin and Gloria mouthed 'thank you' to the catalyst, Peter. He blushed, unaware that he had achieved the breakthrough, just happy to be cementing his place within the group.

"Let's go and get comfortable, we need to come up with a solution," Kurt said and led the way, reaching the 'Authorised Personnel Only' door he pushed it and it wouldn't move. It took a split second to understand that Debbie had blocked it with office equipment and the fury ignited again. He slammed into the door with his shoulder, it opened an inch and he could see the edge of the desk with heavy monitors and boxes of paper stacked on it. She appeared, looked first at her failing barricade and then looked at the hatred in Kurt's eyes. Seeing the desk would not keep them out, she started to move the stationary and computer screens, trying to ingratiate herself.

"Hold on, I am moving it. I just wanted to be safe," she complained as Kurt battered against his side of the door, spilling objects on the floor.

Kurt had cleared a gap that would allow him access and he squeezed through, catching his life vest which only fuelled his burning anger. Debbie was stepping backwards, afraid of the coming confrontation, she reached the edge of a desk and could go no further.

"You evil whore!" Kurt growled and grabbed her around the throat, squeezing. "If we needed to get away in a hurry, we would be dead right now." He squeezed harder, her face reddening and her thin arms beating ineffectively against his copper plated and padded forearms.

"Kurt, don't!" Sarah cried out and tried to pull him away from the gasping form of Debbie. John joined her, then Peter, finally the boys, and they succeeded in breaking his grip, but he still flailed to reach her.

Debbie choked and gasped, trying to catch her stolen breaths. She tried to play the victim, crying and reaching out for the group. They just ignored her. Kurt may have overreacted, maybe not, but he was right in his accusation that her actions could have had deadly consequences for them all.

John stepped over and helped her to her feet. "Thank you," she rasped, mistaking the gesture for kindness. He just marched her to the door and pushed her through, before replacing the desk.

"You bastard!" pierced through the door, her voice nearly back to normal. She hammered and tried to force it open but lacked the weight or strength. Gloria looked at John with a mildly reproachful look but understood Debbie had burned her second chances with her actions.

"Leave her. I'll open it in a while. She needs a taste of her own medicine," John instructed and they moved off to the comfort of the leather suite in the Director's office.

"That's good soundproofing," Kurt commented as the Director's door closed on the main office, silencing the banshee wail of their unwanted guest from the stairwell. He opened it, closed it, opened it again and let it swish shut, nodding his appreciation. The bemused looks on the faces of his companions caused him to laugh, "Sorry."

"We don't have enough shells, we don't have enough ball bearings, we are surrounded and the chance of us hacking our way through over a thousand hungry corpses is zero to less than zero. Any suggestions?" John asked, totally out of ideas.

Braiden walked over to the windows and looked out upon the scene. They really were surrounded, hundreds were intent upon the tasty morsels within the building and more were leaving the caves that had been excavated. Kurt joined him, putting an arm around his shoulder while the rest of the group bounced ideas around.

"Sorry I called you Dad, Mr T," Braiden said with embarrassment.

"You call me whatever you want, I am proud to call you Son," Kurt answered with sincerity, pulling him close.

"Ok... Dad," Braiden tried it once more and it felt good.

"What do you suggest then? You always come up with great ideas," Kurt complimented the youngster.

Zombies reached skyward, seeing their quarry. The pair watched the mayhem. The dead were drawn to the flesh like metal filings to a magnet.

"We could always feed them Debbie," Braiden half joked, a dark glint in his eye that Kurt caught. He couldn't deny that he had also given the macabre option some thought. Being a self-centred bitch was not a capital offence, yet.

"I can always make a run for it; draw them away to buy you time to escape," Kurt suggested.

"Over my dead body!" called Sarah, who was eavesdropping on the conversation.

"If we don't do something it may well come to that," Kurt responded.

"Can't we just run them over with the bulldozer?" Peter suggested. "It's heavy and the caterpillar tracks would squash them flat."

"A couple of problems with that," John said, "We don't know how to drive one and the second we open the door they will overwhelm us."

"Oh, sorry." Peter looked dejected. Paige gave the back of his neck a rub.

"Don't be sorry, we need any and all ideas, Peter, we just have to think through them all," John added and Kurt smiled inside, it was normally himself that was subject to the condescending tone. Hearing it directed at someone else, Kurt had to admit to himself that it was meant in a kind way, not as a means to belittle somebody. Perhaps he had been far too fast to jump to conclusions and rebel against his father's authority. At least he may have time to make amends if they made it out of this bind.

"I know how to drive one," Braiden offered and looked up at Kurt.

"What? How?" Kurt was amazed. The boy looked away, shame in his eyes.

"I broke into a building site one night and came across a bulldozer. The keys were in the ignition. I had a play, knocked a couple of walls down, then the police caught me and I was arrested. Dad had to pay the fine and he broke two of my fingers," he replied, shuddering with the vivid memory of the pain and the snapping noises.

"Well that sorts one of the problems at least," Paige said and walked over, giving Braiden a hug. She had heard from the others about the abuse the poor child had been through, it was anathema to her how someone could treat their own flesh and blood in such a horrific manner.

81

"We can't just trundle out into the open though," John persisted, imagining the roller door rising and the swarm of rot that would pour in.

"Even if they all stood in line for us, which they won't, we can't possibly get them all before they get us," Sarah agreed.

Kurt was at a loss, they had heavy machines to use but the sheer numbers made it suicide. Another zombie stumbled from the cave mouth and fell to the ground in a puff of stone dust.

"I have an idea, it's a long shot but it may be our only chance," Kurt told the others who had all gathered round.

"Let's have it," John urged.

"You see those pillars of stone?" Kurt pointed at the support columns that had been installed at the entrances. "They are designed to hold the hard cap, the layer of solid rock that sits on the mineable stone. The miners would take away the layers below it and form them into square blocks for building. If we could take out those pillars, the entrance may collapse."

They all looked puzzled. "How does that help us though?" Gloria questioned, voicing their concern.

"I have to pull them deep into the caverns, when they follow me you bring the whole section down," Kurt answered.

"Dad, no!" Sam cried and hugged him. Sarah held her hand to her mouth, biting down to stop the tears.

"Whoa, hold on! I don't intend to stay in there, I'm not crazy. There is a shaft at the back that descends to the lower mine and comes out on the next road down, I will head for that and meet you there," Kurt explained, showing them the staggered roads in the distance.

"You bastard!" Sarah slapped him playfully.

"Hey, you didn't let me finish!" Kurt pulled her close.

"Kurt, how can you actually get up to our level, from what I can see the next is about fifteen feet lower than this one," John surmised.

"We will have to find some rope, or I will have to run right round until I get to the ramp for this road." Kurt shrugged. There were so many variables, so many things that could go awry and he just wanted to get it done. Fate would decide the outcome.

"Don't be stupid, we can do better than that," John said, the hated tone coming through. "We plan it step by step. It's not as if we are in a rush. The first problem is how do you even get out and past them so they follow you?"

"We could always make a commotion and that would clear the rear of the building, you could use the fire escape over there." Sam nodded at the clearly marked door that Kurt had missed, it would lead down to the ground and he could skirt the zombies before they gave chase.

"Great idea, Sam. Next, when you get in there, how do you know the shaft hasn't been blocked up?" John asked and there was no easy answer.

"Then I really will be trapped. We have to take the chance though," Kurt said, resolute. John closed his eyes in frustration and knew that his son was right. They didn't want to end up like the lost souls that took their own lives in this tomb.

"Ok, what if bringing down one of them isn't enough? Braiden how fast does the dozer move?" John asked.

"They aren't quick, I can probably destroy one, but if I'm seen they could be on me before I get the other pillar," he admitted. That one time, while joyriding in the machine, he had tried to push it but it had barely reached the speed of a slow jog.

"I don't like this, there must be another way," John grumbled.

"I could always drive the digger," Peter suggested and John looked at him.

"Do you know how?" John asked suspiciously.

"Kind of, I used a smaller version to dig the foundations for our garden wall. It's just getting used to the levers again," Peter said, sure of himself. "There's nothing stopping me getting behind the wheel in the garage area and trying it. If both Braiden and I hit two separate supports, the chances of it collapsing are that much greater."

"Dad, what choice do we have?" Kurt questioned, but John knew there were very few.

"I just don't like it, why don't we use the distraction to lure them away from the roller doors and we try crushing a few? The cabs are high enough that Peter and Braiden will be clear of danger as long as they keep moving," John suggested, he wanted to thin the numbers a little before they tried to pancake the remaining zombies.

"Won't their weight just cause them to stall?" Sam asked.

"How do you mean, mate?" Kurt replied, unsure if he was talking about the machines.

"I remember you mentioning before that we couldn't drive through the zombies, that if you get enough blocking the way the van couldn't push through their combined weight," Sam explained.

"We won't have that trouble; the power of these machines will roll right over them," Braiden told his brother. He had loved all things mechanical as he was growing up and knew the capabilities of the metal behemoths.

"If we use the windows to entice them over and to spread them out a bit, then when the doors are clear we begin the mayhem," Peter laughed sickly, going pale. He was terrified of the task at hand but he owed it to his new friends to brave the horde.

"Ok, when do we do this?" Gloria asked, checking her watch. It was only mid-afternoon. They still had about four hours of daylight before the night fell.

"We will be cutting it close, if anything goes wrong and we end up on the road in the dark, we will be in real trouble."

"Right, we do it at first light. We use the time to check the equipment, and you two," Kurt looked at Braiden and Peter, "You practice with the controls."

Activity resumed and the doors were thrown open, the shrill cries of Debbie were heard again. The desk was dragged clear and she came stumbling through the unblocked door, sweating profusely from the battering she had given the door. Her knuckles were bloodied and they could see spots of it on the fitted door sign. Kurt grabbed her, pinning her against the wall.

"Are you going to play nice, or do I lock you in a cupboard?" Kurt held his face inches from hers. Her feeling of isolation was compounded by the drumming coming from the door at the bottom of the stairs, a single inch of metal separating the dead from her tender body.

"I'm sorry, please don't do that," she said softly, contrition in her voice. How long it would last they had no idea.

"Come here." Kurt pulled her to a chair and pushed her into it. She was expecting more violence but he walked off, took the small first aid kit from his bag and returned. He dabbed at the torn knuckles with antibacterial wipes, removing the blood and passing her a small bandage. "Wrap this around it."

"Thanks," she said as the group moved off. She quickly bound it around each hand before taping the ends down to hold it in place, then rushed after the others.

Their decision to postpone the mission was further validated by the fact it took over an hour to find the keys to the two mining appliances. They were tucked away in the back of a desk drawer that seemed to have nothing to do with the maintenance of the machines. If it had taken much longer they would have given up and tried their hand at hotwiring the vehicles. Braiden and Peter mounted up and the dry atmosphere of the workshop had kept the contacts and wiring free of moisture. The engines coughed into life and the high set exhaust pipes belched out black smoke, the rain covers flapping madly. Standing well clear of the tonnes of poorly controlled metal, the others watched as the two wrestled with the controls. Braiden was a lot quicker in remembering the functions of the levers, moving forwards and backwards as well as utilising the blade, twisting and raising it. The throttle increased and decreased as he adjusted the power, getting a feeling for the yellow dozer.

"What about the exhaust fumes?" Sarah shouted over the din of the engines.

"The workshop is huge; we should be ok for a little while. If anyone starts to feel tired, just yell," Kurt answered, sniffing the air and smelling the burned diesel.

Peter was taking more time, the excavator had many more levers and functions. The movement was fine as he rolled forwards and backwards and gave them a smiling thumbs up. The success was short lived. The digging buckets were flying all over the place, clattering against the tool chests and surrounding work benches. His smiled faded and was replaced with a look of concentration. They chuckled and laughed at the wildly flailing arms; he saw them and shook his head in apology. It was their turn to return the thumbs up in support. In less than ten minutes he was reasonably competent and would probably not kill them all when he next climbed behind the wheel. He stopped the engine and climbed down.

"Sorry, that was tough," he apologised again.

"You did great," Paige complimented him and they all agreed.

"Took you about fifteen minutes to master it, I'd say that was a bloody good effort," added John.

"I don't know about master, but I should be able to smash that stone pillar." He grinned.

They searched the small kitchenette and found no food, but plenty of powdered milk sachets, coffee granules, and Typhoo teabags.

"Oh my God, I would kill for a cuppa, even one with awful powdered milk," John pined for the warm liquid.

"Let's take it up. I'm sure we can heat some water. I will boil it on the engine of the digger if I need to," Peter volunteered and John clapped him on the back.

"Bless you, lad," John thanked him, grinning.

They blocked the upper office doorway completely. The heaviest obstacles were laid side by side to stop anything getting through. The thin staircase would not allow any real pressure to be brought to bear by the dead should they gain entry. With a metal waste basket and a champagne bucket they had found in the director's office, they were able to light a small fire by an open window and boil water. The hot brews were most welcome after the chill of the workshop and they bedded down for the night. Even Debbie joined them, some of her obnoxious attitude had departed and they could only hope it would last.

***

"Braiden, are you awake?" whispered Sam quietly so that he didn't disturb the others.

"Yeah. Can't get to sleep anyway. Too psyched for tomorrow," he answered.

"Can I ask you something? It's a bit weird," Sam said, trying to think of the best way to word it without sounding too childish.

"Boys, you need to get some sleep, we have a busy day tomorrow. It's going to be dangerous enough without you both being tired," Gloria said, rising from her modest bed of chair cushions.

"Sorry, I just can't get to sleep. I'm a bit nervous about tomorrow," explained Braiden, which wasn't a complete lie. He wasn't worried for himself, only the chance that he might lose someone close to him if anything went wrong.

"Ok. Let me make you some hot cocoa, there were plenty of sachets left over from earlier. I will be back in a jiffy," she said.

"No, it's ok. Don't worry, you need your sleep too," Sam apologised, feeling guilty that he had woken her in the dead of night.

"Nonsense. It will take me five minutes and then, hopefully, we can get you two to get some rest. We need our fighting men strong," she declared. Standing up, she carefully lifted the tray that had all the leftover drink packets and stepped over the other sleeping figures.

"Thanks, Miss, you're the best," Braiden said graciously. He still couldn't bring himself to call her Gloria. He had tried on occasion, but the entrenched teacher and student relationship was still foremost in his mind. He also thought it showed more respect which was a thought he would have never countenanced before the horror.

"Be right back," she replied, gently rubbing his head as she moved past.

Honey took the opportunity and followed, seeking a far corner to relieve herself. The spark of a lighter flashed in the offices and then dulled as the small flames in the bin took hold, warming the water through.

"What did you want to ask, bro?" Braiden continued now they were alone again, except for the sleeping forms of the others.

"I don't really know how to say it. I mean, I know the words, but I don't want you to think I'm a pussy." Sam tried to think of the best way to articulate his problem that wouldn't leave Braiden disappointed in him. Their new brotherly bond was sacrosanct and Sam suddenly wished he'd just kept his mouth shut.

"It's about that night isn't it?" Braiden didn't need to be a mind reader to see it was troubling him.

"Yeah, how did you know?" Sam asked, amazed at how in tune they were with each other.

"I've seen the way you have changed. It's like you aren't as talkative as you used to be, before it happened," Braiden explained. "You have tried to ask me before, but then just clammed up instead."

"I was going to mention it the other night too, until Dad interrupted us," Sam replied. Braiden smiled at the word Dad, and the way he had come to use it as if Kurt was truly his father.

"I know. You were nearly bursting." Braiden wasn't pushing. He waited for Sam to get to what was really bothering him.

"I can still hear their screams when I close my eyes," he said with barely a whisper, "I see his burnt face in the rubble, looking at me."

Braiden held out a hand and squeezed Sam's arm. "So do I."

"What do you mean?" Sam asked with disbelief. "You are always so cool about it."

"Doesn't mean it doesn't stay with me. I can still see HP's eyes when he realised what I had done, the way he was swallowed by the attic hole. I see it in slow motion every night," Braiden added.

"So it bothers you too? I remember you trying to tell me that you were a bad person and dangerous, that we should get rid of you." Sam was dubious whether Braiden was just trying to make him feel better.

"I thought so too, until you convinced me I wasn't. If I was evil, then I wouldn't wish I had never met those fuckers. That way I wouldn't have needed to kill them, but make no mistake Sam," Braiden gripped his hand tighter, "You did what had to be done. That's why it was only laying there worrying that you would get hurt, that made me tell on you."

"So you aren't happy about killing that fucker?" Sam asked, still feeling a bit awkward swearing in the presence of his parents.

"I didn't feel happy killing him, no. What I felt was justice. Payback for all the hurt that people like that do to others, just because they can. One thing you can be damned sure of, though, because of what we did, they will never hurt another family again," Braiden stated with conviction.

"So in a way, we are heroes. Like in the comic books, tackling Evil and fighting for Good," Sam said with excitement. Then he thought about the ripping and screaming of the men he had killed and the grin vanished.

"In comic books, the heroes always win. In real life, it's normally the other way round," Braiden replied. He had seen the misery that men could commit both before and after the outbreak. It often went unchallenged, until now.

"I guess you're right. Thanks, Braiden. I thought I was going to go mad," Sam said with relief.

"You want to know what I do when they come back to haunt me?" he asked.

"Yeah, sure," Sam replied with interest.

"I picture all your faces, smiling. And I know that I have done something to protect you all," Braiden said sincerely. The door opened and the drinks had arrived. Honey scurried through the closing gap and made herself comfortable with Peter and Paige, turning in a circle repeatedly until she finally settled.

"Here you go, boys," Gloria offered the two steaming cups of delicious chocolate drink to the boys. "Careful, they are hot."

"Thanks," they replied in unison, blowing the frothy top to cool it a little.

Sipping in the darkness, Sam felt as if he had released a compressing vice of guilt in his chest. The screams of pain in his mind were replaced with the resounding laughter of his new family. Sleep took him shortly after and Braiden smiled to himself at how, through all the horror, he had found such happiness.

Gloria lay quietly, praying for sweet dreams to take the young boys far away from all the misery. The cocoa worked, and after fifteen minutes the boys were snoring quietly, showing no signs of fear in their slumber.

CHAPTER EIGHT

They awoke and ate, fuelling their bodies for the upcoming trial. Braiden took Peter to one side, huddling and psyching him up.

"We got this, follow my lead. The dozer will be slower than your digger, so I want you to cover my back, crush any that look like they are going to be able to catch up. I don't know if they can climb, but the maintenance steps could give them a chance." Braiden held Peters gaze, feeling strange that he was instructing a grown adult and even stranger that the adult was riveted.

"Right, got it. I won't let you down." Peter was nodding furiously, getting himself in the zone.

"I know you won't, you are a part of us now," Braiden said confidently.

"Thanks, I've never really belonged before. Debbie wouldn't let me see people." Peter was humbled by the sentiment.

"Fuck her; she is a dead weight slowing us down. I'm amazed she hasn't been killed or got us killed yet," Braiden fumed, shooting a hateful glare at the pathetic creature.

"I know, but I'm all she had. She was all I had too," Peter said, regretting his life choices.

"Now you've got Paige, you can forget about that horrible bitch," Braiden stated.

"What do you mean?" Peter asked, butterflies bouncing around in his stomach.

"She is crazy about you. She is always looking at you and smiling when you aren't paying attention." Braiden grinned and they both looked over at her, she was petting the dog, showing her deep well of love. Looking up, she noticed their attention and blushed, but not before giving Peter the familiar smile. "There, see." Braiden clapped Peter on the shoulder.

"I don't know what I should do, Debbie would go insane," Peter whispered, torn between excitement and anxiety.

"I'm fifteen, how the hell should I know?" Braiden exclaimed with a wide grin. "Let's do this!"

They moved the desk and gathered in the workshop. Peter and Braiden climbed into the driving seats and started the engines, giving them a chance to warm up. They wanted to minimise any chance of failure that a cold engine may provide. Grinding to a halt in the midst of one thousand festering carnivores would result in a bad day for everyone.

"We need to search all this equipment. There could be some good gear to take," Sam declared, pointing at the scattered tools and engine parts.

"Later, we have a job to do. Sam, go up to the rear of the building, open the windows and start shouting. Debbie, would you mind doing the same from the other end?" Kurt was extending an olive branch.

"Yeah, ok," she replied, taking it with less ill will than Kurt was expecting.

Peter and Braiden turned their ignitions off once the engines had heated and the hollering started, carrying through the floor and steel doors. The noises of the dead battering on the metal diminished and finally stopped altogether. Kurt was nervous, he desperately wanted to take their place, but he didn't have the skill to pull it off. He would just as likely crash into the other vehicle, killing them both. Or roll straight off the edge of a precipice, falling to his death on the rocks below in a tangle of twisted metal. Swallowing his pride, he waited patiently for the zombies to move away and the all clear signal to be given by John.

"*Go!*" His father shouted.

"Now," Kurt called to Gloria and Sarah who pulled on the door chains, opening them to the daylight.

"Good luck!" Gloria yelled as the two rolled past her, giving her a nervous wave.

91

They squinted into the bright morning sun and as soon as they were clear the doors closed, sealing the openings like two closing eyes. They were on their own now, they would lead the crowd as far away as possible when they had, hopefully, been successful and the doors would blink open again. Peter felt like he was going to be sick when the flood of bodies rounded the building and made directly for them.

"Fall in line!" Braiden shouted, beeping the deep horn of the dozer and pointing to his rear. Peter nodded and pulled in behind, following the tracks of the heavier machine.

The horde was filing around their base which worked in their favour. Braiden drove to the far side of the open area and doubled back. The snaking line of horror was perfect and Peter assumed that Braiden would roll straight down it, killing most of them in one pass. Braiden took the safer option, he trusted the vehicle, but there was no room for error. He cut to the left and then sharply right, intersecting the pustule riddle procession, cutting through it. The heads and bodies connected with the massive blade, splattering gore and blood indiscriminately. The heavy caterpillar tracks dragged the dead down and crushed them, innards spewing from mouths and noses before the heads were pressed into the gravel, exploding from the forceful pressure. Braiden was cheering as the machine trundled on. Peter aimed the excavator, mopping up as many as he could that gave chase. The half squashed bodies that had escaped the full weight of the bulldozer reached out, unable to peel themselves from the gravelled ground. The tracks of Peter's vehicle finished them off, compressing them like half rolled tubes of toothpaste. Braiden turned and cut another swathe through the lines, the smell of spilled decomposition was getting through the windows, making his stomach churn.

"Doing great!" Braiden whooped, looking back at Peter and punching the roof of the cab with excitement.

The enthusiasm wasn't shared. Peter felt increasingly nauseous at the stink and the sights he was following, the glistening piles of ruptured meat and splattered blood, still retaining their basic human shape but squeezed to an inch thick. The mass of figures was getting thicker, the line converging on the exhaust snorting monsters. Some tried to find purchase to climb, but the rotating metal tracks brushed them aside and they too fell under the massive weight.

"Oh no!" Peter muttered fearfully. When Braiden had slowed to make a turn, the zombies had scrambled onto the rear of the cab. They were trying to get at the youngster who was oblivious to the impending threat because of the noise. The sudden turn tumbled one sideways and he was dragged into the churning cogs of the tracks, gradually being minced as they continued with the carnage. Peter accelerated and raised the digging arm, stretching it out. Matching the pace of the dozer he dropped the metal bucket and pinned the corpse, scraping it clear in a smear of green ichor which dripped from the rear.

"Thanks!" Braiden yelled, still smiling and putting his thumb up. How could he be so cheerful? Peter wondered.

They were getting close to the main building and Braiden swung away, leading the gathered horde towards the furthest point, readying himself for the final run into the waiting garage. Hundreds had fallen beneath the tonnes of steel. The caterpillar tracks drew crazy wet lines between crushed piles of the dead.

"You did awesome Pete!" Braiden called out as they waited, engines idling while the crowd converged on them. He gave three heavy blasts on the horn, signalling they were making their return journey.

"Can't hear you," Peter shouted, pointing at his ears. The JCB was saturated with unspeakable fluids and fragments of splintered bone that had hit against the cab. Struggling not to vomit, he focused on the steel doors, watching as they opened welcomingly.

"Ready?" Braiden mouthed to him and Peter nodded. They revved and punched forward, hitting the incoming tide with a sickening crunch, slime and blood splashing upwards like a wave hitting a breaker. Bouncing and rocking over the huddled bodies, the tracks started to slip on the dozer and it ground to a halt atop a pile of vileness. Braiden gunned it but the machine just churned the flesh into a paste, he didn't have time to free himself, the zombies were already surrounding the stricken dozer. Peter hesitated, staring at the safety of the garage and the solid doors, the new friends he had made were waiting for him. The inner coward almost won, but with a bestial shout he turned, crushing more of the dead.

"Just go! Get out of here!" Braiden was shouting, pointing madly at the open doors.

Peter ignored him and raised the arm once more, dropping the toothed bucket and grasping the dozer blade with a resounding clang. Shifting into reverse he pulled as Braiden pushed and the vehicle came free, much to the disappointment of the hungry corpses who gave chase. Instead of repositioning himself Peter stayed in reverse, watching over his shoulder and breaking loose of the other machine at the last minute and backing it expertly into the waiting mechanical bay. Braiden parked up and the doors came clattering down just in time, the sounds of fists on metal quickly commencing again.

"Bloody hell that was intense!" commented Braiden, jumping down from the cab and grabbing Peter in a bear hug. "You saved my life, Pete. I won't forget it."

"None of us will, you were fantastic," Paige complimented him and joined the embrace.

"You would have done the same for me," Peter said, blushing. He would keep his momentary weakness from them, he was ashamed at himself. It was the kind of shit Debbie would pull.

"Look out!" Kurt yelled and swung his hammer. The half minced zombie had pulled itself free from the cogs and was reaching for Paige. Peter pulled her away and they fell on top of one another. The steel hammer head punctured the brain and it collapsed, the entrails stretching in a disgusting trail from the dozer.

"Thanks, you saved me again." Paige smiled up at Peter; she saw his face and the smile changed to confusion.

"I... I ..." Peter didn't finish, instead vomiting his breakfast all over Paige's hair.

"That's gross!" Sam said, trying not to laugh.

Peter looked devastated. He was frantically trying to clean his mess, pulling bits of food from her golden tresses. She started laughing underneath him, unfazed by the sickly smell and sticky hair.

"Oh God, I am so sorry," Peter was apologising repeatedly as Kurt and John helped him to his feet.

"Bend over, dearie," Gloria instructed, pouring clean water over her head, washing most of the larger debris away.

"Hang on!" Sam said and ran off, returning quickly with a handful of soap from the press dispenser in the toilet. "It's not great, but it's got to be better than that." He shrugged, rubbing it into her head. They poured more water, washing the suds away onto the concrete floor.

"That's a waste of our water," Debbie scolded.

"Yes, but necessary," Kurt agreed grudgingly. Paige couldn't have been expected to have vomit dripping from her. "Let's get the last of the water from the chiller, and then we get our breath back. I want to head out within the hour." It was as much to get it over and done with as anything. The sight of the JCBs wreaking havoc was one thing, but he would be on foot.

"We need to get these scraped off first," John argued, indicating the limbs, guts and blood that covered the machines. It was unlikely that the gore would cause a malfunction but why take the chance? John picked up a broom and started to poke through, dislodging lumps of viscera that hit the bottom of the inspection pit with a wet splash. Peter looked over, retched and looked away.

"You sit this one out, mate. We will finish up," Kurt advised and Peter raised an appreciative hand before staggering off to lie down.

Three more incomplete zombies were ground up and wedged in between the main body of the vehicles and the hydraulics. They gnashed and moaned before being dispatched without ceremony, ramming jabs from the last crafted steel spear ending their loathsome existence. It was more difficult to shift these larger objects and Kurt had to reach in, hacking away with the hatchet until the remains dropped onto the growing pile of meat.

"I think that should do it," John said, dripping sweat.

"Fancy a cuppa?" Kurt asked, wanting a steaming mug of coffee.

"Sounds like a plan," John replied and they returned to the upper floor, igniting the fire in the bin to boil more water.

"You ok, Pete?" John questioned, kneeling by him on the sofa and offering the hot fragrant brew.

"Yeah, sorry it was just the smell. I'll be good to go again shortly." Peter took the mug, savouring the delicious coffee.

"Good man, you were terrific. Rest up a while longer." John patted his shoulder and retrieved his own drink, before walking to the window.

95

The broken bodies were strewn across the gravel, some still alive, now immobile and stuck to the ground. Several hundred had been wiped out, making Kurt's task slightly less daunting. They were still a sizeable force to take on.

"You ready for this?" John asked when Sarah and Kurt joined him.

"Nope, but we don't have a choice. I'm the only one who knows the mines a little," Kurt said and Sarah held him tight. His youthful exploration into the lower level had been short lived, his bravado in front of his female companion quickly disappearing when mournful wails had echoed down the tunnels. It had probably been a lost animal but they had not stopped running until they were safely back in his rusty car, panting and laughing in equal measure.

"We should go and sit down, get our strength back. This nervous pacing is doing us no favours," Kurt stated and they settled onto the sofas. They talked and discussed as much of the coming plan as they could think of. It didn't go unnoticed that the closer Paige got to Peter, the further Debbie moved away, both physically and mentally. The hateful looks that she regarded the pretty blonde with were beginning to grate on Kurt. Just as he was about to explode again, the time had come.

"Shall we? We still have to reach the pub," John asked, aware of the shadows moving on the carpet with the slow crawl towards night.

***

It all had to be executed perfectly to give them a chance at survival. Kurt was poised by the fire exit; a quick peek had revealed about forty zombies to the rear of the building. None had climbed the metal fire escape staircase yet. Debbie was positioned at the window above the main entrance and Sam was below, they were to make as much noise as possible and tempt the horrors away from the rear as well as the steel roller doors which housed the two massive machines. Peter and Braiden were seated and locked in the cabs, engines idling, ready to trundle out on caterpillar tracks and crush the horde under a hundred thousand tonnes of compacted limestone. The interior doors had all been wedged open to give uninterrupted communication between them. With one final prayer, Kurt gave the signal and all hell let loose. Debbie screamed and shouted, baiting the zombies toward her position and Sam was beating on the door with a metal chair, resounding clangs echoing up the stairs. Kurt was poised like an Olympic athlete; hand on the push bar that would open the exit. He took deep breaths, attempting to keep his composure and waiting for the shout.

"Go! I love you!" John shouted, seeing the last of the dead rear guard head towards the entrance.

Kurt pushed through and saw the way was clear. He carefully descended, remembering the pain of his ankle from the last time he had rushed. More was riding on this than his own life and if he failed they would soon be joining the new species that ruled the world. The fence separated the two areas, beautiful peace and tranquillity on the lake and chaotic horror in the mines. He envied the swans as they bobbed around on the quiet water, carefree and lacking the faculties to understand the new order. The corner was reached and Kurt readied the hammer, with his short hatchet ready to be pulled from his belt in an emergency. Across a space of three hundred yards the dark mouths of the cave openings waited, still housing potential dangers that he would only discover when he stumbled across them. One more breath and he pinioned his arms, sprinting across the short distance. His terrified mind started to play tricks and the gap seemed to elongate, stretching away into the far distance. Panic started to grip his heart, but it snapped back to normal as he was suddenly at the cavern opening. Shining the torch into the deep recesses he saw that it was safe as far as the beam would penetrate. Who knew what lurked within? His pause threatened to drag into permanent paralysis, but a shout brought him back.

"Get a fucking move on!" Debbie screamed, back to her usual charming self. He was grateful though for the kick in the pants. She and Sam both fell silent and now it was his turn.

"Hey, you putrid bastards! Grubs up!" Kurt yelled, "Come and get it, fresh and red, come on!"

He watched the massive swarm turn as one and commence their slow march for him, his bowels shrivelling. Talking through the plan had not prepared him for the reality as thousands of weeping eyes fixed him with their dead gaze.

97

"Sweet Jesus," he muttered and backed into the black opening. His mouth was dry and he had to force a whisper. "Get a grip on yourself."

He looked at the building that housed his whole life, clenched the hammer tight and carried on calling out. "Over here! Hey, come on!"

The hunger was upon them. Kurt backed away fully, knowing he had their undivided attention. The flashlight cut to and fro, picking out more columns that were set throughout the cave. The ceiling was moist and huge stalactites hung from the stone, dripping water that penetrated the limestone and forming sharp spears of mineral deposits. Similar spikes rose from the floor, one mistimed step would throw him onto one, impaled and ready to be devoured like an aperitif. Graffiti was sprayed on the stone by young vandals; intricate lettering and artistry in a multitude of colours, a modern take on the ancient pictures of hunting and survival. This particular mine had been long abandoned after all the easy rock had been extracted by craftsmen hundreds of years ago. The pillars were fragile.

An arm grabbed him and he stumbled, falling far too close to one of the stalagmites where he hadn't been paying attention. The corpse was female and only the upper trunk remained, trailing intestines and guts behind her. Her arm had tripped him and she was frantically crawling, determined to mount and feed on Kurt. He kicked out and the flesh peeled away, revealing the rotting skull underneath. The zombie was undaunted by the blow and it climbed his legs, trying to bite, but the angle was wrong to find purchase. It continued up his body, aiming for the tender area between his legs. Kurt aimed with the hammer, missed and hit his own thigh, the pain shot through the limb and the half zombie took its first bite, catching the zipper and chewing down tight. Kurt screamed and hammered indiscriminately, trying to maintain his manhood. If he had to be a walking corpse, please let it not be as a eunuch. The final blow connected and the brain was destroyed, the head sagging into his groin; a welcome gesture from his wife, but not from the putrid half mess. He pushed it away in disgust, felt his genitals for reassurance and thanked God or whatever power had saved him.

The thronging mass was navigating the caverns, sensing his presence rather than seeing him. The torch had been thrown clear and the bulb was out, only the faint reflection of the light from the entrance catching the glass showed him where it lay. He grabbed it and fumbled for the switch, pressing the button and it blazed into life. The rear of the cave beckoned, empty and bleak. He knew where the shaft was, the iron rungs that had been embedded in the rock face for emergencies would take him to safety. Running toward the ladder he passed a bizarre sight; half burned black candles littered the floor and there was a pentagram drawn in the compacted dust of the floor. Satanic rituals had taken place at this spot and Kurt nearly laughed. He hoped that whoever they were, they were satisfied with their work. This really was a Hell on earth.

Barriers were placed around the ladder hole to prevent errant trespassers from falling in. The opening beckoned Kurt.

***

"Ok, *Now!*" shouted John.

Sarah and Gloria heaved on the chain runners that opened the shutter doors. They rose, inch by inch, and Peter and Braiden revved their engines and crawled forward, ready to burst forth into bright daylight. The machines were clear and rumbling across the main courtyard, aiming for the solid stanchions. A small number of the dead remained nearby and Gloria raised the shotgun, aiming at the nearest. The barrel blazed and the skull was obliterated, she swung and the gun bucked against her shoulder, dropping another corpse. She cracked the stock, pulled the two cartridges out and threw them away. She loaded two more and readied herself, watching the spreading pools of festering green blood from the headless bodies. Sarah was joined by Sam and John and the three followed the JCBs picking off any stray abomination.

Braiden and Peter straightened out, matched each other's speed and hit the cavern entrance columns at exactly the same time. Stone crumbled as the machines pressed forward, scattering the supporting pillars deep into the cavern. They backed away quickly, not wanting to be buried with the dead and waited. Nothing happened, the capping rock stayed put.

"Shit, shit, shit!" Peter yelled, looking at Braiden for ideas.

"Hit it again!" Braiden shouted back, opening his window to be heard over the growl of the engines. He raised the blade, shifted into forward and accelerated. He hit the hard cap with a massive thud and was quickly followed by Peter who did the same, crashing into the rock face. Cracks started to appear in the stone, splintering noises heralded the roar of an earthquake as the whole structure dropped into the void. The slowest of the dead who were returning to eat the drivers were pressed flat instantly; gore pouring from their openings before rock met rock. They reversed and watched the spectacle, seeing the whole outcrop sink, sagging and fracturing as the cavern was slowly filled with Kurt still inside.

"Please be safe, Kurt!" Sarah begged, shielding her face from the plumes of dust that billowed from the forever closed cave mouths.

***

Kurt heard the shattering impact of the first strike and climbed down into the hollow opening. After his near miss it felt like he was crawling into the throat of a waiting beast, ready to close its jaws and eat him whole. He watched in shock as the dead closed on him, totally oblivious to the unfolding destruction behind them, the inner columns were exploding under the pressure of the collapsing roof. Debris was tearing through the massed bodies and shredding flesh from bone. The ceiling would be on him in any moment so he scrambled down, concentrating on speed as well as safety, gripping each rung tightly. Something hit him on the head and he thought the whole shaft was collapsing upon him. He was going to be buried alive!

A wet, crunching noise rose from the bottom and he was hit again, on the shoulder this time. Looking around he caught sight of the zombie dropping down, still reaching for him as it fell. Kurt looked upwards at the moving rock, several more bodies toppled in before it closed the shaft off forever, spilling a thick torrent of green juice from the squashed dead. He grasped the wall, trying to minimise his target but an outstretched leg caught him hard on the head, causing starbursts behind his eyes and threatening to pull him loose. The moans from below led him to think of two scenarios, either the shattered bodies of the jumpers were still alive, or the lower tunnel was filled with the dead, waiting to greet him.

"How the Hell did I not think of that?" Kurt asked, trying to stop his vision swimming.

He held out the torch, reluctant to aim the narrow beam down to reveal the answer, but procrastinating would get him killed just the same. The torch illuminated the broken pile of festering pus. There was nothing else at the foot of the shaft; what stalked the tunnels he couldn't know until he was down, so he descended. Nearing the base, one of the rungs broke free, loosened by the shifting rock. Kurt lost his grip and plunged backwards. In slow motion he seemed to plummet, arms outstretched trying to grab at thin air. The fall was only nine feet and the soft, flexible pile of meat saved him from any fractured bones, but his wind was knocked out. Snapping mouths writhed under his body, biting at his life jacket and he flung himself clear, jumping as if electrified, struggling to fill his stunned lungs. The hungry eyes followed him with desire, but luckily their injuries kept them immobile. The mine stretched into the distance, the burrowed rock scored and chipped from the activities of the men and machines. Light bulbs were fixed along the ceiling, but without power they were just pretty baubles. The rumbling from the cave in was too loud for Kurt to know if there was a threat waiting ahead. He stood by the pancaked evil, trying to separate the sounds.

"Just move, get your ass in gear," Kurt ordered himself and stepped around the slopping mess of gnashing teeth. At the first intersection the torch beam blinked out, the damage from the two drops finally breaking the bulb. The darkness was absolute; he tried to hold his hand in front of his face but there was nothing there. The sound of scuffing came from his right and he had no way of knowing what caused it, he held out his hand and it sunk into a wet, spongy, mobile obstacle. It groaned.

***

"Wow," Braiden said, awestruck at the collapsed mine entrance.

"Braiden, Peter, get back here, we need to load up the bags and get Kurt!" John yelled from the building.

Peter rolled backwards, turned, and headed for the door. The stragglers had been destroyed by the family before they could attack, the roar of the engines was an irresistible beacon to the dead. With the way clear, they hopped between clear patches of gravel and grabbed the bug out bags.

"The bucket!" Sarah shouted to Peter and he curled it, providing a perfect place to stow the bags while they rescued Kurt.

The group gathered behind the hulking beasts, the noise of devastation had brought dozens more zombies from deeper mine shafts that weren't part of the huge, original excavation. Arms raised, they descended, hungry for the moist flesh. Braiden and Peter pulled together to protect their family, making a steamroller eighteen feet wide. It met the small crowd in battle, battering the bodies aside and dragging them underneath the wide metal tracks. Those on foot hung back, taking cover like soldiers following tanks during war. Using the cleavers from the farmhouse they hacked at the fallen dead, severing heads and slicing brains. They reached the first branch of road that snaked downwards, following the line of the concentric circles that had been blasted into the deeper rock. A sheer drop of more than fifteen feet separated each tier and around the edges were similar cave openings. The one which Kurt should be escaping from was just ahead. More cadavers were struck, falling from the precipice and bouncing from the lower ledge before continuing down in a sickening spiral of shattering bones and spilled guts. A couple just fell to the first ring, suffering only minor injuries and standing up outside the mouth that Kurt needed to exit the depths of the caves. Sam raised his slingshot and smashed the skull of the female while Gloria picked up the gun and shot the second. The spreading buckshot pulverised the face and head, causing it to pinwheel backwards, falling to join its splattered friends at the mine floor a hundred feet below.

"Where is he, he should be here by now!" Sarah yelled, frantically looking around for any sign of her husband. The others could only look on, hoping against hope that he would appear soon.

***

Kurt screamed in surprise within the confines of the tunnel and it echoed back to him, fainter each time. The zombie clutched at his arm, pulling him forward and trying to bite. He could hear the mouth snapping shut in the absolute blackness of the mine and held out his protected forearm, buying himself time to think. The teeth scraped the metal surface of his copper arm guard and Kurt pushed hard, forcing the zombie back to the wall. Slamming with his arm again and again he heard the crunch of pulverising skull and all strength left the animated corpse in an instant. A sudden rumble brought with it fresh shaking and Kurt stumbled, falling to the hard ground. The torch would probably have another bulb ensconced within, but he had no time to search the floor with his hands to retrieve it. He withdrew the small lighter he had pocketed when they left the farm house and prayed the falls and knocks hadn't broken it too. Striking the flint, it lit the tunnel and he could see another fallen horror struggling to rise, it was horribly chewed and torn from the waist up. The gas didn't ignite, so he rolled the flint again, and again, over and over. The monstrosity was caught in the strobe effect, like an old TV puppet show that required changing the pose each time, it stood and turned.

"Work, damn you!" he ranted at the lighter, fingering the adjuster on the side and striking once more. The gas burst forth, released finally, and rose brightly from the nozzle. His hand was shaking so badly that he blew the first attempt out, plunging him into darkness again with a line marked indelibly on his eyeball from the flame.

Kurt switched hands and reached into his belt, igniting the flame and raising the small hand axe. The zombie advanced with mouth gaping and he was horrified to see the tongue had been chewed out, only a ragged stump flapped in the back of the orifice. He took a calming breath, waited until the monster got within range, and struck downwards, embedding the blade through the front of the face and wedging in the top of the chest. He wrenched it free and the bloodied mess fell.

"Where are you?" Kurt asked the madly dancing shadows as he twisted around, trying to find the torch. It was tucked into a small niche and he pulled it free, putting it between his legs as a clamp and twisting the top off. It had a spare bulb, somewhere, just not in the torch. The small spring holder was empty and looking through the thin glass he could see the incandescent element had been burned out, it was not the new type LED torches. He decided against throwing it away for now, they may be able to secure a replacement in a hardware shop. The barking crack of the shotgun bounced down the cave on the air, helping him with his orientation. If he went right the tunnel would run for approximately two hundred feet as the crow flies.

Stepping slowly, all too aware of the fragility of the flame as the air currents pulled and tugged at it threatening to extinguish his lifeline, he made his way toward the noise. Rounding the bend he saw a figure stretched out on the ground, it was a dead zombie. Looking up he could see the brackish green blood dripping from the hanging stalactite. The flickering lighter banished the shadows and Kurt looked at the face and the split skull, the pierced brain on display. The death was fresh.

"Hah! Way to go rock," Kurt said, giving a mock high five and pressing his palm to the cold, wet stone. The cadaver must have come blundering down the tunnel and ran its own head through on the pointed tip of the mineral deposit. It was one less for Kurt to fight at least and he moved on, the darkness receding as he neared the tunnel opening. The light improved as he turned the final corner and the bright daylight of the entrance revealed the small group of dead that had stumbled from his tunnel. They were reaching and each gunshot blew another to hell, but it was an awful waste of the ammunition. Kurt crouched low and rushed forward. Breaking into the daylight he heard the screams of joy and fear as he wielded the sharp blade, quickly dispatching the last of the zombies in a frenzy of swipes. He looked up, almost overcome with happiness to see the waiting faces of his loved ones.

"Kurt, look out!" John shouted down and he turned to the right to see thirty or more festering shamblers were nearly upon him, only forty feet away.

"Oh God," was all Kurt could muster.

***

"Where the hell is the rope? You were supposed to bring it!" Sarah screamed at Debbie. Why had they relied on her? It was obvious she was not one of them.

"Sorry, I forgot," she answered nonchalantly, pulling a face that indicated she was anything but sorry.

"You bitch!" Sarah yelled and punched her straight on the chin, laying her out flat on the ground. Debbie's eyes fluttered in her unconscious state and it was only the shouts of the others that stopped Sarah from dragging her to the edge and feeding the zombies with the poisonous bitch.

"Peter, there!" John shouted as he noticed two dead were getting near while Peter was looking down at Kurt, trying to think. He pulled the levers and swung the cab, brushing the bucket sideways and batting the zombies from the edge to go sailing to the scattered rock at the bottom of the mine. The bodies impacted and splashed in all directions, like a water balloon filled with rotted spinach coloured paint.

"What do we do? We have to help him!" Sarah was going crazy, the rope was too far away now and the clean cut, smooth sides of the cliff would prevent Kurt climbing.

"We can't destroy that many in time!" Gloria shouted, watching the large group as they closed on Kurt.

"I can try something!" Braiden called, leaning out of his cab.

"Please save him! There are even more now!" Sam pleaded with his brother. More had started to pour from the lower shafts, converging on Kurt from both directions.

Braiden nodded and his engine roared. The dozer lurched forward, breaking lines with the excavator that Peter piloted. He continued and then pulled to the right, aiming for the edge of the cliff, the fifteen foot drop to the lower level and the sheer drop beyond. He opened the cab door, still giving full power to the machine as he readied himself for the jump. He prayed that he would make it. The faint cries of his companions didn't break through his focus, he watched as the dozer reached the brink of the rock and the ground started to crumble under the weight of the trundling beast. Braiden roared his hatred at the dead and leaped free of the machine, hitting the gravel and rolling clear. The ground was cracking towards him, threatening to drag him down to certain death. He scrambled backwards on his bottom, kicking clouds of dust in his desperate attempts to clear the fracturing ground.

***

Kurt looked both ways, seeing the dual hordes that would devour him. The cliff edge beckoned. The rush of air and feeling of flight, followed by instant death upon impact would be infinitely preferable to being eaten alive. He looked up at his family, ready to say goodbye, but they were preoccupied by the raging noise coming from further down. The blade of the dozer appeared over the edge above the closest group and it kept coming, the rock face shattered and collapsed, joining the dozer in a massive tumult, crashing down and sweeping the whole road clean and out into the chasm. The roar of the avalanche rung from the canyon walls, the sound of the machine hitting the bottom was like a thunderclap, causing Kurt to cover his ears.

"Watch out!" Sarah shouted down, the danger of the second crowd was growing with each step.

Kurt looked around. The upper road had been broken beyond repair, it would be suicide to try and cross the uneven surface. The loose stone would likely pitch him from the edge in a second rock slide. Stepping away towards the perilous edge, he backed into a metal surface with a gong of steel on skull. He clutched at his head and turned, seeing the lowered bucket of the digger.

"Grab it, quickly!" Peter called and Kurt gripped two of the solid 'teeth'. Peter sat down, still watching from the cab, and pulled the lever slowly, raising the arm and Kurt with it. The bucket was fully extended when Kurt held on; if he had been closer Peter could have scooped him up like a pile of dirt and pulled him to safety. They weren't so fortunate, and the wet teeth could still cause him to fall, which was why Peter took it slowly, desperate not to break Kurt's tentative grip.

"Be careful!" Sarah shouted at Peter, but he didn't need to be told. Kurt dangled from the arm, his feet swinging in mid-air, only inches from the clawed fingers of the dead who had reached him. Peter's heartbeat pulsed in his head, drowning all other noise out. He stared at his friend, gaining strength from the look of trust in Kurt's eyes as he rose, ignoring the cannibals beneath.

Kurt was losing his hold on the teeth. The moisture from the previous disembowelled Hellspawn and his sweaty hands combined to slide his grip free, millimetre by millimetre. The arm started its sideward swing, the edge was so close Kurt could taste it, but he was not going to make it.

"HOLD ME!" John bellowed. He reached out over the void; Sarah held his vest, while Sam held hers, Braiden then took hold of Sam and the human chain stretched as far as possible. With a cry of fear, Kurt swung, his fingers slipping completely and plunging him down toward the waiting horde. John caught the handled collar of the life vest and held on tight, the sudden weight pulled him and he dropped to the ground, hitting his chest on the hard floor. Kurt was trying to find purchase on the cliff edge, wanting to take the strain from his father's arm which must have been agony. Peter carefully moved the bucket and provided a platform for Kurt to stand on. They paused, John still holding tight, yet able to draw breath now the pressure had been reduced.

"Thanks, Dad," Kurt said, his heart racing. He held out his hand and cupped his father's head, caressing the stubbled face, ecstatic to be alive. John smiled down at his only son, proud beyond words of his bravery and selflessness.

"You're welcome. Now stop messing around and get up here," John stated.

Peter slowly raised the bucket until Kurt could step onto their level to safety. They all jumped for joy, hugging and crying, the close calls were becoming habit and sooner or later their luck would run out. Debbie stood away from them, alienated once more and rubbing the lump on her chin and the back of her head where it had struck the ground.

"Peter, keep us covered. A quarter of a mile will take us to the boundary. Whose idea was it to come through the mine again?" Kurt questioned.

"You suggested it, silly!" Sam reminded him and Kurt grabbed his son in a headlock, mussing his hair and laughing.

They moved on, the path clear in front but the zombies below were still agitated and gave chase. That was until they reached the damaged section of road that Kurt didn't dare cross and the remaining stone tumbled away, taking the bodies with it. More splashes coated the bottom of the ravine and the remaining bloated, rotten monstrosities surged forward regardless of the danger, one by one toppling into thin air and dropping to the waiting rocky bottom.

"Dumbasses." Braiden gave voice to their thoughts, brushing his clothing to get the dust off.

The occasional zombie would cross their path and Peter duly crushed them, protecting the friends who followed closely. Within ten minutes they had reached the emergency entrance and the digger just rolled straight through the gate, tearing it free and throwing it to the ground, the chain link clattering against the tracks.

"Where to now?" Peter climbed down to talk to the group.

"Straight through there." Kurt pointed at the woodland in front of them. "It takes us to within throwing distance of the Beachwood Pub."

"We have to leave the digger then," Peter said with sorrow, the grumbling hulk had saved their lives and now it would be left to rust. He climbed into the cab, turning the key and silencing it forever. "Goodbye old girl, you did us proud."

They picked their bags up, shouldering the burden again. Weapons were readied for the perilous journey. Staring at the thick tree line, the autumnal chill had stripped the trees bare, deep piles of yellow and brown leaves coated the ground. The wind blew through the skeletal branches, which resembled waving fingers, beckoning them to enter.

"I have a bad feeling about this." Sarah shivered.

"It's either this, the Lavant road," Kurt looked at John and the involuntary shudder was enough to put them all off, "Or the Motorway." No one needed to be reminded about the miles of stationary cars and the occupants who haunted the open spaces between.

"Let's go, I want a pint before bedtime," John urged and they moved off cautiously.

CHAPTER NINE

The trees provided cover from the wind, breaking the chilled breeze before it could reach them. The ground was a kaleidoscope of colour from the shed foliage. Browns, yellows, and greens provided a crisp blanket for their passage. The noise of the crushed leaves was matched by the swaying branches, masking their progress for any awful entity that may be listening.

"Keep close, pass each tree slowly. They may be hidden," John whispered, his breath pluming in the cold day.

Honey explored, disappearing for minutes at a time as she scented the local wildlife. The piled leaves were a constant fascination to her and she leaped and frolicked, scattering them every which way. Sam and Braiden smiled, before rushing forward, kicking at the huge mounds while laughing. Sarah and Kurt watched their children, glad for the brief moment of high spirits amongst the horror that was their existence. Honey's demeanour changed instantly, her playful exuberance was replaced by snarling. She bared her teeth at the boys, who stopped and tried to calm her.

"Sorry, girl, we only wanted to join in." Sam held his hand out and had to snatch it back, barely missing the chomping jaw of their yellow pet. She started to bark furiously, spittle flying from her cheeks.

"Sam, get away from her!" Kurt shouted, wincing at the barks that could be drawing unspeakable danger toward them.

"Kurt, we have to quieten her, she will get us killed," John hissed, raising his cleaver, meaning permanently silence.

"No!" Braiden yelled, getting between them, "You won't hurt her!" He raised his screwdriver, making it clear he would defend the dog, despite the danger.

"Get out of the way, lad. This has to be done. I was worried she would create a scene at the wrong time. Thank God she did it when we were in the middle of a forest, and not in a town," John said, stepping forward menacingly, ignoring Braiden who had moved between them yet again.

Gloria was torn; she knew what the animal meant to them all, what she had done to save them and bring them together. The change she had wrought in Paige was remarkable. But the fact remained that this sudden change in nature meant they were at risk from both the dog, and whatever she alerted to their presence. Carefully moving to the side, she raised the gun, aiming at the crazed animal, curling her finger over the trigger. Braiden was focused on the standoff with John, neither willing to back down, which gave her the opportunity she needed. Closing one eye, she sighted the pet and took a breath. The large deposit of leaves behind her moved, stirred, and fell from the two forms that had stood up in the middle. They wore thermal clothing, possibly in an attempt to survive the cold, but hunger or dehydration had done what the weather could not. There were only the first faint signs of decay, small pustules on the white skin and darkened veins from the dead blood.

"Oh my God!" Gloria said while training the gun on the new threat as the two zombies kicked their own way through the leaves, imitating the actions of the youngsters.

Honey whirled, snarling and barking. The din created a diversion and the dead reached for the nimble animal, but she danced out of the way.

"Don't shoot!" Braiden told the teacher, motioning for her to lower the gun. Silently, he stepped up behind the corpses as they followed their four legged feast. Stabbing upwards, taking each zombie in the base of the skull where it met the spine, the screwdriver penetrated into their brains. They dropped to the ground, becoming one with the dead leaves.

"Good girl, you are such a brave girl," Braiden cooed, kneeling and stroking Honey's head. She was silent now, satisfied to receive the attention and fussing.

"She was only protecting us. We would have stood right on them if she hadn't barked," Sam stated. They waited, listening to the sound of Honey's tail disturbing the dry leaves.

"We were lucky. She could have brought hundreds down on us," John grumbled.

Braiden stood, eyes narrowing. Stepping forwards, he still had the dripping shank of the screwdriver by his side. "Don't you go near her again. Ever," he growled menacingly.

"Are you threatening me, boy?" John asked, meeting the gaze.

"Damn right I am," Braiden replied.

"Stop it, both of you!" Paige cried, getting between them. Sam pulled Braiden back, and Kurt did the same with his father.

"Braiden, calm down," Kurt told him. "Dad was right to do something, you know that. We couldn't know that she was protecting us. Now we do, ok?" Kurt looked at him and Braiden looked away, nodding his agreement, although not happy.

"He'd better not try anything like that again, I won't be so understanding next time," John muttered and Braiden reared up again at the threat, marching forward.

"Dad, shut your mouth!" Kurt pushed his father away and stopped Braiden in his tracks with a look. "You won't do anything! We are all in this together. She is a part of our family, she has bled for us."

"She's a bloody animal," John grumbled.

"And we are only alive because of her, remember that!" Kurt hissed, tiring of the attitude that his father displayed towards the heroic hound. "Don't forget who told me to stop and think, before acting rashly. What were you about to do to her?" Kurt pointed at the grinning furball.

"She still put us in danger," John finished, knowing Kurt was right, though too proud to say.

"Happy family," Debbie chuckled with derision.

"Let's see how happy you are when you are left behind." Kurt rounded on her and the smile died, to be replaced by the usual scowl. "Yeah, thought so."

"Peter, you won't let them leave me, will you?" Debbie asked, looking for support where there was none. Her bridges had been burned.

"You did this to yourself," he replied quietly, going to Paige, who was also petting Honey.

"Fuck you, you snivelling weasel. I don't know what I ever saw in you," she blustered, furious.

"Well, now you don't have to worry about it anymore, do you?" Peter answered back, signalling the true end of their dysfunctional relationship.

"I… I…" she could barely speak, her face reddening. Debbie was getting ready to explode, and to hell with the consequences.

"Shut up!" Kurt whispered and grabbed her from behind, putting his hand over her mouth, cupping the scream that escaped into his palm.

More rustling noises bounced from trunk to trunk in the murky woods, making it difficult to pinpoint the cause. Honey was still, sniffing and pricking her ears to locate the source. It could be the renewed grasp of the wind, disturbing the trees and causing the last of summer to fall from the branches to nourish the soil. Honey growled. It wasn't wind.

"Move, this way!" Kurt ducked and made his way east, toward the bridge that led to the Beachwood Pub.

They ran, careful to step where the foliage was thinnest, wary of twigs and their echoing snaps. Between fleeting glances of the forest floor, they caught sight of figures in pursuit. The dead were aware of the new flesh and wanted a taste, blundering around in their haste to reach the family. A rotting male stepped out from behind a tree, directly in Kurt's path. It reached out and was knocked to the ground, Kurt landing on top with a sickly eruption of decayed liquid.

"Help him!" gasped Sarah, stifling the scream of shock she nearly unleashed.

Kurt didn't need any assistance. He clutched the throat of the zombie, pinning it to the ground, ignoring the gelatinous feel of the peeling skin. He raised the hammer and punched a neat hole directly into the forehead, a bubbling green mixture spilling from the crater.

"Are you ok?" John whispered, helping him to his feet.

"Yeah, let's go, we are nearly there." Kurt was mindful of the crashing from behind, made by the converging dead.

The onset of stronger draughts indicated the end of the woodland; the frigid air was no longer filtered by the thick tree trunks. They took several moments, knowing they were being followed, but fearing the open stretch of road approaching the bridge that crossed the flowing river. It would leave them out in the open, fully exposed for anything else that was watching.

"When will we catch a break?" Peter groaned, looking upon the scene. The bridge was blocked with cars. There was crushed metal and broken glass from one side to the other where people had tried to push through, desperate to escape the horde. The paint had been scratched and furrowed where bones had grasped for the occupants, clawing at the cars. Thick puddles of blood lay on the road, the rain unable to wash them clean. Piles of unidentifiable gore were strewn everywhere, spilled from the dying. They had an unenviable choice, the fast flowing, freezing water of the River Lavant. Or traversing the uneven, wet, zombie infested car crash on the bridge.

"What do we do?" Paige asked with fear in her voice. She could count at least thirty on the bridge, some still in their cars, but able to reach through broken windows.

"Dad, what do you think?" Kurt asked. "The water will be safer, but cold enough to cause hypothermia if we can't get into fresh, dry clothes quickly."

"You mean if the pub is overrun, or surrounded?" John looked at Kurt, voicing his fears.

"The bridge will mean we stay warm. We just have to climb over the wreckage, the broken glass, and sharp metal. If we slip we will be cut to ribbons, if we get grabbed we will be eaten. I just don't know!" Kurt was weighing the options, the zombies from behind were close, visible at all times and not hidden by the trees anymore. Honey chuffed and ran down to the river's edge, wagging her tail.

"Looks like she has made her mind up. What about you?" Kurt asked the group. No one looked pleased about the choice, but they were out of options. Zombies in the forest, zombies in the wreckage, or the cold water.

"We have life jackets, so we probably won't drown," Sam piped up, trying to cheer them up. He failed.

They hurried away from the tree line, rushing around the blood and viscera. They waited on the bank of the river, surrounded by reeds and bushes that thrived on the moist earth. The water passed by, lapping at the bridge supports. It wasn't too deep which surprised Kurt. Normally at this time of year it would be chest deep. They would likely be submerged to the tops of their thighs, which was still bad and enough to cause loss of feeling and life threatening illness.

"How fast is it moving?" Gloria asked while keeping a wary eye on the dark woods, knowing festering horror would soon break cover.

"Quite fast. We will need to keep hold of one another as we cross. Take it slowly or we will be pulled down," Kurt warned.

"At least we won't drown, just freeze to death," Debbie moaned, pulling the fasteners on her life preserver to make sure they were tight. No one corrected her, for once she was right.

The horde was clear of the trees. Five, then ten, then twenty, more and more came into the daylight.

"We couldn't have survived against that many," Kurt said to no one, just thinking out loud. He stepped down, the water parting for his foot and filling the shoe. It bit into him like a thousand shards of glass as his leg sank into the water. Hissing his discomfort, he tried to maintain his composure and waded deeper. In the back of his mind, he knew that if they couldn't find sanctuary, this would be the end of them. He was young and fairly fit, but the cold was enveloping him, numbing the muscles of his legs. He wasn't sure he would even be able to walk once they reached the other side. Honey jumped in and paddled for all she was worth, reaching the other side in seconds and shaking off, watching the rest as they prepared for the crossing.

"This won't work, we will die." Kurt stepped back to the bank, dripping weeds and icy water. He had been submerged for ten seconds at most and already felt like he was missing the lower extremities.

"Jesus," he gasped, squatting several times to get the blood flowing. They looked at him expectantly, wondering why the plan had changed. "It's far colder than I thought. We would be crippled if we even made the other side. We clear our way through the cars, slowly and carefully."

"We need to be quick!" Gloria stated, watching the group of dead get closer. They had less than a minute.

"They aren't the problem. As soon as we get a car between us we are safe, I am worried about those," Kurt pointed, then rubbed at his drenched trousers, trying to massage the unresponsive muscles. The zombies in the crash were conscious of their quarry, although they couldn't get to them. As soon as they started the dangerous manoeuvre, all bets were off, one slip or errant step would mean death.

"Sam, take that one out for me," Kurt indicated the closest cadaver, standing in a small enclosure that would safely house them all while they took a short while to plan the route. Sam loaded and aimed, releasing the steel ball with a sharp twang. The zombie's head whipped back as the bearing ripped through, flinging it against the protective barrier of the bridge, then toppling it into the water below. The splash caused Kurt to shiver in sympathy, regardless of the corpse being twice dead. They watched the body bob down the river for a few seconds, spinning lazily on the surface.

"Good shot. Get over there. I will throw the gear to you," Kurt told them, teeth chattering in his head like a jackhammer.

"No, you go, your legs are icicles. If you stay, you may not be able to reach us," Sarah ordered and Kurt started to protest. "Now!" she demanded.

She was right, he couldn't lift his legs properly, so instead he laid his back onto the bonnet and rolled over with less grace than he would have liked. One by one they jumped over, filling the small space left between the crumpled cars. John remained, throwing the rest of the bags at the group before making good his escape. The pack reached the spot John had vacated, moaning with inhuman desire for the meat they could no longer reach.

"Do we destroy those first? The fewer walking around the better." John signalled the small crowd that had pursued them through the forest.

"No, we will waste time. Kurt needs to get dry," Sarah explained. Kurt was shivering and his lips were turning a dangerous shade of blue. "Get those trousers and socks off." Sarah started pulling at his belt.

Kurt turned away and undressed from the waist down and no one looked or made any comment. Sarah wiped at his damp skin with a blanket, getting most of the moisture off before helping him pull fresh clothes on. It wasn't ideal but the best they could hope for at that time.

115

"That's better. I couldn't even think straight, thanks, Love," Kurt said. He was still shivering, but the change of clothes would delay the hypothermia.

Surveying the scene, they saw that no route was without its risks. The occupied cars would need to be cleared first, lest they get pulled in by the zombies. The small numbers who were trapped between the shells could easily be picked off by the slingshot, but the sharp edges and glass was Kurt's primary worry. To clear the bridge, they would be traversing the carnage of fifty tightly packed vehicles, going either over, or through, depending if doors could open wide enough.

"Right, follow my lead," Kurt said, climbing over the second bonnet, dusting the crushed glass onto the ground with his discarded wet trousers.

"Gloria, come on," Kurt beckoned.

"No, you all get over. I will maintain the rear guard," she replied, turning to face the vocal group that hammered on the car, only feet from them.

"Ok, kids, hop over. Mind the rest of the glass," Kurt ordered and they obeyed. Gloria followed last, helped by John and Kurt.

"Good, this is going better than I expected," Kurt declared. "We go through this car."

He opened the door. It hit the closest vehicle and the gap was sufficient to squeeze through and crawl inside. They formed a human chain to pass the bags and blankets through, placing them in the back of an open van which they used as a tunnel to reach the next safe area. Just in case, they shut each door after using it to prevent anything following too easily.

The day was growing darker; they had only an hour of light at most. The tall lights on the bridge walls would be forever dark. Torches would need to be used, which would make the journey more perilous.

"Through this one too, but careful, the next car has a zombie strapped in." Kurt opened the door and a quiet gurgling moan issued from within. He had mistaken the empty front seats and lack of thrashing movement to indicate the car was abandoned, but in the back seat was a baby carrier. The tiny child was clothed in a padded coat and blue baby onesie; it wasn't big enough to have teeth or be a danger. Kurt hesitated and looked in the eyes of the monster that couldn't possibly understand what it hungered for. The arms flailed like a newborn; uncoordinated, with fingers flexing spastically without real control. The poor baby must have been sealed inside during the accidents, and then protected from being consumed by the vehicle barriers. Any of the walkers on the bridge could be the parents, perhaps they had gone to assist before falling victim to the plague themselves.

"What's the holdup?" John asked, looking past Kurt. "Oh."

"Don't let her see, Dad," Kurt whispered back. John stood and Kurt vacated the car, closing the door.

"Why are we not going through?" Braiden asked. John caught his eye and tried to slyly nod at the back seat, praying he wouldn't push the issue. The youngster cocked his head, saw the baby carriage and was quiet. He positioned himself to block the view of Paige, who was still oblivious to what was going on.

"There's too much blood inside. We go over," Kurt said, climbing the metal bonnet. Stepping down the other side, he trod on something and fell, hitting his head on the wing of the next vehicle whose tenant went wild. Stars danced before Kurt's eyes, swirling and dizzying him. His leg was grasped and an arm started to pull at him from beneath the car he had crossed. Little by little he was dragged closer to the waiting mouth, only the friction of the tarmac slowing the process. The body had been run over, crushed beneath the car and left to die in the tumult, alone and in agony. Kurt's resolve was hardened, but he still felt immense pity for the plight of the cadaver that now wanted to eat him, and the poor baby as it starved in the seat.

"Mind your leg!" John shouted. Kurt shook his head, clearing the fuzziness of the blow. He pulled the limb back, exposing the rotting arm and John hacked clean through, leaving the hand still clasping his ankle. With its other arm splintered, the zombie lacked the means to extricate itself. It would stay embedded into the chassis of the car forever.

"Are you ok?" John inquired, helping Kurt to his feet.

"Yeah, just a bit dazed. Let's keep moving," Kurt told them all, rubbing his head.

The zombie in the next car was hammering on the dashboard, a distraction, not a threat. They would have to ignore the noise. Taking it

117

slowly, they soon reached the halfway point. Underneath the vehicles were checked as well, but only the previous victim was trapped beneath, all others were clear. Sam used his skill to destroy any active, roaming corpse with his lethal bearings. The cars were cleared by slowly opening the doors, allowing the zombie to fall out, and using their combined weight to pin it while they rained axes and machetes at their exposed heads. It was an effective method and they were soon within three cars of reaching the far side of the bridge. One zombie was left, pinned between a car and a van, the lower body crushed and compressed, vital fluids and innards expelled through the open mouth.

"I've got this one!" Peter wanted to help and he jumped up onto the car.

"Pete, no. Let Sam get it with the slingshot!" Kurt warned.

"It's fine, trust me." Peter smiled back, failing to notice the zombie's shredded waist and the last strings of flesh holding the trunk to the pulped groin and legs. With one more desperate lunge the upper half of the body came away, thumping onto the car and crawling for Peter who shrieked and slipped. He fell backwards awkwardly and hit the bridge railing on his side with a sickening crunch, breaking ribs. The momentum carried him over and down, into the icy water below.

"Peter, *no!*" screamed Paige, who leaped forward and cleaved the zombie skull in two with her curved billhook. Heedless of the danger, she jumped over the last vehicles and ran down toward the bank, watching as his unconscious body floated past.

"Paige, don't! I will go in!" Kurt called. He was already cold and it would be better if the rest of the group stayed dry. He would struggle on until they reached the safety of the pub.

Paige looked back at Kurt, but ignored him, plunging headlong out into the water, reaching for her new friend. She stumbled on some sunken obstacle and fell beneath the water, then erupted from the frigid surface with choking coughs. Peter was almost out of reach and if she failed to catch hold of him he would drift away, drowning on the surface. The cold would do its worst regardless, so she lunged forward, grabbing at the leg and going under again. Her hand hooked on his trouser leg and she broke the surface again, before turning him over. Honey dived in at full run, paddling furiously until she reached them. She bit down on his life preserver and added her own kicks to the battle to get him to safety. Kurt waded out and helped them pull him in, all three now frozen and suffering from violent shivering tremors. Only the dog seemed unfazed, shaking herself and splashing the rest of the group as they ran over.

"Get him on the bank, quickly!" John called.

"I'll do CPR," Sarah said, readying herself to start the resuscitation.

They dragged him completely free of the water and Sarah wasn't needed. Peter coughed and vomited a small amount of water onto her legs, then clutched at his ribs as the involuntary spasms sent waves of pain down his damaged side.

"We have to go. Now," Gloria declared. The soaked clothing, coupled with the icy gusts of wind, would be their end if they did not reach shelter soon.

Debbie was stood to the rear, nonplussed at the near death of her ex fiancé. She had switched her feelings off, if indeed she ever had any for him in the first place. Gloria was certain her personality lacked the quality to love, or even feel. She was a dangerous person to be in the group and, despite her earlier misgivings, Gloria would be glad when Debbie was in their past.

"Braiden, can you help Paige? I've got Peter," Kurt asked, lifting Peter to his feet and placing his drenched arm over his shoulder. John took the other side, ignoring the feel of the wet fabric on his neck.

They shuffled and stumbled, the cold proving to be a worthy adversary. John's teeth were chattering from the contact of only one wet arm. He hated to think of the discomfort of the others, who were saturated. Luck was on their side for once, the roads were clear of cars or zombies as they neared the fork in the road that was the site of the Beachwood Pub.

CHAPTER TEN

"Shit!" Sam exclaimed when the pub came into view. The front garden area was occupied by a dozen undead. They would need to be cleared before they could gain entry. The zombies were also beating on the front door, fruitlessly it turned out, as the door was thick wood with heavy locks. This meant that people were inside, another complication which could mean a violent showdown if they refused entry.

"Wait here," John told them, rushing off after taking the short axe from Kurt. Sam and Sarah followed, entering the seating area in the front garden. As before, the distraction helped their effort and, taking more pleasure than they should, they butchered the dead from behind. They fell without even knowing they were about to be destroyed.

"Come on, quickly!" John called out, seeing they were no longer alone, many more were appearing from the road and undergrowth surrounding the premises. He tried the door handle, it was locked.

"Is anyone in there?" he called through the wooden door. Nothing.

"Please, if you are in there we need your help!" Sarah begged and heard hushed conversation from within.

"If you don't let us in then we will have to break in, and that will mean we are all in danger. Please." John didn't want to hack through the door, leaving the pub vulnerable for anything that wanted to get in. They heard more raised voices, a male and a female, arguing.

"Dad, what's the holdup?" Kurt asked, reaching the door.

"How do we know you won't hurt us?" came an angry male voice from the other side of the door.

"We are a family. We don't want any trouble, just somewhere to get warm. We have been in an accident," Sarah pleaded. Gloria stepped forward, preparing to blow holes in the lock to get them to safety, but with a final curse, the door rattled and opened outwards. A man and woman stood in the dusty light of the bar.

"Oh, thank you! Thank you so much!" Sarah said to them smiling, as the man closed and locked the door again once the family had all entered. The lady was happy, but the man was scowling at the intrusion. Kurt couldn't blame him; they had barged in unannounced and brought even more death with them.

"Get your clothes off, quickly," John told the wet trio, who needed help to do the task. Their fingers were numb and unresponsive to the signals their brains sent. "Do you have a fire, or any form of heat?" John looked at the man and woman who exchanged glances, bemused at the crazed stripping and activity that had replaced their peace.

"We have a log burner but we don't use it, it will bring more of those things," the man explained, crossing his arms defiantly.

"Listen, we know you are scared, you have every right to be. But trust me, the fire won't cause any attention, the smoke will be blown away before anything can see it," John explained. The surly man just stared back, unhappy at the unintended insult.

"Come on Mike, we can at least get a fire going, look at them all," the woman told her gruff partner, who just shook his head in disgust. "It's this way, in the other bar area." She gestured for them to follow.

They left Mike to his own devices and gathered in the back room.

"Thank you so much, I am Sarah, they're my sons, Braiden and Sam," Sarah explained and the rest of the introductions were quick.

"I'm Jodi Ussery, pleased to meet you all," she replied, concentrating on stacking the kindling to get the fire alight. The iron wood burner had a pivoted door with a glass panel on the front, to close when the fire was burning sufficiently, causing the steel casing to warm the rooms. Sparing their new acquaintances blushes, they had all left their underwear on, wrapping blankets around themselves as the fire took hold.

"Don't get too close, you can't get warm too quickly or you could go into shock," Sarah explained to the three who looked longingly at the flames, wanting to move closer.

"She's right. The widening of the blood vessels would cause a rapid drop in blood pressure that could be fatal," Jodi confirmed the fact. "Please, sit down over here. The heat will build in time and then you can get as close as you want."

"Thank you, Love. We may not have made it without you," John remarked, indebted to the stranger.

"You're welcome. I can't tell you how good it is to see survivors, we thought we were the only ones." Jodi beamed, genuinely happy to have company. "My friend there is Mike Arater, we own the Beachwood Pub."

"Nice to meet you, Mike," they all said, seeing that he had appeared at the archway. He didn't smile or answer, just nodded. It was plain to see that he didn't share the same feelings of companionship as Jodi.

"Ignore him, he is just pissed he will have to share the drink now," Jodi joked, causing another frown from her business partner.

"We really are sorry for the intrusion," John tried to placate Mike, approaching him and asking, "How solid is the front door? It seemed to hold well."

"It's solid enough. Things were built stronger back in the day," Mike answered, staring across the room at Debbie. There was a look of... recognition? John couldn't be sure and the contact was swiftly broken. Mike was six foot, stocky and tattooed, with a closely cropped shaved head, dark stubble growing through. He exuded an air of hostility that was the polar opposite of Jodi, chalk and cheese sprung to mind. John ignored it, putting it down to the end of the world and their untimely intrusion.

As the air warmed gradually, the family took in their surroundings. The bar was centuries old, with low ceilings and a hard stone floor. The gnarled joists that supported the upper floor were darkened with smoke and time. The underlying smell was of ingrained alcohol, combined with the usual fragrances of a drinking establishment; wood, leather, cigarettes, and food. Tables were still laden with checkerboards from the older patrons, as well as a dart board and pool table for the younger generation. Over the years, countless punters had watered themselves at the stained bar, from doctors and teachers to the outlaws and cutthroats of yesteryear. The pub was a sanctuary from the outside and a welcoming sight for a weary traveller.

"Would anyone like some food? The meat has turned, I'm afraid. We still have some fruit and vegetables left, pastas and rice, plus bar snacks," Jodi asked. She was about five feet three, with long brown hair tied back in a pony, greasy and lank after the past few weeks of not being able to wash. Kurt's decision at the outbreak to buy these dietary staples had proven sensible, they lasted well.

"We don't have enough to share, Jodi, you know that," warned Mike.

"Don't worry, we have our own supplies, we don't want to burden you further." Kurt stood, looking at Mike. He opened their bags and took out the food they had packed, passing the tins out to the group.

The worst of the chills had passed, the room was cosy and they hung the wet clothes on the back of creaking chairs to dry. Peter was struggling to breathe, the fractured ribs moving around painfully in his side. The dark, purple bruising was testament to the force of the impact. They could only pray the splintered bone had not pierced anything vital. He wasn't coughing up blood, which was encouraging; a punctured lung would mean certain death without medical aid.

"We can at least offer them a drink," Jodi admonished her partner, her smile now gone. "Why are you being like this? The first human faces we see in a month and you act like a dick." She pushed past him, opening the hatch and returning behind the bar.

"Honestly, we are ok. You don't have to do that," Sarah smiled, trying to break the tension. Mike was glaring at Jodi, and she was glaring back.

"I insist. We have all sorts of ales and soft drinks. I'm afraid the lager is out because we don't have power for the pumps," Jodi stated, doing her best sales pitch. The group were excited at the prospect of a drink with flavour. Water sustained life, but it could never titillate the taste buds.

"Should we really be drinking, what if something happens?" Kurt asked.

"One drink won't hurt. We deserve a tipple after what we have been through. It will steady the nerves," John answered with a grin. Mike snorted and walked away, angry at being embarrassed by Jodi in front of the strangers.

"Sorry about Mike, he is normally friendlier than this," Jodi apologised, pulling the pints of ale. Sam and Braiden looked at the frothy brews, then at Kurt who nodded. They hurried over and sipped at the drinks, before wrinkling their noses.

"It's an acquired taste, lads," John chuckled, swallowing the sweet brew.

"Sorry, could we please have a soft drink?" Sam pushed the barely touched pints back to Jodi, who put them to one side, before passing two bottles of cola to the boys.

"So, what on earth brings you to our establishment?" Jodi had finished pouring everyone's drinks and gave herself a double measure of scotch whiskey.

"You wouldn't believe us if we told you," Sarah laughed.

"Try me. Zombies have taken over the world, I'm sure your story won't be as crazy as that," Jodi replied.

"Sam, would you care to enlighten our new friend?" Sarah asked, seeing the excitement in his eyes.

"Well, we are looking for the old smuggler tunnels that lay beneath Chichester. This pub was the end of the line, before they loaded the contraband for delivery to the rest of the country," Sam grinned.

"I have heard the tales. There is only one problem, Sam, we don't have any tunnels I'm sorry to say. We have searched high and low too," Jodi said sadly, sorry to bring the youngster down.

"But there must be…" Sam was no longer smiling. He had advised his family to make the journey, and now it was proving to be a stupid mistake.

"She's right. It's a load of bollocks, designed to get people to visit the pubs in the area." Mike had returned, picking up one of the drinks that Sam had abandoned and drinking deeply.

"So what do we do now?" John asked the group, and then turned to Jodi and Mike, "We were trying to reach St Richard's Hospital, taking the underground route. The army have set up a base there for survivors," he explained.

"The only way will be cross country, and then we have to head south toward it, going through the Orlits housing estate," Kurt said quietly. The estate was home to several thousand people, not counting the hundreds of thousands that resided in the city limits. It would be swarming with the dead.

"That sounds like fun," Debbie chimed in, smiling at the difficulty they now faced. Mike laughed at her snide comment and she grinned even more at the approval. He turned away and carried his drink into the other bar, isolating himself again. Debbie stood and followed, sensing a bond with the unfriendly character. Kurt was glad to see the back of her, even if it was only briefly. Honey had lain down by the fire, absorbing the heat and falling asleep. She was dreaming, issuing small chuffs, legs twitching as if she ran from something. The river water had washed some of the dirt from her coat, and she was now more yellow than brown.

"You are more than welcome to stay as long as you want. My home is your home," Jodi offered.

"That's very much appreciated. But we need to find somewhere secure for our family," Sarah replied. "We are hoping to reach Hunston Nunnery, or Arundel Castle if the hospital doesn't work out."

"Bloody hell. They are miles away, surely there is somewhere closer," Jodi cautioned, hoping the group would reconsider the suicidal mission.

"We have to try, anywhere like this could be overrun at a moment's notice," John added and Jodi looked around, thoughtfully. She listened to the banging on the main door from the new arrivals. Perhaps John was right, it couldn't hold forever, nor could their food or water.

***

"What do you want?" Mike said, watching Debbie approach.

"Just wanted to say hello, and thanks for the drink," she replied, raising a toast to him.

"Bah, I wouldn't have given you anything," Mike dismissed her gratitude, but she sat down next to him anyway.

"There's no need to be like that," she purred, moving closer, her leg touching his.

"What are you doing?" Mike asked, knowing the game she was playing.

"I thought you could do with a friend. Jodi seems like a real bitch, insulting you in front of them," Debbie whispered.

"Them?" Mike raised an eyebrow.

"I'm not really one of them, they are all bastards, look what they did to me!" she pointed to her black eye and facial bruising, fishing for sympathy.

"So they gave you a slap, are you telling me you didn't deserve it?" he sneered.

"Fucking arsehole. You're as bad as they are!" Debbie complained and went to stand up until Mike held her wrist, squeezing.

"Now I see why you got the slap. Come, sit back down," he coaxed, patting the seat, smiling.

"That hurt!" Debbie muttered, massaging her wrist, meeting his gaze.

"Don't tell me you didn't like it," Mike continued.

"Well that depends who's doing it, doesn't it?" she said seductively, rubbing against him.

"Yes it does," he smiled, but there was no mirth in the grin. "So what's your story, how the hell did you end up with them?"

"Peter, the square with the broken ribs, was my fiancé," she answered with a grimace.

"Was?" he said, stroking her leg.

"Yeah, he is a pussy, letting them treat me like this, so I dumped him. He can go to Hell. I'd hurt him if I had the chance," she growled.

"Now, that's not very nice," Mike said with mock disapproval. "What would you do to him?"

"I'd cut his balls off and feed them to him," she grinned.

"Ouch," his hand was roaming higher up her leg, closer to the cleft of her jeans. "What else?"

"I'd cut his throat and feed him to the zombies. I'd kill all of them," she stated and their eyes met.

"Really?" Mike's hand came away and she mistook this for condemnation.

"No, I was only joking. I'm not a psycho," she blustered as he stood.

"Hmm, that's a shame." He locked eyes, and then walked away, back into the warmer room, leaving her alone and confused.

***

"Where do you both sleep?" Kurt asked, expecting them to share a bed as a couple.

"There are two bedrooms and a lounge upstairs, with another door to separate it from the pub. It means if those things got in, we would have plenty of warning before they ate us," Mike explained, staring intently at Peter who didn't notice. He was too absorbed with his pain.

"Can we sleep down here?" Paige asked, wanting to keep Peter warm. The colour had returned to his face, the blue tinge gone from his lips.

"Of course you can. You can stay upstairs with us though if you wish," Jodi offered.

"No thanks," Kurt declined. "Would you mind showing me around."

"Why?" Mike narrowed his eyes.

"Just in case we have to leave in a hurry," Kurt explained.

"You mean, if those things you brought with you get in here?" Mike demanded. The rest of the group shuffled uneasily at the new tension and Jodi sighed.

"They were outside anyway, or have you forgotten?" she said. "We are no worse off than before, except we have new friends now."

"They aren't my friends," Mike answered, looking at them all with mistrust.

"Mike, what the hell has gotten into you?" Jodi challenged him.

"Nothing, everything is rosy," he replied, then finished his drink and walked out of the room, heading for the upper floor.

"We will leave tomorrow. I'm sorry that we complicated things for you both," Gloria apologised.

127

"No, I'm sorry. I don't know what his problem is. Ever since the shit hit the fan, he has been talking about making a break for it to find his brother, who's in prison."

"It must be hard to not know what has happened," Kurt commiserated, feeling guilty he had caused more uncertainty. "Do you have family?" he asked Jodi.

She looked down and answered softly. "I have a mum and dad, but I think they are gone. They lived in the middle of Chichester; I don't think they could have survived this."

"Don't lose hope, Love," John tried to comfort her, "They could be safe and secure, you never know."

"No, it's better if I think the worst; their home is not very safe. I have grieved for them already." Jodi was welling up and Kurt felt like a total idiot for even asking, what were the chances she hadn't lost people?

"I'm sorry, Jodi, I can be such an ass at times." Kurt wanted the ground to swallow him up.

"Don't be silly." Jodi wiped her eyes, smiling again. "You couldn't know. And it's probably better they don't have to struggle through this. They weren't in the best of health. Anyway, let's do the tour."

***

"The toilets are through there," Jodi explained unnecessarily, the stick figure of a man and woman showed the way. "They are self-contained; no way out so there are only two other doors we need to worry about."

Jodi signalled for Kurt to come into the other bar area, and he saw another reason the front door was still standing. The old brickwork was inlaid with four iron brackets that held two sections of timber, laid across the door itself to brace it. They had been put in hundreds of years ago, but the thickness of the metal kept them strong. Originally they were designed to secure the property from raids by the authorities of the day, protecting the illegal booty. Now the thick planks sat in the iron holders, dissipating some of the force of the zombies.

Jodi lifted the bar hatch for Kurt and he walked under and into the serving area. The bottles of spirits hung from the rack ready to pour, backed by mirrors that reflected Kurt. He was shocked at the visage, dirty, straggly haired and days old stubble that would soon be a full blown beard. Before the horror, he had never countenanced growing facial hair, but with each day the dark hair lengthened, insulating his face from the cold. He felt for the women, but they wouldn't look as good with it, a scarf would have to suffice.

"This is where the magic happens," Jodi laughed, walking down towards the rear door. "Business has been a bit quiet lately though, the customers aren't as friendly."

"How safe is the other door?" Kurt enquired without much concern. Jodi and Mike had survived here since the outbreak of the dead.

"It's as strong as the front one, plus we have wedged a heavy freezer against it. Our kitchen doesn't have windows, so we haven't even heard them out there," Jodi explained, holding the door open for John, who had joined them.

They walked into a small corridor, with a staircase to the right that led up to the bedrooms. Set in a small alcove there was an open trapdoor in the floor, revealing a set of wooden steps that led down into a pitch black void.

"The cellar," Jodi said over her shoulder, walking past and pushing the remaining door open.

The kitchen was small but well equipped with highly polished stainless steel counters sat in the middle. To the left was the freezer pressed against the rear door. The deep sink was full of dirty dishes since to the water supply was no longer running. She caught the look of amusement on their face.

"Sorry, we have been using our bottled water to live. Our hygiene has taken a back seat," Jodi shrugged nonchalantly.

"We are not as fresh as daisies either." Kurt smelled his own armpits; the odour would have curdled milk.

"There's nothing like a zombie outbreak to take us back to the dark ages, we could really do with some plague, that would top it off," Jodi said and the men chuckled.

"At least we are secure. How do you get the kegs into the cellar?" John enquired, leaving the kitchen and making for the trapdoor, taking out a small pencil torch.

"We had a lift installed. It was the only modern thing in the place. There used to be a ramp that they would roll the barrels down, but we blocked that up. You won't need the torch, we have a couple of Coleman lanterns." She reached into the darkness and retrieved one. Opening the glass, she lit the wick and the flame drove back the shadows, showing them the cellar floor.

They descended to the bottom of the ancient stairs. The basement was typical of the era, with hard impacted dirt instead of other floor finishes. The wine racks stretched off into the distance, there were fifteen feet of cobweb covered bottles. Fat spiders skittered on the webbing, retreating from the light, preferring to hunt in the dark for whatever poor insect was unfortunate enough to become their prey.

"The kegs are back here." Jodi took them between the ornate, carved bottle holders. Kurt pondered the loss of the skills that had gone into making the beautiful racking many years ago. The uprights had vines, leaves, and fruit chiselled in the grain, reaching from floor to ceiling. Their wine rack at home had comprised strips of timber glued together, lacking any character, mass produced for a throwaway culture.

"Have you checked behind the racks for a door?" Kurt asked, trying to pull himself out of the bout of melancholy at the thought of his lost home.

"It's all solid. The racks are fixed to the stone itself," Jodi answered as she reached the open area for the barrels. The ales and lager were stacked in neat rows on each side, with an old hydraulic system for the hand drawn mead and electric pumps to provide pressure for the lager. The walls of the room were also stone, with no visible cracks or splits that would signal a hidden door.

"Shit." Kurt was angry that he had fallen for an obvious marketing scam. The local tourism authority had probably thought visitors would be intrigued by the old tales of highway robbery and skulduggery. The masked raiders like Dick Turpin, a legend even to this day.

"I'm sorry it didn't work out for you," Jodi apologised.

"It's not your fault. It was bound to be pie in the sky. We just have to come up with another plan," John said as he was reaching between the metal cylinders, rapping on the stone, still hoping for a hollow echo to signal the way.

"Is that the ramp?" Kurt asked. There was a sloped tunnel, roughly two and a half foot square, with a wooden trough full of sand embedded in the ground to stop the barrels from rolling away at the bottom. No sliver of light penetrated at the top.

"We had it sealed properly, to deter thieves. It's all bricked up now. This was the replacement." Jodi showed them the lift, a small version suitable for only two kegs at a time. It was designed for alcohol, not people. The top was made up of two steel shutters, which would be unlocked and laid open for the drink to be loaded. They would stop anything getting down into the cellar and Kurt finally relaxed, satisfied of the precautions for now.

"There is nowhere else is there? No hidden areas?" Kurt asked, just in case.

"I'm afraid not. Why don't we go have a look around the bedrooms?" Jodi walked off, the lantern illuminating the wine storage, plunging Kurt and John back into the gloom.

"I think one bedroom is like another, we should get back to the family. I think Mike could do with the peace and quiet anyway," John suggested and Jodi agreed.

"Listen, I will make you some food, not canned stuff," Jodi offered, defying her partner. She extinguished the lantern, placing it back on the shelf and left them for the kitchen.

John took advantage of the isolation the corridor provided.

"Son, we are in a bind. You know we will never make it through the northern housing estates, there will be thousands and we will be out in the open," John articulated his fears.

"Where can we go then? Back to the farm, find an isolated place to hide out?" Kurt was frustrated too, their lives depended on him.

"We don't know how they act. We can't be sure that they won't migrate when the food runs out. Even if a quarter of the population of Chichester heads toward us, that's thirty thousand corpses," John pointed out. The possibility of a swarm of that magnitude finding them made Kurt understand the gravity of their plight.

"We need somewhere with thick walls," Kurt announced. "We need the castle."

***

Jodi brought the food through and they ate, relishing her culinary skills. They sat in the warmth, ignoring the occasional stomping coming from the upper floor where Mike signalled his continued displeasure. Jodi shook her head in apology.

"More have joined the party, there are forty or more out front and round the side of the building," Braiden told them from the window, the heavy curtains shielding him from view.

"We will need to lower that number before we move out. We will come up with a plan in the morning to get out and leave Mike and yourself safe once we are gone." Kurt was thinking about using the upper floor for Sam to hone his slingshot skills. It may be disgusting, but they would benefit from reclaiming some of the ammunition after it had mashed brain tissue.

"Thank you for dinner, Jodi. It was lovely." Sam smiled. "Where do you want me to put the plates?"

"That's ok, I'll take them," Jodi replied, stacking the plates expertly on her arms, displaying her waitressing skills. The group clapped quietly as she gracefully used her elbow to lift the hatch and open the door, finally bowing before making her exit.

"I like her," Paige said and Honey looked up from the warm carpet, wagging her tail.

"Why doesn't that surprise me," muttered Debbie. "Two kiss asses together."

"She is worth ten of you," Paige smiled, politely insulting Debbie.

"You're welcome to her. I will be staying here, with Mike," Debbie spat back.

"No, you won't," Kurt stated, watching the fire through the glass. Debbie turned her attention to him, glaring her usual venom.

"What the fuck do you mean? You don't get to tell me what to do," she snarled, standing up. Kurt did likewise and stood nose to nose with her.

"If you think I would inflict you on that lovely woman, you are sadly mistaken. You will be coming with us, even if I have to tie you up and drag you behind me like a dog," Kurt spoke quietly, the threat not needing to be shouted. She searched his eyes and knew that he meant it. Backing away, she pushed past him, going to find her new 'friend'.

"Mike won't let you take me, I'll make sure of that," she sneered.

"I'm afraid he won't have a choice, sweetie," grinned Gloria, stroking the black barrel of the shotgun.

"Fuck off!" Debbie shouted and ran out, crashing through the bar door and nearly knocking Jodi over in her haste.

"What was that all about?" Jodi enquired. She knew something was up between them all and the dark haired, angry lady. Kurt let Peter explain the long and arduous journey, her evil outbursts and general vile demeanour. Jodi was shocked to find out that Peter had lived with the woman and had been betrothed. As time went on, Peter found himself asking the same questions, how he could have ever come close to formalising their awful pairing with a wedding? Looking across at Paige, she smiled at him and his heart skipped a beat. This was the lady he wanted above all others. Hopefully she felt the same.

"It's getting dark; we should all turn in for the night. Thank you so much for opening up and letting us in, you saved our lives," Sarah suggested, noticing the yawns and bleary eyes of the group. First light would allow them to think clearly and decide how to best extricate themselves from the pub, and their next destination.

"I agree. You look like you all had a hell of a day. If you need anything, please just tap the ceiling there." Jodi pointed to a section in the other bar area. "That's where my bed is, I will come straight down."

"Thanks so much, Love, we are in your debt." John shook her hand, the grip was firm and John respected the lady even more.

"Sleep tight." She smiled and walked off, the sounds of her creaking footfalls climbing the stairs carrying over the noise of the undead outside.

The family drifted off quickly, only Peter remained awake. The discomfort that had been somewhat numbed by more painkillers and a couple of shots of vodka, yet would still ensure he remained awake most of the night. He wondered where Debbie was and what she was doing. He didn't feel any emotional attachment toward his ex-fiancée, only guilt at the thought of leaving her alone somewhere. Maybe this was the best place for her. Thoughts spun through his mind, if they could convince

Jodi to come with them, the decision would be easy. She seemed strong and resourceful and would make a great addition to the survivors group. The noises of creaking from above caught his attention, but this wasn't footsteps. It was constant, rhythmic. Debbie was having sex with Mike.

CHAPTER ELEVEN

Sam awoke with an aching bladder. They had drunk several bottles of cola and water during the evening. Honey looked up, acknowledged his quick stroke and fell back to sleep. He stepped over the rest of the group and pushed through the swing door into the toilet. The smell of pine disinfectant was on the air and fresh urinal cakes were in the troughs. The door swung closed, blocking the soft glow of the wood burners' fire. Sam held his arms out and walked forward, feeling for the tiled wall. He found the cold, smooth surface and unzipped, aiming at the point where he knew the bowl to be. The sound of him emptying his bladder finished and was replaced with a quiet grumble. It wasn't his belly, it was more a vibration, difficult to pinpoint. It seemed to come from all around him, were there that many zombies outside? The vibration increased in intensity, it was like a steady drone, not at all like the sharp hammering of dead limbs on surfaces. He zipped up and pushed back through into the bar, happy to be in company again.

"Dad, something is going on. There are noises." Sam shook Kurt by the shoulder.

"What, where?" Kurt sat up immediately. The grogginess of awakening didn't seem to affect the group anymore. As soon as they were awake it was like a light switch had been flicked in their minds, triggering instant alertness.

They went to the window and peeked through a small crack. There was indeed a steady vibration, pulsing and reverberating from the walls and glass.

"What the hell is it?" Kurt asked the dark night and walking horrors. Movement from the right caused them to crane their necks and they saw a large garbage truck creep slowly round the bend in the road. It stopped with a faint squeal of brakes and sat there, facing the pub, watchng.

"A rubbish truck? What are they doing?" Sam whispered to his father.

"I don't know, mate, maybe they are just driving around trying to find a place to rest," Kurt answered, watching the metal hulk in the pale moonlight. A few of the dead had broken off to go and investigate this new stimulus. The driver of the vehicle didn't seem concerned as they reached him, banging on the side panels and moaning. The truck was put in gear and started to roll forward, crushing two of the intrigued cadavers under the wheels. Kurt strained to see into the dark cab but the moon only provided a shadowy outline of a person. It could have been a man or a woman.

"At least they will draw a few of them away," Kurt commented as the rear of the van passed them, closely followed by the chain of walking death. Another squeal of brakes broke the silence and the reversing lights came on, blinding in the night. The sound of the reversing beacon shrilled, warning the unheeding zombies to move out of the way. The driver floored it and swung the wide back directly at the pub, picking up as much speed as possible.

"Everyone, up. Now! Some lunatic's going to ram us!" Kurt called backwards, rousing the group as he frantically dragged Sam away from the windows. Both father and son grabbed tables and held them facing the impending impact, scattering checkers all over the floor. The grinding crash reverberated in the confines of the bar. Brickwork and glass shards bounced from the table tops that Kurt and Sam held, shielding their loved ones as they gathered their meagre belongings. The bright lights blinked out when the driver shifted to forward, bringing another rumble of breaking masonry and snapping wooden joists from the upper floor.

"It's coming down, get out of the way!" shouted John, pulling them all toward the safety of the toilet block. The ceiling protested with more rending snaps as unsupported weight was brought to bear on centuries old wood. The crashing noises subsided when a structural support landed with a thud on the solid bar, giving them a small window to escape through the four-foot-high gap.

"*Go!*" screamed Kurt, seeing the thick timber start to bend in the middle, threatening to snap at any moment and drop the whole roof onto their heads.

John went first, ducking low and encountering the first of the outside dead. With a single slash the top of the skull was split open and the creature dropped back outside. More were coming now that the van had disappeared into the distance, cheating them of their meal.

"Faster, get behind the bar and through the door." John was ushering them past. They were all coughing from the dust that was swirling in the area, eyes stinging and red.

"Who the fuck was that?" wheezed Kurt.

"I have no idea, but they want us dead," John answered while severing the head of a female zombie that had stepped over the rubble. They both fled into the small corridor to join the rest of the group and try to get to those trapped upstairs before the whole place collapsed. Incredibly, Jodi, Mike and Debbie were already waiting. Jodi looked scared but Mike was furious, he stepped forward and grabbed Kurt by the throat.

"Look what you've done to us. You and your fucking family!" Mike roared, slamming Kurt into the wall.

"Not so brave are you now tough guy?" Debbie laughed and danced with joy at the spectacle.

"Mike, leave him alone, what are you doing? It's not their fault," Jodi screamed at her partner.

The others were reluctant to hurt Mike. They had been the catalyst for the devastation and felt guilty their home was now in ruins. Braiden felt no such compunction, he stepped forward issuing a sharp head-butt straight into Debbie's face, breaking her nose with a crack and a gush of blood. Slumping to the ground she wailed, clawing at her face to try and rip the pain away. Braiden passed John and Peter who were wrestling with Mike, trying to break the stranglehold. He withdrew the sharpened screwdriver and stabbed at Mike's buttocks, penetrating the muscle. Blood ran down the steel shank and Mike dropped to the floor, screaming and holding his pierced flesh.

137

"You're fucking dead!" screamed Mike at the young boy who stared back at him, wiping the bloodied driver on his trousers.

"Want me to finish the job?" Braiden asked, taking a pace forward and raising the weapon, ready to follow through with the threat.

"Ok, sorry," Mike groaned in pain, holding up a hand to ward off the attack, "You didn't have to stab me though."

"It's only your arse. Fat and muscle, no major blood vessels. It will hurt like a bastard though. My dad Lennie used to do it all the time with a box cutter on people who owed him money. He called it striping, I guess because of the scars afterwards. We can call yours spotting. You shouldn't have hurt my dad," Braiden said, cowing Mike with his stare.

Mike stood up and his bottom muscles flexed, sending white hot pain through his body. He would pay Braiden back for this, with interest. Debbie came over and tried to help but he just pushed her away.

"Get the fuck away from me," he snarled.

"I was only trying to help," Debbie complained, fresh tears running down her cheeks but not from the broken nose this time. The family were shocked. A similar rebuke from Peter would have been met with vitriol and screaming.

"Let's go, we go out through the kitchen door. Jodi you said it was clear?" John asked as they bundled through into the cooking area.

"Oh no," Sarah moaned as the sounds of hammering greeted them from behind the door and heavy freezer.

"Jodi, are there any other ways out?" Gloria asked desperately.

"No, I'm sorry," she said with a look that spoke of understanding. They were trapped and the only way out would be to fight. She reached into a small nook and pulled out a Louisville Slugger aluminium baseball bat that she used for training sessions with her old softball team; the Chichester Wildcats.

"We have to go through them," Sam declared, trying to carry off the bravado. The fear in his eyes betrayed the truth; some, or all, would die here because of his childish fantasies.

"We can't, we are too disoriented. I can barely see from all the dust in my eyes. We would be slaughtered," John reasoned, trying to blink away the tears.

"The cellar is safe, we will hide out and decide what to do when we are more prepared," Kurt directed them all down the wooden staircase, watching the bar door for signs of movement. They just made it down and closed the hatch after themselves as the first rotting monster entered the hallway. It was oblivious of the floor and hook mounted within it, so it just shambled past into the kitchen they had just vacated. More came, many more. The pub had never been busier.

***

Sarah convinced Mike to drop his trousers so she could wrap some sterile bandage around the buttock from their first aid kit. Debbie mothered him, fluttering around like a hummingbird, wiping his sweaty face with a cloth, which only soured his mood further.

"Leave me alone for fuck sake!" Mike shouted, grabbing the fabric and throwing it into a dark corner.

"Sorry," Debbie whispered. She was now the weaker member in the partnership, no longer able to bully. It was a remarkable transformation in personality, abuser to the abused.

Jodi ignited the lanterns and placed them on the floor. They had all moved away from the collapsed end of the building, John had worried that the weight could drop into the cellar at any time. The lager barrel area with the lift was brightly illuminated with flame glow. Candles from the bug out bags were lit and placed evenly on the floor.

"Can we get out through there?" Braiden asked, pointing up at the twin steel doors of the lift access.

"No, it's got a heavy duty padlock. We could smash through, but the noise would mean they would all be waiting for us," Jodi explained.

"So we really are trapped," Mike complained. "Great work."

"We've survived worse than this. Don't worry, we will be fine," Kurt said, massaging his neck.

"Did I say I was worried?" Mike said, glowering.

"It's obvious you're worried, that's why you were hidden away in here," Braiden stated, trying to get a rise out of the tattooed bully.

"You little bastard! I'll rip you apart with my bare hands!" Mike stepped towards Braiden, ready to take him on even with the screwdriver.

"I don't think so," Sam said, raising the slingshot and aiming it straight at his face. Gloria had the shotgun aimed at his crotch and the rest got between them with razor sharp blades at the ready. Honey growled deep in her throat, daring Mike to move. His bravery faltered at the group's anger and his shoulders slumped in resignation. In his inner mind he thought; *They will pay for this, each and every one of them. They won't even see it coming.*

"One more word and I will kill you, do you understand?" Kurt asked, clutching the hatchet. Mike just stared, refusing to answer, trying to regain some confidence. Sam loosed the bearing and it tore through several bottles of fine wine, shattering them and spilling the sweet smelling contents onto the earth which absorbed it like a dry sponge. He reloaded in one fluid motion before Mike had finished ducking and flinching at the passage of the metal.

"Jesus, you could have killed me!" Mike shouted.

"Yes, he could have, but he didn't. Now calm down so we can get out of here. We never wanted to cause you both any aggravation." Sarah was trying to placate Mike. Any conflict within the group would leave them all vulnerable. They may not like each other, but survival depended on cooperation.

"What we may have to do is raise the hatch and kill them one by one as they fall down the stairs. It isn't the best idea, but it's all we have that I can think of." Kurt had calmed down and lowered his weapon.

"The place is swarming with them, are you crazy?" Mike wasn't too happy with the plan.

"It doesn't matter; the hatch will provide a bottleneck. They can only get down one or two at a time which is more than manageable," John explained. "We could even hide by the side of the staircase while someone acts as bait. Then we destroy them from the shadows."

A rumble of movement caused them all to duck and cover their heads. Streamers of dust fell from the ceiling where the bar area had now been buried by the upper floors.

"If that lot comes through, we will have dozens down here with us," Gloria said, listening to the settling of tonnes of wood and brick onto the cellar ceiling.

"That doesn't look like dust." Jodi pointed to a puffy cloud that was being drawn down into the darkness.

"You have got to be shitting me. Again?" Kurt groaned, holding his head in his hands. Everyone looked at him with confusion.

Realisation dawned on Jodi when her lantern banished some of the darkness, "It's smoke. The wood burner must have been damaged. The pub is on fire."

"What do you mean, again?" Mike demanded, already feeling the oppressive weight of the burning building.

"Not now. We have to smash the lift and take our chances," John shouted.

"I would shoot it, but the ricochet from the steel could kill us." Gloria lowered her gun, ignoring the impulse to blast through the plate to get at the lock.

"Jodi, how thick is the wall up there?" John asked her, pointing at the blocked barrel tunnel.

"Only a single layer of bricks. It blended in so well no one would even know there is a hole there to get down here," she detailed.

"Breaking that out will be quicker and quieter, what do you think?" Kurt asked his father.

"Let's do it, Jodi can we borrow the lamp please?" Kurt held his hand out and she passed him the glass covered flame.

John and Kurt crawled into the small opening and climbed. The face of the brickwork was illuminated and Kurt started to hammer away at the barrier. Hopefully the noise of the fire and collapse would help to mask some of the dull thuds of the tool. John watched while holding the lantern over Kurt's shoulder to help him. The glass door on the lantern had opened on the ascent and the flame started to waver, flopping around inside the vessel. Goosebumps rose on his arm with a cold breeze that washed over the exposed skin. John frowned, there was no opening yet, so the air should be still. Kurt wasn't swinging with sufficient force to cause a draft of that power. Looking to his right there was a small section of wall that was crumbling. It didn't match the surrounding stonework of the tunnel, so John poked at the cement, which fell away, increasing the cold air.

"Kurt, stop. Look at this." John showed his son, who then swung the hammer at the older surface. The wall crumbled, exposing another small tunnel into the surrounding ground.

"Do you think this is it?" Kurt asked, ecstatic they may have a safer means of escape.

"Sam, you were right," called John. "We have found the smuggler's tunnels."

"I told you they were here!" he called out excitedly.

Kurt crawled forward, the air of ages swept past him now that the area was clear. It was faintly unpleasant and he held his nose. It was the smell of decay, but thankfully not the decay of flesh. That scent was now so well-known they could detect it easily, like a bloodhound. After a short distance, the tunnel dipped downwards, dropping several feet lower before opening up into a wider storage area.

"Come through, it's safe," he called out and their bags were passed down. The family joined him in the small cave, surveying the scene with interest. The room was twelve foot square, with a low ceiling. Most of the group had to crouch within the confines.

"People were shorter back then, they would have been fine in here," Sam told them.

Wooden struts were wedged at intervals across the area and then continued into the tunnel that led from the room. The air was rank with the smell of mould, the timber was moist and where Kurt touched it, soft with decay.

"We need to be careful, or it could all come down," he said, leaving it alone.

In the corner were a dozen green bottles, still corked and containing a dark liquid. A few wooden barrels were broken in the corner. The damp air, coupled with the alcohol inside, had corroded the wood, leaving the rusted iron cask bands behind. They resembled a stack of rotten wedding rings, suitable only for the dead.

"What is that?" Braiden asked with awe. Against a wall stood an ancient rifle, merging into the wall itself with the passage of time. The long barrelled gun was a flintlock type, old and valuable if it had not been in such poor repair. Laid next to it was a pistol, similarly corroded and becoming one with the floor. The young boys couldn't help but let their imagination run wild, who had held these weapons? Smugglers, criminals, highway robbers? The romance of the era was compelling. Not the romance of love, but of the outlaw. The adventure of being outside the law, always running, dodging the gallows for the next big score. The reality had probably been far less thrilling, the existence had often been hard and ended with a short drop with a hemp rope around the neck.

"Wow," Sam uttered and tried to pick up the guns. They just crumbled in his hands and a look of disappointment crossed the boy's faces.

"They have been down here a long time," Paige commiserated.

"Dad, do you have the compass?" Kurt asked John who reached into the backpack and withdrew the small plastic instrument. The needle swung wildly, before settling on north.

"We don't have a proper map unfortunately, only Sam's handout sheet from school. But if these tunnels are like a spider web, we should be able to head north-east as much as possible and reach the pub by the hospital. As long as we maintain the right heading we can't go wrong. My only concern is the fragility of the tunnel supports, there may well be cave-ins that we will need to go around," John told them. A roar of devastation bounced through the small hole they had crawled through, the pub had fully collapsed and fallen into the cellar. Small cracks started to form in the ceiling of the cave, dropping soil onto their heads.

"Move it, into the tunnel!" Kurt whispered urgently, ushering them away from the crumbling danger. The mouldy wood started to sag, no longer able to support the weight of the dirt it held aloft.

They filed down the narrow tunnel, careful to avoid the remaining struts, lest they snap like toothpicks and crush them in an avalanche of soil. After fifty feet the rumbling subsided and the worst of the settling was over. Kurt slowly walked back and the room, plus about twenty feet of tunnel was now cut off, buried beneath a thousand tonnes of crumbled earth.

"Fucking marvellous, now we are trapped in here." Mike was sweating and fear cast a pall over his face.

"Mike's claustrophobic," Jodi explained.

"Yeah, so what? It's like being in a coffin down here." His breathing was becoming ragged, gasps instead of proper inhalations.

"Mike, calm down. You will have a panic attack," Jodi cautioned, trying to make him see sense.

Debbie was watching with concern. Mikes face was going red from the lack of oxygen and he was close to breaking point. He would flee headlong down the tunnel and career off of the walls, killing them all. Sarah stepped forward and took his face in her hands.

"Mike, look at me. *Look at me!*" she shouted, gaining his attention. "Slow down, take a deep breath."

Kurt looked at the ceiling with trepidation but the echoes of the yell died and nothing fell onto them. Mikes eyes were still wild, looking round for a means of escape that didn't exist.

"No, here. Look here," Sarah continued, meeting his gaze, "That's good, now keep the breathing slow and steady. That's better, nice and slow."

Mike's face was returning to a healthy colour. He closed his eyes and continued the breathing, slowing his heart which galloped like a stallion inside his chest. The rest of the group had been gripped by their own fear at the near meltdown of Mike. The reality of their subterranean endeavour impressed it upon them fully. They would have to move slowly and carefully, assessing each step.

"I'm ok now. Thanks," Mike said begrudgingly. He didn't see John put away the hatchet that he had pulled out, ready to stop a crazed outburst with one swing. Debbie, however, had seen it and would bring it up later when they were alone. Her poisonous mind was fabricating plans on dividing them so she could have Mike to herself. If she could take some revenge at the same time; that would be the icing on the cake.

CHAPTER TWELVE

They moved in a steady line, Kurt ahead with one lantern, and John following behind with the other. The torches would have been better for lighting the way, however, the flame served an extra purpose. If the oxygen had dropped to a dangerous level, the flame would falter and die, allowing them to retreat and find another route. Much like the canaries that would be taken into the coal mines back in the day; if the bird had fallen an alarm had been raised to evacuate the shaft.

"Everyone ok? How you holding up Mike?" Kurt asked, looking back. He wanted to repair some of the damage their arguments had caused, but he only received a grunt in reply. It looked like both he and Debbie would have to part ways with the others at some point soon.

"How about you Peter?" Gloria continued. He was being assisted by John who held him up with an arm around his waist and Peter's arm over John's shoulder.

"I'll survive," he answered, wincing with each step.

They had been travelling for about five minutes when they came across a weakened section of tunnel. The timber had broken free and some of the ground had cascaded down, partially blocking their route. Kurt looked back and held a finger to his lips; even noise could bring the remaining weight down on them. He stepped through, ensuring no contact was made with the fragile walls. Turning to light the way, the others followed safely. When it was John's turn, Debbie was nearly crazed with conflicting emotions; she could bury the bastard right now, in front of his family. But there was no guarantee the whole passage wouldn't follow suit. She opted for caution, reining in her murderous impulse and moving clear.

Ten more minutes of careful travel and they came across the first open area that provided eight more tunnel branches to take, excluding the one they had arrived from. The space was much larger, over twenty feet wide and twelve long. The supports were thicker and more frequent, spaced much closer than anything they had seen before.

"This must be where they would store stuff and sleep, look." Sam's finger pointed out perished blankets. He toed the fabric and it disintegrated instantly, turning to dust.

More items were stacked haphazardly, bottles and boxes. Mike picked up a bottle and smashed the neck, sniffing at the contents. He recoiled and threw it into the corner with disgust.

"Whatever it was, it smells like rotten eggs and vinegar now," he said. The smell was spreading and the others moved away, seeking fresher air.

"Dad, what's that?" Sam pointed at a pile of black chippings and powder in the corner. They had spilled from a barrel that had weakened over time. "Coal, maybe?"

"I doubt it. They wouldn't transport coal in barrels," Kurt mused. Gloria grabbed at Kurt's wrist as he held the lantern out to get a better look at the material.

"I think we should keep away from that. If I am not mistaken, it is gunpowder," she warned.

"Oh shit!" Kurt backed away, respectful of the potential for a detonation from the volatile material.

"Dumbass," muttered Debbie.

"Sorry," Kurt shrugged, letting the slight go. He had been a dumbass.

"Which way now?" Sarah asked and John looked at the compass.

"That is the most north easterly tunnel, we should try that one first," he answered. "I'll take the lead now, ok?"

"Go for it," replied Kurt.

They all followed the older man as he ducked through the entrance. It became surreal and monotonous. The underground shaft stretched into the distance, seemingly infinite. Timber, then rooted soil, timber, and then rooted soil, the pattern never changed. Mike was struggling again and only Sarah seemed to be able to keep him from freaking out. He resented that fact, fuelling the hatred in his heart. A pungent odour became apparent, the smell of sewage wafted down towards them on the air current. Rounding a bend, they saw that the floor was inches deep in fetid, stinking water. The yellow tinge and astringent scent told them it was stale urine. The wall to the left oozed unspeakable liquids. Small mushrooms and fungi grew on the disgusting, but bizarrely nourishing, mix of water and human waste.

"That's awful," complained Debbie, holding her arm to her nose, trying to dilute the smell.

"There must be a sewer close to the tunnel," guessed John.

"I'm not walking through that!" Debbie said adamantly.

"We don't have a choice," sighed John, carefully stepping through the noxious water.

"You are totally useless, aren't you?" Mike taunted her, pulling a face of derision.

"Fine, fuck it," she declared and splashed through like a child in a puddle, drenching her shoes and inner legs. "Happy?"

Mike grinned at the power he had over the woman.

"Come on, let's get to our destination. If this is the right way and we have been walking at about three miles an hour, we should be there in about fifteen minutes," John told them all.

"Gross, it's soaking through my socks," Debbie moaned, gagging at the smell she was giving off.

"Tough, you shouldn't have stomped through like a cry-baby," Mike laughed. She looked on the verge of tears again, eyes reddening the same shade as her bruised face.

"We can get you a change of clothes as soon as we get above ground," Gloria offered. She could feel the tension rising and Mike teasing the unstable girl could only end badly. The small act of kindness acted as a safety valve and Debbie was appeased, turning to follow John.

They moved silently for five minutes but they came across a problem, the tunnel had collapsed where thick roots had grown around the supports and crushed them. They couldn't try digging through, the earth looked too unstable. As they watched another small clod fell away and joined the growing hill on the passage floor.

"What a great plan this turned out to be," Mike mocked them.

"No problem, we go back and find another way," said Kurt. He was starting to lose his patience with the constant sniping.

"My arse is killing me, no thanks to that cunt. I'm not going anywhere until I've rested," he informed the others. Braiden grinned and fingered the screwdriver by his side.

"Fine, stay here. But we are going." Kurt handed a small torch to him but Mike just batted it away and it broke on the floor.

"Come on." John pushed Kurt past Mike and the rest started to trace their way back, following them. Mike and Debbie cursed and then caught up, scheming in their inner minds.

***

Kurt recognised the fractured beam that was close to the subterranean bed chamber. He faltered in his step, holding his hand in the air. Moans echoed from the walls, masking the true numbers that were approaching in the tunnels. Their conversations must have brought them; the darkness had probably slowed their advance or they would have already fallen over the dead.

"Which way are they coming from? The pub collapsed!" John asked, looking at the random openings that awaited them.

"The sound isn't coming from that way. There must be a breach somewhere else in the tunnel system. We can't fight them down here. We will be buried alive," reasoned Sarah, listening intently.

Kurt was thinking quickly, his mind free of the fear for now. They only had one choice; the sewers. "Go back, I will wait here and stop them with the gunpowder. Break through where the smell is, it will be a drainage tunnel at this depth. It will be horrible, but it will take us to the surface. I will be right behind you,"

"Be careful," warned John, hugging his son. Sarah and the boys did the same, afraid but no longer trying to prevent Kurt doing what needed to be done.

Their footfalls came back to him from the tunnel for a few minutes, to be gradually replaced by the increasing volume of walking horrors. Kurt flicked his Maglite on, shining it down the various openings. They poured from one of the entrances across from Kurt. Seeing their prey for the first time their arms raised in anticipation of feeding. Kurt spat on the floor and tossed the lantern underarm at the spilled explosive, before turning and running. Even as the burning torch was spinning, passing the putrid zombies, Kurt was sprinting. The glass broke, spilling the kerosene, which burst into flame a fraction of a second before the gunpowder exploded. The zombies were blown to pieces and then buried under countless tonnes of settled dirt. Kurt was running for all he was worth, feeling the chain reaction of implosion that he had triggered. The rumbling went on and on, deafening him and drowning out his laboured gasps as he ran, accompanied by crazed torchlight from his pinioning arms. The way ahead grew brighter with the glow of the second lantern.

"Run Kurt, *Run*," called Sarah from the freshly formed hole in the wall. Piles of brickwork and mud lay covering the urine pool and his wife reached out from their new vantage point in the sewer. She could see the falling tunnel as it crept ever closer to her husband's heels, it would be a miracle if he made it. Against all odds, a support that was slightly less rotten than the rest, held for a second before splintering into a hundred slivers of wood. Sarah held out her arms and Kurt jumped through into the quagmire of human excrement just in time, a cloud of dust burst from the hole and engulfed them. The roar of the passage collapse faded as it continued onward, finally reaching the blockage and stopping.

CHAPTER THIRTEEN

The sewer was roughly ten feet in diameter, with raised walkways on either side for inspection and maintenance. The sluiceway was in the process of drying out. Where once a fast flowing torrent of water and effluent would race down, the lumps had started to congeal and solidify. All manner of disgusting objects greeted them; used condoms, tissue, nappies, differing sizes of shit. They had broken through a section where the walkway had sunk into the smuggler tunnel, only twelve inches needed scraping away before they encountered the soft brickwork. The acidity in the urine had weakened the blockade, otherwise they would all now be dead and buried, rising again, but forever trapped.

"Christ, that was close," gasped Kurt, resting on his knees and drawing deep breaths.

"Now we are really in the shit," joked Sarah, making him stand to hold him tight. She was certain the tunnel would claim him as it closed like an eager mouth in pursuit.

"What's the plan now then, genius?" Mike challenged, stretching his aching leg out to try and minimise the pain in his buttock.

"Now it's easy, genius," Kurt answered with contempt. "We can use the access hatches to plot a course through the drains, looking quickly for our position."

Mike harrumphed, angry that he had been made to look small. The rest of the group gathered their belongings and made ready to move off. Honey was fascinated with the awful odours. She sniffed here and there, paying special attention to a nappy and the smeared contents.

"Honey, away!" Sam commanded and the dog gave it one last sniff, and then turned away with a guilty face. He did it to keep her safe, who knew what bacteria and diseases were rife in the vile paste of the drain.

"I'll look through that one, wait here," Kurt jumped the waterway and walked down toward the ladder. He climbed and paused at the top, listening for movement. Shuffling noises were close, the unmistakeable movement of the dead. Kurt knew the weight of the iron cover would drop back into place if there was any danger. The zombies had shown no sign that they would be able to think independently and raise the lid. He pressed the top of his head to the iron and gently pushed upward, revealing a sliver of dawn light. The scene was carnage. Broken, burned cars, piles of fleshy detritus, and bloodied smears over every surface from the running battles that had taken place here. Kurt recognised their position; they were close to the main fire station in Chichester, the hospital was situated a further half mile away to the north.

"Dear God," Kurt whispered. The sheer number was enough to take his breath away. Thousands lined the streets as he took in a full three sixty-degree view. The site was close to central Chichester, so it stood to reason that it would be swarming. The involuntary shudder he gave off caused the iron to rattle in the frame and the nearest corpses saw his face peering out. They gurgled and moaned, coming for Kurt, so he dropped the lid back. The cold, dead fingers began clawing at the iron, unable to lift it as he had surmised.

"Kurt, what is the matter?" asked Gloria when she saw the unhealthy pallor of his face.

"There are so many," Kurt said, without explaining further. They all knew what to expect from a major city, but the sight was beyond all powers of reason. The horde at the army barracks had been separated by water, and the distance lent it a strange disassociation. The knowledge of what shambled around, ten feet above their head brought reality home with powerful force.

"What's the plan, Kurt?" John asked, shouldering his backpack.

"We go north. We are near the hospital. It will only take us about fifteen minutes through the sewers," he answered and they followed John as he led the way, taking the direction that led the most northerly.

Reaching an area with railings, a huge, circular sump was absorbing the surface runoff from the rainfall. Water roared within the confines, pouring into the vast basin. Bobbing on the surface, like white marshmallows in a hot chocolate, were dozens of zombies. Their skulls had been rubbed clean of flesh by the circular motion of the water, bouncing them from the sides and smoothing their bones like pebbles. The macabre scene was disturbed by two more victims who came barrelling down the sewer channel. They reached out at the last second upon seeing food, but went over the waterfall and landed in the mass of dead, unfulfilled.

"We need to go round, that opening there should take us close." John pointed, watching the compass needle. Fortunately, it was a 'foul' sewer and dry with no one left alive to flush the toilets.

After eighty feet they came across another ladder and Kurt repeated the process. They were under the road that curved left to the main public carpark of the hospital. The distance from the centre of the city had thinned the herd; only hundreds walked the streets amongst the destruction. Homes had been breached, doors and windows broken to reach the succulent meat within. Kurt dropped the lid and informed the others how close they were to journeys' end.

"We need to get as close as possible to the main building, that way we can see the soldiers and raise the white flag before we get shot," Kurt explained.

"You can stick your head above the parapet first," grinned Mike without humour.

"I wouldn't dream of asking you to risk yourself. You're a survivor," Kurt replied, adding an inflection on *survivor* that really meant *coward*.

"Yes he is," smarmed Debbie, missing the insult. Mike hadn't and stepped forward, ready to attack Kurt and no amount of guns would stop him. Kurt ducked the punch and pushed, preferring not to use his axe. Mike was caught off balance and stumbled over the raised concrete siding of the sewer culvert. He fell backwards and landed on the top of the partially hardened faecal matter. The squelch rebounded from the concave walls of the passage and Kurt knew he would have been better using the hatchet to finish him. The look of pure hatred chilled Kurt's blood. There would be a reckoning for the insults and this humiliation.

"Take my hand," offered John, reaching out. Mike was sat in the depression his weight had created. The only other way he could extricate himself was by pushing off of the drain floor which would mean his arms sinking into the quagmire. With a scowl, he clasped the outstretched arm and pulled free with an audible pop. Braiden laughed, which increased the animosity and Kurt winced internally. The decision would be his whether to defuse the coming confrontation with a pre-emptive strike, or wait and see. Despite the bullies' abrasive personality, he was reluctant to commit cold blooded murder. If being an arsehole was punishable by death, Debbie would be six feet under already.

"Get out of those clothes, you could get infected." Debbie pulled a new pair of trousers and jumper from Kurt's backpack. He didn't resist, looking at his father, who could see what was coming too.

After peeling the layers off, careful to keep his fingers away from the brown slime, Mike said, "Let's get moving." His tone of voice spoke of violence repressed. But, like a pressure cooker, it would explode at some point. The question was when.

153

CHAPTER FOURTEEN

The drain was reached and the excitement had built within the group. Even Mike and Debbie were smiling at the thought of having some well-trained protection. Kurt did his best impression of a human submarine periscope and wished he hadn't. The scene of chaos sunk in, removing all hope of salvation.

"What do you see?" asked Sarah with excitement. Kurt looked down and the smiles instantly died on their faces, like a switch had been flicked.

Kurt scanned around. The hospital entrance had been chosen as the site of the army outpost. Treble stacked motorway dividers had been placed against the brickwork, reaching nine feet into the air, funnelling anyone - or thing - toward the waiting soldiers. Sand bag placements had been built and spaced out to provide cover for the machine gunners. Each gun lay silently, pointing toward the sky. Their operators were pacing in the carpark, dressed in combat fatigues which had been shredded by ravenous mouths. Thousands of spent bullet casings littered the ground and glittered in the rising sun. Scorch marks and overturned cars indicated grenade detonations, with piles of unidentifiable flesh intermingled. Hundreds of zombies lay dead across the vast carpark, victims of the final stand of the army before they were overrun. Several army vehicles had been parked to the side to provide covering fire, as well as a means of escape. The Foxhounds were armoured land cruisers, suitable for fast travel and strong enough to resist explosions. Some of the troops had fled into the safety of the vehicles. They were beating at the reinforced glass, now turned. The drivers had tried to force through the crowd, corpses on the pavement that had been partly crushed attested to the fact. Tyre tracks marked flattened heads and torsos, sticking the victims to the ground. In their desperation, the driver of one had grounded the Foxhound on a pile of bodies. They must have sat there, wheels spinning uselessly as they had been surrounded, until the fuel or engine died. The zombies had been unable to gain entry, but the troops had been trapped. Finally succumbing to dehydration or blowing their own brains out, painting the windows red.

"They are all dead," Kurt said, looking at them each in turn.

"Ok, what are our options?" Sarah asked. Crying over what could have been was pointless; they needed to keep moving to find shelter.

"There are guns all over the place up there; assault rifles, pistols and machine guns. We could really use the firepower," Kurt explained.

"Does anyone know how to use them?" questioned Gloria. Blank faces met her enquiry and Kurt's Rambo act was at an end. They were untrained and would be just as likely to hurt themselves as the zombies.

"The hospital grounds are quiet. I counted about sixty in the area. I will go and set a car alarm off from the other sewer cover, then when they leave, we can hold up inside for a while. We could use some supplies anyway, things like medicines and bandages," Kurt told the others and took the slingshot, plus a small number of bearings, from Sam.

"Wait here, I'll be right back." He hurried off.

"Why the hell are we risking our lives for some pills?" Mike asked Debbie who smiled.

"I know, it's crazy. We should find a nice safe place and build our strength," she said, fawning over him.

"You will be grateful for the medicine if you ever get sick. We are here now, we should at least have something to show for it," Gloria reasoned.

In the distance a car alarm started to shrill, the sound coming to them though the iron cover. Kurt returned at a slow jog and handed the weapon back to his son.

"I go first and make sure we are clear. Then we all take cover by the sandbags and concrete beams. If we are seen we will have to get back down here, if not, we get inside and clear the place out until we get to the pharmacy. Understood?" Kurt clarified and was about to ascend, ready for battle when Mike piped up.

"Do I get a weapon? Or do I just use my fists?" The challenge was in his eyes. He would love to use fists and a weapon on the group, but necessity demanded cooperation for the dash into the abandoned hospital.

Braiden shook his head, John shrugged, and Gloria looked down at the shotgun, showing she would act if necessary.

"Ok, here." Kurt handed over one of the hatchets. Mike weighed it and nodded, they were ready to go.

Kurt raised the sewer lid and laid it gently to one side. The noise had been minimal and none of the remaining dead noticed. He climbed through and made a *'come'* gesture with his finger. One by one they reached the surface and took cover behind the nearest machine gun placement. John followed up last, covering their rear in case any of the sewer zombies managed to get clear of the swirling water. He hoisted Honey carefully over one shoulder and she lay there unprotestingly as he climbed. The trapped zombie soldiers had seen the survivors from inside the vehicles, and their dull thuds as they beat against the walls of their metal coffin drew the attention of a dozen more zombies.

"Quietly now. Get inside; we will take them the main foyer." Kurt ushered them ahead and they pushed through the first set of double doors that led into the main hospital building.

"Look, there's some chain that the soldiers must have used to seal the main doors. Let's get it back on the handles." Mike crouched and picked up the steel links.

"No, leave it," Kurt said and pushed their belongings out of the kill zone.

"Why can't we just shut the door?" Debbie asked.

"Their hollering and banging will bring more. We need to keep a low profile or the whole of the city will be on us," Kurt explained and Mike dropped the chain.

"Sam, pick as many off as you can, we will deal with the rest," instructed John. The others positioned themselves in the shadows to the side of the doors, weapons poised to strike those that got through the main entrance.

Sam stood in the light that reflected from the few remaining patches of polished floor that weren't covered with dust and debris. He took a calming breath and loaded up the slingshot as the dead skirted the first sandbag wall. Their straight advance gave him a perfect target and his growing proficiency filled him with much needed confidence. The bearings glinted in the morning light before ripping through bone and brain matter. The zombies came on, crumpling to the ground as Sam destroyed them one at a time. Out of the twelve, only five made it into the hospital. The blades and hammers swished as they cut the air, erupting from the shadows and rending the dead brains.

"Good work, everyone, let's try and get the bodies outside." Kurt crouched low, using the high bagged walls to shelter from the view of any passing cadaver. He took the sleeves of a young female zombie. She had only suffered a single bite wound to the neck before bleeding out. Opting to place the dead out of sight to the right of the entrance, they dragged the carcasses out quickly. Mike was waiting with the chain. He looped it round the solid handles and pointed at a heavy duty padlock that had fallen under one of the chairs. Debbie scurried over and brought it to him but Paige could see a problem.

"Wait, where is the key?" she asked, looking around with one of the torches.

"Who gives a shit? We need to lock the doors." Mike fed the bar through the links and as about to snap it shut when John stopped him.

"Wait. The second you do that we are trapped in here. Let's see how safe we are before we lock it, ok?" he said to Mike. The temptation to lock it as a big 'fuck you' was hard for Mike to resist. The overriding emotion proved to be self-preservation, however, and he let it fall loose.

"I will stay here. The second I see one of those fuckers coming for the door, I lock it," Mike insisted, leaving the padlock in place, unlatched.

Listening intently, they discovered that the large open space of the foyer was as quiet as the proverbial tomb. The reception desk was to the right, abandoned now, when in better times it had bustled with queries, ringing phones and tapping keyboards. Kurt wasn't the only one to have a mild flashback at the scene; they had all used this hospital at some point in their lives. Four corridors led off to different parts of the main

157

building, with colour coded dots stuck to the floor for people to follow to reach their destination. Two vending machines had been looted, the hinges broken and the glass doors lay open. One had contained canned soda drinks and the other assorted unhealthy treats. It had always amused Gloria that something that promoted obesity would be overlooked for the financial income it generated. Hypocrites. A few cans had split and spilled their contents on the floor. It was now a sticky puddle of differing colours, all mixed together like an artist's palette. Honey took advantage and licked at the sweet covering, wagging her tail with pleasure.

"Honey, leave." Paige gently drew the dog away so that she didn't become ill.

"Where are all the bodies?" Braiden whispered. The walls were riddled with bullet holes and blood of both red and green was pooled around the site of the shooting.

"They must have moved them," Kurt said.

"Or they moved themselves," Braiden added which was probably closer to the truth.

"We need to clear the wings to make sure we don't get attacked without knowing ahead of time. They will have to break through the main doors which we would hear. I don't want to get caught again like we did at the pub," Kurt told the group and Mike glared at the mention of his destroyed bar.

"I'm staying here. I want to be able to lock this up if I see any coming," Mike said and Debbie went to his side.

Kurt wanted to keep them separate, he could see the developing relationship and the conspiring whispers when they thought no one was looking. "Ok, if you two get in trouble, lock up and follow the dots." Kurt handed one of the fresh bill hook machetes to Debbie for protection.

"We do orthopaedics first, red dots," John instructed and the rest moved off silently down the hallway, leaving Mike and Debbie alone.

CHAPTER FIFTEEN

"**F**ucking wankers," Mike grunted as the rest of the group disappeared from sight.

"I know, I hate them so much," Debbie responded.

"You hate everyone. I need to try and sit down somehow, my ass is killing me standing here." He pushed her away and lowered himself carefully onto the waiting room chair, favouring the undamaged left buttock, facing the door to keep a wary eye on the entrance.

"I don't hate you," she complained, hurt by his attitude. She sat down by his side without invitation.

"Jodi has been my business partner for eight years, I can't believe she has dropped me like a hot potato," Mike said to himself, trying to justify his growing detachment and anger at his once friend.

"They do that to people. Myself and Peter were happy until they showed up to 'rescue' us. After that, he treated me like dirt and is now fawning all over that Paige bitch!" Debbie scratched her own arm, drawing blood.

"Didn't you say that you wanted to kill him, that being together was a mistake?" Mike looked at her.

A look of disorientation passed over her pinched features. "Umm, yeah I know that, it was. I hated him, he was weak. You aren't weak."

"So you mean you couldn't control him any longer, and you resent that?" Mike deduced and she looked down at the trickling blood on her forearm.

"It's not like that, I..." she started to protest but he had hit the nail on the head.

Mike turned to her and lifted her arm, licking the blood clean. "Hey, I'm not judging." He changed tact, cajoling instead of abusing, "I need strong people like you around for what's to come. The strongest will rule this world, people like us."

Her eyes lit up at the thought of the power they could wield. "Do you really mean it?"

"Of course. When we reach my brother, we will be unstoppable. He is serving time for murder and controls the prison, drugs, phones, and women. Everything," Mike explained.

Debbie's mind went into overdrive. She would be at the top of the food chain, the mistress of Mike Arater. No longer vilified and abused for exercising her right to control people. The very thought was enough to make her moist and Mike wasted no time, unbuttoning her jeans and reaching within.

***

The signs of damage were everywhere. Glass was broken and shell casings lay on the floor where the soldiers had encountered the Hellspawn. The group used Honey to guide the way after tying a short length of rope around her collar. They cleared the first three rooms and then cut a length of duct tape to put over the door and frame. If anything went into the rooms they had taped, they would know ahead of time and wouldn't be surprised by an attack. The fourth room was a small examination suite and they guided Peter to the bed before he collapsed. Paige offered to stay and look after him. As they moved away they heard the sound of Paige dragging heavy furniture into place to block the door. They reached the children's section and Honey sat down and started whining. The group saw the bloody trails that streaked the floor, running under the magnetically sealed security doors. With no electricity, the locks were no longer working and John pushed the left hand door open an inch. Honey growled and whined at the same time.

"We need to clear it out," John reasoned, knowing the fallen children were the hardest to deal with.

"Dad, I can't," said Sam, thinking back to the mystery house and the child zombie that had nearly killed him.

"I understand. Myself, John, and Braiden will clear it, the rest of you watch our backs," Kurt offered. He hated the young ones too, but it needed doing despite their sensibilities.

They pushed through and the play area was revealed that sat just inside. Sarah remembered waiting with Sam here, watching him as he played after suffering a bad knock to his head. The toys had perked him right up, and after a couple of stitches and some medicine, he had been right as rain. He had even wanted to stay and play for a while longer, much to the amusement of his parents. The door closed and ended the memory.

Honey scratched at the door, she wanted to be with the men. From inside came the unmistakable groans of the zombie children. Quiet patters of shoes on the floor were silenced with the horrific sounds of meat being cleaved. The noises of a butcher's chopping block carried under the doors and only Gloria didn't cry. She was too stoic, although inside she was breaking apart. Teaching was her whole world and the suffering of children caused her to question her faith. How could God allow such heinous evil to be unleashed on the Earth? Movement at the door ended her inner dialogue and Kurt emerged, covered in green gore.

"It's done," he said quietly and placed the length of tape over the door. Gloria took the roll and cut one more strip, laying it vertically on the other piece, forming a cross.

"God protect the little children," she prayed and made the sign of the cross. In her heart, she was struggling to justify the action.

"Amen," came the chorus from the rest, who had bowed their heads solemnly.

***

Mike pulled his fly up and looked at Debbie who was sweaty and flushed. She smiled at him and wiped her brow. She could still feel the heat in her core and the burning sensations where he pulled her hair and raked her back with his nails. She shivered with delicious memories.

"Why can't we just leave right now?" Debbie asked, while straightening her bra.

"I have to get payback, Braiden is dead before we leave," he said with malice.

"I don't like it. They have guns and watch us like hawks. What if we don't get an opportunity?" She didn't like the odds. Hopefully she could convince him to abscond in the night.

"Leave that to me. Tell me a bit more about yourself, you look so familiar," he pondered, staring at her face.

"I come from Leigh Park, the Bosmere estate. I was adopted when I was a baby after my parents gave me up," she replied bitterly.

"That must be it. I lived on Middle Park way, in the centre of Leigh Park. My older brother Craig is the one that got locked up," Mike explained and her face creased in thought before her eyes opened wide with recollection.

"Craig Arater? Wasn't he the one that beat the man to death in the street?" she asked.

"Yeah. The guy owed my brother money for drugs. Instead of paying up, he got mouthy and got what was coming," he answered.

The story had been front page news at the time. The victim had been a prolific offender and nobody mourned his passing, but the media had eulogized him, focusing on his younger years as a successful student. The mention of his later drug dealing and violent tendencies had been ignored, as was the wont of news reporting to get the most dramatic headlines. Mike had been there when it had all erupted over the drug money. When the punches had started being thrown, Mike had intervened and knocked out two of the victim's friends who had wanted to break it up. They lay on the ground, one unconscious and the other nursing his broken jaw. After nodding his thanks to Mike, Craig had punched Aaron to death. The blows had caused a brain bleed and he died on the side of the road, in front of a crowd of gawkers. Craig was sentenced to fourteen years in prison, and Mike had taken over his drug business.

"So why do you work behind the bar in Jodi's pub?" asked Debbie with bewilderment.

"It's not Jodi's pub. We bought it together, fifty-fifty. It's what I used to distribute the drugs and legitimize the cash. The pub was a total failure, but Jodi never asked why we were so popular with the younger punters as long as the doors stayed open," Mike explained.

"And she never knew what you were doing?" she asked.

"I think she might have known. How could we possibly make money when the only normal customers were over seventy years old and only had one drink all afternoon?"

Debbie laughed. "What a dumb bitch."

Mike slapped her across the face and grabbed her around the throat. "Don't you ever talk about Jodi like that, do you understand?"

Unable to speak from the pressure on her throat, Debbie simply nodded. His fury barely abated with the nod. She was starting to black out and clutched at his hands, trying to free the deadly grip. Mikes arms were like iron and she would be able to do nothing to stop him killing her. A look passed over his face and the compression eased, allowing her to take gasping breaths.

"I'm sorry. Just don't speak about my friend like that," he said, then stroking her bruised face. Though his voice was calmer, his eyes were still angry and fevered. Debbie said nothing.

***

Kurt and the group reached the eastern entrance to the hospital. The doors were blocked by more concrete barriers, sealing that side of the hospital. No amount of walkers could move the blockage. They checked in on Peter who was fast asleep, then returned to the main foyer to take a break before clearing the western block. Mike and Debbie looked like children who had been caught in the cookie jar, shifty and guilty looks were on their faces. Kurt was fearful for the coming hours and days and what the pair planned. After eating and resting they were left to follow the yellow dots into X-ray and the dining areas.

"Follow the yellow brick road," Sarah sang as they went down the corridor.

"I guess that makes you Dorothy, Mum?" Sam joked.

"I would say Wicked Witch of the West," Sarah laughed, "And that's Toto." She pointed at Honey who grinned at the attention.

"I'm the Scarecrow," said Braiden, "He's dumb too."

"Hey, don't you say that. You are as smart as anyone I know," Kurt rebuked the self-deprecation. Braiden smiled and blushed.

"I would be the Cowardly Lion, I'm always scared," Sam muttered.

Kurt grabbed both boys and held them close. "Sam, you are braver than me, I would never have gone out alone in the dark to get payback. Same goes for you, Braiden. You two are the backbone of this group, we wouldn't survive without you."

The boys were happy with Kurt's confidence in them and moved low through the next doorway into the dining area. Unfinished food had gone beyond mouldy. The food had dried or had fur covering it. The smell was beyond awful. More blood had been splattered in the room and bodies were laid where they had fallen. Shattered brains were spilled over the tables and chairs from the high calibre bullets that the soldiers had used. Whatever clean-up had been put into motion had been ended before they could finish the job, as the children's wing and the food hall attested.

"Honey, anything?" Sarah asked the dog who was interested in the bodies, but showed no outward signs of fear.

"Ok, let's go," Kurt ordered. They stepped carefully over the human debris and broken furniture. Behind the serving counter, more rotting food was still under the heating lamp. The pre wrapped sandwiches were all green, and the fruit had shrunk and withered in the display bowls.

Kurt signalled to the rear doors and whispered, "Kitchen." He pointed and put his fingers to his lips, telling them to be quiet. They all nodded and Sam took Honey's lead, walking her to the entrance. Sniffing around the door lining, she still seemed unperturbed at the area.

Gloria swung the door open with the shotgun barrel and Kurt glanced inside. The glass skylights in the ceiling cast pools of sunlight onto the reflective counters and appliances like the spotlights of a theatre. No matinee was taking place, only the silence and abandoned feeling that was so pervasive. By nature, humans are social creatures and they all felt more of the loneliness that would accompany them with each day of their new lives.

"It's all clear. Come take a look at this," Sam said, poking at a pile of food on one of the counters.

"What about it, Sam?" Gloria asked. The food was unremarkable; the whole area was covered in it. She gave an 'I don't get it' shrug.

"Look how fresh it is, how long do you think the other stuff has been sitting for it to rot like that?" he added. The food had barely started to fester; the first signs of mould had just appeared on the surface.

"You're right! Which can only mean there are people in the hospital," Kurt stated. None of the group showed any excitement, the disappointment of their previous finds had left them cautious.

"Everyone keep your eyes peeled. I haven't seen any other signs of the living which may mean they have left already," John explained.

"I hope they are nicer than Debbie and Mike," said Braiden without tact.

Jodi saw the others were hoping she didn't take it the wrong way and smiled. "No he is right, I don't like what this whole thing has done to Mike. I always knew he had a troubled past, but his behaviour is totally beyond the pale."

Wary of surprises from both the dead and living, they exited the dining room and turned left towards the x-ray department. More holes riddled the walls at head height and the chunks of brain and scalp were still embedded by the bullets. The army had a hell of a battle within these tight, winding hallways. Ultimately, for all their firepower and training, the unsleeping, remorseless advance of the dead had prevailed. Kurt looked at the meagre weapons they held, and felt the immensity of their predicament. The x-ray's red warning lights were mounted outside the examination rooms, forever dark. Kurt pushed at the first door and met resistance from the other side. It wasn't a lock, because when he and John put their shoulders to the door it opened a fraction with a grind of protest.

"Gloria, get ready," John said as the gap opened wide enough to allow them through.

"I will go first, stand back," she answered and disengaged the gun's safety. She sidestepped through, prepared for an attack. The room looked empty; however, with no other doors in the room it was obvious that the equipment had not moved itself to block the entrance. The end of a mattress could be seen projecting from the protective barrier as they moved further inside. The room filled with the others and the only place a living person could be hiding was behind the shield that the doctors would use to protect themselves from radiation.

"You, behind the counter, come out now. We won't hurt you," called Sarah and they waited. The faint sound of movement came from behind the panel and a blonde head peered out with fear.

"It's ok, you can trust us," Sam tried to coax her out and the sight of the family was enough to assuage the fear of the gun. Gloria raised it to the ceiling and reengaged the safety to show their harmless intent. The rest lowered their machetes and Kurt put his hammer into the waistband of his trousers.

"I'm Kurt. This is Sarah, Sam, Braiden, John, Jodi, and Gloria. The yellow wagging machine is Honey," he said to the lady.

Honey couldn't resist and ran behind the screen to lick the new lady. She took a couple of steps back at first and held up her hands, fearing she would be bitten. Nothing could have been further from the dog's mind and she jumped up and lavished licks and kisses to the woman who immediately started laughing. Walking around to them, stroking the excited dog with one hand she held out her other and shook theirs each in turn.

"I'm Dr Hargis, but you can call me Christina." She smiled warmly at the group.

"A doctor. That's fantastic news, we figured that we would never see another medical professional," John exclaimed.

"You all look like you have been through the ringer. Where are you from and, more importantly, how on earth did you make it here safely?" asked Christina in quiet admiration.

"It's a long story. We are from Emsworth, I will tell you how we got here later, when we are all settled if that's ok?" Kurt answered. In truth, he would only give a brief breakdown of the travails, the destruction and horror that they had witnessed wasn't something Kurt wanted to relive unnecessarily.

"Of course," she said, smiling warmly, "I assume you came because of the soldiers?"

"Yes. We were told that they had secured the hospital, what happened here?" John asked and a look of anguish wiped away the smile.

"They held out for as long as they could, I will tell you all about it later too," Christina replied and said no more.

"We could use your help, we have a couple of injured people," Sarah said, changing the subject. She didn't want to take advantage of the lady's skills when they barely knew each other, but Peter needed to be checked.

"I must emphasize I am technically an anatomical pathologist. I have still had extensive medical training so I will do what I can, where are they?" she asked with concern.

Kurt sent the doctor and Sarah off to check Peter over while the rest continued their task to destroy any remaining zombies in the last section of the building. Gloria said a silent prayer of thanks. Just when her faith was being tested to breaking point, He seemed to respond in mysterious ways. Moving slowly, Sam used the slingshot to pick off the stragglers so they didn't need to take unnecessary risks and go hand to hand with the dead. Reaching the final entrance they found that the army had also blocked this one with concrete which meant they only had the front door to watch.

***

They met back in the main foyer and Kurt gave Mike the nod to lock the door properly. The snap was a welcome sound for the group and they felt safe, for a little while at least. Christina returned from Peter's room and gave him the all clear from a punctured lung.

"I have listened to his chest and, though painful, the broken ribs haven't penetrated his lung. He will be in considerable pain for a few days so I have given him some morphine. He is currently singing to Paige so it seems to be working," she explained. Debbie's face reddened and she looked like she would explode. Christina missed it; she had no previous knowledge of the complicated twists in the group's relationships. She assumed that they had always been a couple, the same as Debbie and Mike.

"Thank you for that, we really appreciate it," Kurt said.

"Mike, are you ok?" the doctor asked him with a worried expression.

167

"I'm fine. I'm just tired," he muttered in response.

"Would you mind if I took a look at you? You look really pale and sweaty," she continued.

"I said I am fine, now fuck off!" he yelled and picked up his things. As he stormed off they watched as Debbie followed to heel like a well-trained dog.

"Sorry, I just wanted to help," Christina apologized and the group explained in greater detail the dysfunctional relationships and problems they had encountered with the pair. They made it plain that they would be parting ways as soon as possible.

"Anyway, how the hell did you manage to survive here for the past few weeks?" John asked with genuine amazement. There was obviously more than meets the eye with the friendly doctor.

"It was a bad day, one of my closest friends had just died," started Christina, her eyes took on a faraway look.

CHAPTER SIXTEEN

The chilled room of the morgue was bustling with activity. The smell of pine disinfectant hung on the air, disturbed and swirled by the ventilation system. The floor was highly polished white tile, designed to be easily cleaned in the event of a spillage. Two stretchers were in use, both holding the covered, deceased bodies that were due to have a post mortem.

In the corner lay Dr Keston, who had passed away the previous evening after a short battle with cancer. The death was expected, so the tests had been rudimentary. Blood was taken, followed by any organs that would be suitable for experimentation by the trainees. Dr Keston had been a well-known figure among the staff. He had been a friend and colleague to them all while serving in his position as the previous Head of Anatomical Pathology. Even in death he would continue to help the hospital.

She had trained under Dr Keston and had loved him dearly for twenty years. He was not only her mentor; their relationship had developed into a solid friendship. Despite an age gap of thirty years, he had possessed a sense of humour very similar to hers, derived from the often macabre nature of their work and a defence mechanism against the emotional toll. Dr Christina, as he had affectionately called her instead of her surname, had often spent time at the doctor's Sussex home, sharing meals and learning more about the profession, fascinated by the depth of knowledge he carried. His wife, Janet, was a lovely woman too, quick to laugh and generous in nature.

"So here we are, old friend," Dr Christina said, trying to maintain the emotional detachment that he had instilled in her on the first day of work after completing her medical degree. Her tears were evidence that it wasn't working at the moment. She knew that the body was only a vessel, and his soul had moved on to whatever came next. Placing a hand on his cold brow, she moved a stray wisp of hair from his face.

"Are you ok?" Jenny asked, paying her respects. Jenny was the new medical student, twenty-two years old and as keen as mustard. She had only been lucky enough to work with Dr Keston for two months. A sore throat of Dr Keston's had been diagnosed as aggressive oesophageal cancer. The illness had claimed him seventeen days after first diagnosis, the lack of suffering a blessing in some ways. He had often spoken of his desire to die quickly, not wasting away and becoming someone different as his faculties failed one by one.

"I'll be fine, thank you for asking," Christina answered, removing the tubes from the veins and covering him to protect his dignity. "Actually…"

"Yes, Doctor?" Jenny asked, eager to please her boss.

"Would you mind preparing him for viewing? His wife Janet will be here soon and it's going to be hard enough, without me dressing him too," Dr Christina said, struggling with the grief. He had been like a surrogate father to her through the years.

"Of course, here let me," she replied, moving the body on the wheeled trolley and pushing through the side door. It led to the chapel of rest, a viewing room where the families could see their loved ones in a peaceful and tranquil environment before the undertaker collected the deceased.

Dr Christina took a shuddering breath, wiped the tears away with a tissue and put fresh gloves on. The post mortem on Harold Giles would take her mind from the pain and loneliness of her sudden loss. She prepared her table of implements. Rolling the sheet back, she exposed his torso. Mr Giles had been the victim of a drunk driver. The collision between their vehicles had been so severe that his body had to be cut free from the wreckage. Dr Christina sympathised, life was cruel and unfair at the best of times. Taking the scalpel, she placed it at the top of the chest, but was interrupted by the clatter of the main doors opening and two orderlies manoeuvring a new trolley into the room.

"Where did you want her, Doc?" Brian asked. He was a heavyset man, with a hairy chest and body. The polo neck he wore only accentuated the furriness, his coarse, brown hair bristling from the collar. He was a friendly character though and Dr Christina liked him. The same could not be said for the second man. Percy was in his early thirties, single, and had a surly attitude that aggravated everyone. It was only the fact that his mother was one of the governors of the hospital, that he even had a job. His usual tardiness and general aggressive tone would have seen lesser men fired. On one occasion, Dr Christina had found him in the refrigerated storage room. A young female body had been uncovered and the lascivious look on his face was enough to send chills down her spine. Much shouting had ensued between them as she chased him off. Her complaint had been brushed under the carpet at his mother's behest. Their only communication now was looks of disgust on her part, and anger on his.

"She can go in 3 E, thanks Brian," she answered, taking the transfer sheet from him. She signed it and then wrote the name on the tracking board, ignoring the glare of Percy and the way he looked both furious and aroused as he regarded her. Refusing to be intimidated, she stared back, looking him up and down before laughing dismissively. His face reddened and his small eyes narrowed with hatred. Brian pulled the metal handle of the refrigerated door and a cloud of cooler vapour flowed over the floor. The fluorescent lights flickered, blinking off before coming back on.

"Sorry, Doc, that wasn't me, was it?" Brain apologised.

"No, the doors are not linked to the electricity. It's a standard lock instead of the electromagnetic type we use for safety," she assured him and he smiled, pushing the trolley deeper within.

Dr Christina took the scalpel again and made an incision straight down to the man's navel. She then started to cut across the collar bone to the sternum, but noticed movement from the left arm. Pausing, she watched and waited, sure it was just the pressure she had exerted on the corpse. There it was again, the fingers fluttered and flexed.

"Oh God!" she exclaimed and ran to the phone and dialled the emergency line. A matron immediately answered.

"Emergencies, Cathy speaking," came a pleasant voice down the line.

"Cathy, it's Dr Hargis, we have an emergency. I have just started a post mortem but the man is alive! Get a team down here now!" Christina shouted.

"They are on their way," was Cathy's unflustered reply. They were used to dealing with high pressure medical issues, though probably never one as bizarre.

"Brian, Percy, I need your help!" she called through into the darkened room. The heavy plastic strip curtains that hung just inside the door had fallen back into place, hiding the men from view. Turning to administer any treatment she could before the emergency team arrived, she was astonished to see the man sitting. Astonishment turned to blood curdling terror in an instant as she watched his intestines uncoil from her incision, falling from his lap and trailing down to the floor.

"Dear God in Heaven," she whispered, holding her face in shock. The noise was sufficient to turn Harold's head and he regarded her with dead eyes. She had seen enough of them in her time as a pathologist, but none had studied her so intently, and they had never been in the head of someone mobile. The second gurney was also alive with movement and the body sat erect, the sheet falling from its face. The head of the second body slowly rotated, seeking the source of the frantic gasping coming from Dr Christina.

Loud thuds and crashes came from the refrigerator room. Brian and Percy were halfway through placing the body onto the storage shelf when she had started to move. Dropping the young lady, she rolled to a stop at Brian's feet and then reached for him. More impacts echoed in the small chamber as other bodies writhed free of their place of rest. The young woman pulled herself close to Brian and with a lunge; she bit down on his calf, tearing a chunk of muscle away. Brian screamed and pushed the cold body away, watching as it chewed. Another zombie grabbed him from his place on the shelf and tore the left side of Brian's face away in a red spray.

"Percy, help me!" gurgled Brian, as blood poured through the gaping hole in his face.

The younger man looked around, and saw the rising forms of the other corpses. "Fuck you, you're on your own!" he squealed and ran, dodging past a naked man who reached for him and groaned. More of the previously dead converged on Brian and they weighed him down, the gurgling screams reaching fever pitch as his flesh was peeled away from bone.

Dr Christina was moving toward the chapel of rest, the eviscerated Mr Giles was clear of the gurney and only a few paces from seizing her. It was surreal, the entrails glistened but there was no blood. Her legs felt like they weighed a thousand pounds, leaden and sluggish. It was a mixture of fear and disbelief. She was a logical and intelligent woman; this was simply not possible. She almost moved toward the figure again, thinking it must be shock that had numbed him from the pain. Percy hammered through the fridge door, catching the shoulder of the man. The legs of Harold Giles tangled in the intestines and he fell to the floor at her feet, lassoed on his own guts. She rushed forward and reached for the spilled loops, hoping to put them back in.

"Please, Mr Giles, hold still. What are you doing?" she said as he clawed for her, trying to bite at her arms. "I'm trying to help you."

The second deceased body was walking towards her too, arms raised and teeth gnashing.

"Look, the emergency team will be here in a matter of minutes. Umm, just stay put." She turned and flung open the door that led to the viewing room where families could say a farewell to their loved ones with dignity and grace. Dr Keston was feasting upon the young intern Jenny, who was looking towards Dr Christina, eyes glazing with the agony of her ravaged neck and arms. Blood pumped weakly from her jugular and formed a spreading pool around her body. Jenny's fingers clawed at the floor, imploring Christina for help, forming trails through the blood. Her dead mentor pulled more muscle free and she saw its arms raise, forcing the meat into his mouth. Dr Keston's attention was on the red platter as he ate his fill. The horrific last supper caused Jenny's blood to reach the door and flow under it, a sea of red. The dead man behind was coming; the heavy slaps of his hands on the floor were getting closer as he pulled himself along. The pool of blood at the door meant she would likely slip and fall onto her bottom, leaving her at the mercy of the voracious cannibal whom she had once loved.

Jenny died, her eyes losing focus as her neck ran dry. Dr Christina was trapped. Being in the basement level below ground meant there

173

were no windows for her to escape from. The velvet curtains that separated each viewing area would provide some camouflage, but if either monster looked around properly she would be discovered and devoured. The only chance of survival was the empty display coffin that the doctor should have been laying in. The wooden box was lined with soft fabric, embossed with gentle contours and frills for the carriage of the dead into the afterlife. She hurriedly climbed in, the creaking noises masked by the frenzied meal taking place only eight feet away. She lay down, placing her head on the small burial pillow and pulled the lid closed, the darkness taking her. The sounds of screaming began, muffled by the timber and padding of the box. Dr Christina held her breath, trembling in terror. She was sure the abominations could see the nervous vibrations and would pull open the lid, before ripping her to pieces.

The chaos was growing by the second, shouts and screams were followed by smashing glass in the corridor outside. She wanted to jump out of the stifling box, her lungs ached with the stale air and she was certain she was suffocating. The coffin would be her final resting place she frantically thought to herself. Closing her eyes, which were useless in the tightly sealed coffin anyway, she tried to calm down. As a doctor, she knew the oxygen would last for a while, but she was in danger of hyperventilating. Self-preservation would mean nothing in the blind panic that claustrophobia and oxygen deprivation would create. Imagining she was tucked in bed, taking slow deep breaths and concentrating on happier times, she settled her racing heart. She pictured her parents' warm smiles and loving, nurturing embrace. The coffin lurched with an impact and she almost screamed, but held it in. The footsteps moved away, taking the threat with it. She waited silently while the hospital died, the giver of life and care, now a source of spreading undeath.

Hours passed. The sounds of screaming and shouting, coupled with the occasional crash of breaking glass, was gone. The noise of moaning had replaced all other sound, penetrating the pine and padding of the wooden coffin. Christina breathed slowly through her mouth, wary that the rasping passage of air through her nostrils would alert them to her hiding place. Closing her eyes for a moment, she awoke again with a start. The urge to burst forth from the confinement engulfed her. Only by sheer willpower did she still her arms and keep them at her sides. How long had she been out? The noises had diminished to near silence. What she heard could have been her imagination, it was that faint.

"You can do this," she told herself, and opened the lid by a single inch. From her horizontal position she couldn't see the floor, but the room itself was deserted of anything standing. Gradually sitting erect like a Hollywood vampire from the coffin, she verified the room was empty. Taking the phone from her pocket, she dared to make a call now that she was alone. She tried security; nothing. The on call locum doctor; nothing. Her secretary; nothing. Emergency services; engaged.

"That's not good," she whispered, looking at the screen of her phone as it reported another engaged tone. Scrolling through the options she selected *'vibrate'* from the menu to keep the ringtone muted. She considered trying to dial the police again, but she changed tact and dialled her parents instead. After ringing eight times the answerphone picked up. *'You have reached the phone of Gail and Don Hargis, please leave a message and we will get back to you as soon as we can.'* The line beeped.

"Mum, Dad, it's me. Pick up if you are there," she waited. "Hello… hello… Ok I guess you are both out, please call me as soon as you get this."

Christina thought for a moment about phoning her ex-husband. Her fingers hovered above the numbers but she couldn't bring herself to press them. Adam was probably with that slut! Tears welled up in her eyes even amidst the horrific violence she had witnessed, she still loved him and hated herself for it.

"Bastard."

The phone buzzed in her palm which caused her to drop it on the floor in shock. The carpet softened the impact and it lay there, vibrating by her foot. Picking it up, *'Mum and Dad'* was displayed and she nearly dropped the handset again in her haste to answer.

"Hi, Chrissy, sorry we missed you, we were out on a bike ride, you know how your father insists on keeping fit," her mum informed her.

"Thank God you are alright. Mum, something is happening, did you see anything strange while you were out? Have you seen anything on the news?" Christina asked.

"Not while we were riding, no. The TV says there is a lot of rioting going on again. It's those teenagers I bet, ungrateful bloody lot. They don't know how good they have it, back in my day…" she begun the usual diatribe at the youth of today and Christina smiled, imaging her mum stood in the hallway wagging her finger at her dad who would nod in agreement for an easier life.

"It's not teenagers Mum, it's much worse than that. I can't explain it, but people are hurting each other, even killing. I want you both to lock the house tight and stay indoors until we find out more, ok?" she begged.

"We shall. We didn't have any plans today did we, Don?" A muffled *"Didn't what?"* sounded in the background from her father who was probably making a cup of tea in the kitchen. "Have plans, oh… never mind. We will stay here, don't worry."

"I will call you back shortly. I love you both so much, be safe," she said, hanging up the call.

The phone was returned to her trouser pocket and she strained to hear any tell-tale signs of danger. The noises she had heard earlier were not repeated. Other parts of the hospital may be under attack; she couldn't tell from the underground room. The floor was awash with the blood of her friend Jenny. The intern was long gone, either she had been completely consumed, which was impossible, or she was now prowling the area. Using the same caution, she pushed the mortuary door open, listening and checking before committing to the next room. The smell of death was in the air. In itself this wasn't unusual; it was a mortuary after all. This was different though, an unidentified component mixed with the blood and waste. Checking every corner, she then moved towards the freezer. Carefully parting the plastic drapes that served to keep the chilled air within, a naked man was chewing at the body of the friendly orderly. Hearing the movement, the pale fleshed figure stood while swallowing the tender mouthful. She screamed at the grisly sight. Her reactions were lightning quick and only the first chords of the cry were heard before her hand silenced the betraying yell. She backed away and pivoted quickly, ready to flee for the main door. Logic imposed its will and she skidded to a halt just before the exit.

"No," she said to the frosted glass of the swinging doors.

The man had pushed through and walked forward, groaning. The gurney was the only obstacle that Christina could see in the room and she quickly positioned herself on the other side. A loose toe tag flapped on the tiled floor and she couldn't help but think it looked like a macabre price tag. *What does a body sell for in this day and age?* Grave robbery had been a lucrative profession in the Victorian times when the knowledge of anatomy was in its infancy.

"Can you hear me?" she asked Mr Putney, the victim of an aggressive cancer who she had autopsied that morning. A gurgle and a stream of blood poured from the mouth.

"Guess not," she answered herself and darted to the right, playing a game of cat and mouse with the dead man. Round and round the gurney they went, like an old slapstick comedy chase. The motion of the body was causing the stitches to unravel, tearing at the skin and opening like a coat zipper. The organs had been removed for testing and the abdomen flexed and gaped like an open mouth with red, wet lips of sliced muscle pouting. The lumps of Brian that had been consumed had gathered in the empty trunk and spilled out, hitting the floor. Christina was starting to tire but by sheer luck, the cadaver stepped on some of the pooled blood from the entrails dragging body. One leg shot forward and the other backwards, dropping him to the floor in the splits like a gymnast with a sound of tearing muscle.

"Ooooh, that looks painful." She laughed at the absurdity of the whole situation. Standing was proving troublesome for the monster and Christina took the chance to tip the heavy steel table onto the thrashing figure. The edge crashed down, compressing the chest and the mangled ribs crunched as the full weight bore down. Now that the horror was safely incapacitated, she just stood and watched for a while.

"No blood, no vital organs and yet you won't lie still," she explained to the clutching creature. An idea formed in her mind, a crazy one she couldn't deny, no matter how much she wanted to flee.

Pushing through into the freezer, Brian's decapitated body leaned against the racking and his chewed head was upside down in the middle of the room. Christina caught sight of the blinking eyes and the way it opened and closed its mouth, silently screaming.

177

"Oh, Brian, I am so sorry," she apologised without knowing why. It could have been guilt at her survival, or the loss of so many friends in such a short space of time.

Turning around, Christina walked to the entrance and locked all the doors via the magnetic emergency seal, effectively isolating herself in the gruesome room. It was designed for the possibility that she discovered a communicable pathogen or other virus. Her terror had dropped only a couple of notches and her inquisitive nature had climbed several to compensate. She returned to the freezer with an instrument tray, laid it by Brian's reanimated head and gently kicked it onto the shining surface. The tray slid across the tiled floor with the added propulsion of her shoe. The teeth were snapping like a set of joke teeth, chattering away with its need to feed.

"What are you?" she asked with fascination.

Lifting the tray onto the counter, she was careful not to let the head roll in case the champing mouth took a bite. Using a pair of tongs, the head was placed onto the plastic head block. Christina was spooked by the way the eyes followed her wherever she went, like an old haunted portrait painting. Picking up a scalpel she held apart the arteries and veins of the neck, seeing the tell-tale damage caused by teeth. The spinal vertebrae had been gnawed and small chunks of bone were missing. The face was in pieces but the skull and jaw were still intact.

"Zombies?" she laughed half-heartedly. Brian moved his lips but without lungs he couldn't answer.

"What else could you be?" her answer left more questions.

Taking the knife, she cut the scalp and laid the top of the skull bare. The bone saw buzzed into life and it made short work of the bone, which was just as well because even the low hum could bring guests. She levered the dome free with a sickly pop and the brain was exposed. A green hue had formed on the mucus membrane that coated it.

"No pain," she said and held the point of the scalpel by one of Brian's eyes, pressing downward and piercing the orb.

"No fear either, you didn't even blink." She withdrew the razor sharp implement.

"One more test I suppose." She pressed the spongy brain and sliced deeply with the blade. The one good eye rolled back and the mouth was motionless.

"Zombies... you've got to be shitting me."

***

Christina was hungrier than she had ever been. The packed lunches that she had found in the personal belongings of her colleagues were now gone. Two sandwiches, an apple, two yoghurts, and a bag of salted chips was not enough to sustain her through the previous days. The electricity was still working from the backup generator that the hospital utilized in event of a power failure. The magnetic sealed security door had held against the brief, disinterested searching of the zombies as they searched for fresh prey.

The smell of the festering bodies she had autopsied after they had died a second time was held in abeyance by the extraction system that still whirred away in the corner.

"How long has it been now?" she asked herself, looking at her watch. "Two days?"

She wondered if the hospital was totally abandoned. No one had come to investigate the events which meant things had probably gone badly, very quickly. Her stomach rumbled in complaint at the lack of sustenance within.

"I'm hungry too, stop complaining!" she chastised. "Well, I suppose we will just have to see what is out there, won't we?"

She feared running into more of the moving dead, but feared slow death by starvation a great deal more. If she was ever going to get to her parent's house, she needed to get out of the basement and see what was occurring in the 'real world' as she called it. Weapons were scarce; only knives and various bladed implements that were designed for precision instead of damage potential were at her disposal. The only thing that had been catching her eye was the slatted metal siding on the hospital gurney which could be raised or dropped to prevent the patient, or cadaver, from falling off.

179

"Ok, so it looks like I'm going to be a gladiator," she mused, looking for a tool to undo the bolts that held it in place. The metal would make an excellent shield if she could tie it to her arm, leaving the other free for stabbing or bludgeoning in the event she ran into trouble.

Looking through the pockets of Brian's headless body, she found what she was looking for. It was a multi tool that she had often seen him use to clean out his fingernails, not that they had needed cleaning. She had often teased him about the fact he had the loveliest nails in the whole hospital, the envy of secretaries up and down the wings. She missed his chuckle and his friendly manner. The head that sat on the inspection block was a travesty of the kind man he had been in life. Now that it had been stilled, she found herself crying and confiding in it, apologising for her decision to run instead of fight. Deep down she knew he wouldn't harbour any ill will towards her, Percy on the other hand…

"Damn you, you cowardly piece of shit!" Christina cursed at the rotten bastard. She hoped that wherever he was, he had suffered for his actions.

The siding came off quickly and she bound it to her forearm with sterile tape and bandages to act as padding so it didn't restrict the blood supply. Raising her arm, she tested for movement and it wasn't as restrictive as she had feared.

"That's good. Now how about a weapon?" she asked and the only things that could be used were either a stainless steel hammer or a long bladed surgical knife. The hammer was heavy but would need a few swings to do any damage, and the zombies were not known for just laying still while they were dispatched. The knife would serve her needs better and was sturdy enough to pierce flesh and bone if stabbed with sufficient force.

"We have a winner," she said to herself and moved the gurney towards the entrance.

The time had come to do or die and she pressed the door release button with no hesitation. Pulling the door open, she took a quick peek and saw that the immediate hallway was clear of the dead. Their work was evident everywhere though, trails of blood and remains streaked the corridor from the chapel of rest as well as the autopsy room itself. Signs of her previous guests, the late Dr Keston and probably what had remained of Jenny, were on display. The gurney trundled in front, pushed ahead to act as a battering ram and give her some space from any attacker.

The rear wheel creaked with each turn, "You had to pick the bloody trolley with the dodgy wheel, didn't you?" she complained to herself.

Around the corner was the side office that booked in and checked out each body, followed by the staircase that led to the main accident and emergency department. Cecil fell through the doorway of the office, seeking the source of the noise that disturbed his peaceful slumber. He was the guard on duty the morning of the apocalypse and had suffered no visible damage. The windows and door were streaked with congealed bloody mess where the escapees of the morgue had tried to reach him. A faulty heart valve had finished the elderly gentleman before he could be reached and the zombies had left him alone to turn.

"Hi, Cecil. You have seen better days, that's for sure." She felt growing pity at the fate of people she had once called friends.

"I don't suppose you want to let me past for old times' sake?" Christina asked but the growling and look of intense hunger from Cecil gave her the answer. She took a run and the squeaky wheel creaked like mad until she connected with his body, knocking him down. His thick glasses slid across the floor and came to rest against the nearby wall.

"I'm sorry, Cecil. Now hold still," she said, trying to pin his head down and stop him from gaining his footing. His head twisted and snapped, attempting to chew on the exposed meat of her arm between the metal rails.

"Now that's not very nice," she said, her feelings hurt.

She knelt on top of the struggling body and pinned his head to the side, exposing his temple. Carefully taking the knife, she slid it through the skull and Cecil lay still, finally at peace. She closed his vacant eyes, honouring the dead even in their new state of existence. Climbing the stairs she found that the hallway was deserted and she ducked between openings as she made her way silently to the dining area. Her senses were reaching out and she could hear the faint shuffle that had come to embody the approaching dead. Looking through the windows, Christina thought the dining area seemed deserted but had been the site of more violence as the dead had filed out from the mortuary staircase to seek fresh victims.

She pushed through and the doors swished shut on slow close hinges, concealing her from view of the torn and shredded zombie that turned the corner. She duck walked, down low, while ensuring that the trolley rail attached to her arm did not crash into anything as she moved down the aisles to reach the kitchen entrance just as the previous door gave access to the searching corpse.

"Shit," she whispered. There was no alternative but to push through and fight the monster in the kitchen area when it came to investigate. Throwing caution to the wind, she stood and made eye contact with the creature. It had been horribly mauled and was in a worse condition than any she had encountered up to this point. Being used to the frailty of the human body, she had seen her fair share of awful sights; burns that left the body blackened and crispy, falls that had left the poor victim like jelly from the shattered bones. This new desire to be up and walking was taking a bit of getting used to. Clotted lumps of gore fell from the open mouth as it gave chase, reaching out for her.

"Think! Think!" Christina demanded as she scanned the room, "The fridge!"

She ran over and pulled the handle of the large walk in chiller that contained enough supplies to feed an entire hospital of people. The figure that stepped out in the swirling mist of chilled vapour made her scream in fright.

"Jesus, you scared the shit out of me!" Percy scowled and his eyes narrowed. Seeing it was Christina, his lips curled in a grin that left her in no doubt he wanted to commit unspeakable sexual acts on her. Looking past him, the body of a small child lay naked on the floor of blankets he had taken from the supply cupboard. It was bound and gagged with a pillow case over its head, thrashing on the makeshift mattress.

"You fucking animal," she shouted as the door opened behind her, allowing her pursuer in to join them. Percy's grin disappeared with terror and he tried to pull the door closed, but Christina held it open and raked her knife down his fingers, severing the tendons. Percy screamed and clutched at his useless digits while looking around at a weapon to use against her. The jars of food were close to hand and he started to launch them indiscriminately at her across the kitchen. The glass smashed against counters and walls, smearing the delicious contents. Some rebounded against her body when he got lucky, causing her to yell in pain. For some reason the frenzied, hateful throwing fit drew the attention of the zombie and it ignored Christina, choosing to make an attempt to get at Percy. The jars made no difference to the creature. It didn't flinch or shy away, just had creamy sauce dripping, as well as the green tinged blood.

"Help me, you bitch!" he shrieked and pulled the door closed with a loud thump.

"I don't think so, do you?" Christina asked her friend who had lost interest with the steel door and gazed at her again. It lumbered around the kitchen units and she just sauntered away, keeping pace with the slow moving horror.

"We are going to save that poor child from that bastard, aren't we?" she continued, reaching the fridge door. She took the handle and it opened an inch, then slammed shut again with Percy's weight pulling against it. With a strength that rose from the pit of her stomach, a burning hatred that blazed into life inside her, she clutched the handle and wrenched it. Being caught off balance, Percy fell back into the fridge and cowered, holding an arm out to ward off the attack.

"My mum will hear of this, you cunt. She will have your job. You will never work in another hospital again!" he shouted.

Christina laughed in his face, "Do you think your mummy is still alive? Everyone's dead you halfwit."

"No please don't kill me!" he begged. His hands covered his streaming eyes, as if not seeing what was coming would mean it wasn't real. Christina had a different idea come into her mind, an epiphany of sorts. She had heard about his pending child molestation court cases and decided he should suffer for the evil he had perpetrated against the innocent, both before, and after the unfolding apocalypse. Using the bed rail to pin him down, then with a quick flick of the wrist, her blade had cut through his Achilles tendons on both feet. His eyes flared open and he gurgled bubbles from his mouth, the agonising pain not allowing the scream to burst from his lips. She grabbed his dirty hair and started to drag him out through the door, but he fought back and held tight with his one good hand on the shelving.

"Let go!" she shouted and cut at the back of his last good hand, freeing the limb.

She kicked at him and he fell to the cold floor, trying to stand but with no grip and no way to plant his feet he just flopped to the ground. The zombie had seen the easy meal and came around the kitchen for him. Seeing the rotten monster, Percy cried even harder, dragging himself along the ground in a fruitless effort to get away.

"I'm here, sweetheart," Christina hushed the small figure on the floor while keeping an eye on the one sided chase in the kitchen aisles. Lifting the pillow case, the wild dead face of the child snapped at her and a small part of her died in that room. There were no signs of injury on the child that would indicate she had been bitten before turning. Percy would have most likely snatched her in the chaos and taken her to a quiet place, before committing his cruelties.

"There's a hot, dark corner of Hell waiting for you, Percy," she said, lifting the child and marching her toward the other corpse who had now knelt down and started to chew at Percy's stomach, tearing deep and pulling intestines out all over the floor. She took her knife and cut the bindings free, lowering the child monster onto Percy's tortured face. The fingers clawed and raked, pulling lips and skin away which were thrust deep into the eager mouth.

It took Percy minutes to die and Christina made sure the job was done before she stabbed at the two zombies, destroying them. Not waiting for Percy to turn, she stabbed into his untouched brain, denying him the chance to hurt any more people. She removed the bed rail from her arm now that the imminent danger was passed, and to make the next task easier. Using the blankets, she made a burial shroud and wrapped the child tightly. Unable to give her a proper ceremony, she opened the freezer and placed her within, hoping to get the chance to finish the job later.

"He can't hurt you any more, little one," she said and closed the door, head bowed.

Her appetite was gone, but she forced herself to eat a sealed pasta bake that was quickly heated in the microwave. The flavourless food filled her stomach, appeasing the growling organ. She closed her eyes, taking a moment to process the awful happenings of the past few days.

***

Waking inside the fridge that she had slept in, the darkness was absolute. It was morbid to think what had occurred within these steel walls between the living and dead, but she was exhausted both physically and spiritually after killing Percy and didn't want to risk exposure to more zombies. She looked at her phone and the time was twelve past one in the afternoon. The message bar was empty and the battery only had six percent remaining. She hadn't thought to keep it charged after the landline phone signal had died and not returned after the power failed in the surrounding area. She served up a small portion of cereal topped with a huge spoonful of sugar and leaned against the wall, savouring the sweet crunch. The sound of the door being kicked inwards caused her to drop the bowl, which smashed into pieces on the floor.

"Identify yourself! Now!" came the shout from the armed man in the doorway. It had a muffled tone to it from the full face mask that he wore to guard against airborne pathogens.

She held up her hands, "I'm Doctor Hargis. I work here."

"Miss, you should come with us. We have a man down and the medic could use your help," he led the way to the foyer where a dozen men were working tirelessly, stacking boxes and clearing access.

"What are you all doing here, what is going on?" Christina asked the soldier who had identified himself as Sergeant Edwards.

"I have no idea how you survived, Miss, but you have my respect. The whole world is on the brink, we have been ordered to try and set up a refugee centre here for Chichester and the surrounding towns. I don't think we are going to have much luck, all we have seen so far are the dead heads," he explained.

"You can take the mask off Sergeant, this thing isn't airborne or I would be trying to eat you already," she said and he took the heavy mask off with a sigh of relief.

"Troops, we are clear of airborne contamination. Masks are optional, but keep them close in case anything changes," he barked the order and his men complied.

Through the front doors, as she paused to administer aid to the bitten soldier, she could see what they were trying to accomplish. A camouflaged forklift was moving large concrete blocks and a line of men were throwing sandbags to each other, which were then placed in a curved row on the ground. A forward group was firing short bursts from their rifles at the dead. The numbers were growing from the ruckus being created and the point men were glad of the reprieve the first machine gun placement provided. It chattered into life, mowing a path through the growing mass and the other guns took up positions, adding to the waves of bullets that punched through the flesh.

"Sarge, we can't hold them back much longer," gasped a corporal, looking madly over his shoulder.

"Banksy, hold it together! We will have full field of fire with close artillery support in ten minutes. Get out there and give those fuckers hell!" shouted the superior, which served to bolster his flagging spirit.

"Yes, sir!" he roared and ran back outside, triggering a renewed energy amongst the others as he gave orders.

"Quinn, this is Doctor Hargis. What do you need her to do?" the sergeant asked the blood drenched medic.

"I can't get to his artery, can you try and find it while I hold him down?" he said, ripping a syringe free of its packaging and injecting it into his arm. The morphine took effect quickly and his struggles lessened.

"Bitten?" Christina questioned. The shapes of the wounds on his arms and face left no other possible explanation and the medic just nodded.

"They came out of nowhere as we landed. The chopper touched down and we thought they were hospital staff. Maybe they had been... once." He let the sentence trail off as he pinched the artery which was pumping feebly now.

"Come on you bastard, *fight!*" Quinn yelled at his dying comrade.

"Men, lock and load. Get your asses out front, we have a war on our hands!" Sergeant Edwards shouted.

"How can I help?" Christina asked, watching the men as they ran to take up firing positions.

"Hide. Don't come out until we come and get you. If we don't come and get you… keep low and do what you have done best. Survive." He pushed her away and met his men as they rushed for the entrance.

"Sarge, we have really fucked the hornets' nest haven't we?" shouted a young recruit with a terrified expression.

"Yeah, and now we fuck the hornets!" he bellowed in reply, trying to instil courage for the coming battle. His own expression turned to fear when the panorama of thousands met him crossing the car park.

"Grenade out," came a cry and they all dropped low, waiting for the dull crump as it exploded and signalled the start of the fire fight.

Christina retreated into the kitchen and, with each door closing, the sounds of fighting diminished. She unplugged the fridge, hoping to keep the temperature a bit higher until they would come and retrieve her. The motor stopped humming and she kept the door open a crack, listening to the war, trying to gauge which way it turned out. The sounds of faint screams breached the doors and she knew. The door closed, sealing her inside the metal room. Safe, but cold.

CHAPTER SEVENTEEN

They looked at her with amazement. She had survived on her own during the outbreak and been on the frontline of the fight between the army and the massed dead of Chichester City.

"Wow, you have really been through it," Sarah commended the doctor for her resilience.

"I don't think anyone that is still alive can say they haven't. You've had your own struggles by the sounds of it." She returned to compliment.

"Why did you pick the x-ray room to hide if you don't mind me asking?" Kurt enquired.

"It's the most sound-proof room in this part of the hospital. I would lay low to avoid the few that are left in the hallways and when it was quiet I would run to get some food." Dr Christina showed her knowledge and survival skills.

"And you have survived on your own? Remarkable," Gloria said with respect.

"Well I've never really been alone. I have always had the company of the zombies, but they aren't the best conversationalists," she joked.

"On the subject of sleeping, we could do with some rest. Would you mind if we pulled some mattresses in with you?" John asked and Christina was more than happy to have company again. The poor soldiers had been friendly and brave, but totally unprepared for the assault they would face from the locals. She mourned their passing ever since that fateful day.

The group wheeled Peter through the main foyer to relocate him to the x-ray room. It was a shame the power was out; they could have used an x-ray to get a proper look at the internal damage. He was so high on pain medication that he was still singing 'show me the way to go home' as they closed the doors to gather their belongings and more mattresses from the hospital beds. Debbie and Mike were nowhere to be seen, so they decided to leave them to it. The split among the group was taking place properly and the family would need to be on guard against any foul play. Placing candles around the examination room, the scene was gently lit and gave them all a feeling of calm.

"I wish I had possessed some candles; the darkness was the hardest thing to take in here. You are left alone with your own thoughts and memories," Christina told them with a shudder.

"Well you aren't alone now. We all look out for one another," Sarah told her.

"You don't know how grateful I am to hear that," she replied and gave Sarah an unexpected hug. The rest of the group moved in and had a massive cuddle fest, sharing the moment of new companions.

"Hang on a minute," Kurt said, pulling away, "How do you smell so clean?"

"Oh, we still have the operating room showers working. The water is freezing, but by using the soap from the bathroom dispensers I can keep fresh. You all smell like you could do with one," she joked and they all laughed. The muck and filth was ingrained in their skin and, even cold, a shower would be a welcome relief.

"That would be great," Braiden said, looking at the dirt under his nails and skin that hadn't been its natural shade for several days.

**

They lay in the shadows, the single candle barely managing to banish the darkness. It was decided they were too valuable to waste by having a few alight at one time. Jodi had been quiet ever since Mike had left them for another area, choosing to ignore her after all they had been through. Gloria sensed her pain and asked her to explain their partnership.

"We were together when we were younger. He was my first love, but with all the trouble he was getting in to, my parents made me break it

189

off. I went to university and got my degree in business management and didn't speak to him for nearly ten years. I was managing a pub in Chichester and in he walked, as handsome as he always was. We rekindled our romance and he swept me off my feet. I knew within a year it was a mistake, too much time had passed and things just fizzled out. The initial buzz wasn't enough to sustain our relationship. We were lucky that we stayed friends and, one afternoon, he suggested we buy our own pub. I jumped at the idea and took out a loan. I'm not sure where he got his cash from, though I have my suspicions. We got the Beachwood for a great price as it was in financial difficulties and the owners were desperate to sell. After two months I could see why; the main road that passed by had been rerouted and most of the traffic used the new motorway. We had our regulars but they barely covered the cost of the firewood we used. Mike had a word with some friends and suddenly we had a younger crowd in. They drunk a lot more and we started seeing a massive spike in profits. The problem was the numbers just didn't add up. I know the unit price and the profit margins like the back of my hand, but we were way over those. I am ashamed to say that I think he was using the place to hide his brother's drug money. I was so desperate to have a successful business that I ignored it. I am such a bad person," Jodi started to cry and Sarah went to her, giving her a consoling hug.

After calming down she continued, "After a while, the fact we were on top of each other the whole time meant he tried to get back together. By that time, I only saw him as a friend, maybe a big brother, and this really knocked his confidence. He was surly most of the time towards the end, before everything died and, you know, came back to life. I have to confess that I went to him a few times at the start of it all, I was so scared. It left me feeling worse for some reason and I stayed away for the last few weeks. I know I have been messing with his head but I didn't want to be alone. It's my fault that he is being like this now." She felt responsible for the gulf that was growing between them all.

"It's not your fault," Sarah soothed her. "We have to take responsibility for our own actions. Mike has chosen to attack our group for no reason."

"Well you did turn up out of the blue," she tried to defend him. "I'm sorry. I didn't mean that, you had no idea what would happen."

"I'm sorry I stabbed him, Jodi," Braiden offered, although it wasn't true.

"Thank you, sweetheart, but someone needed to stop him from hurting Kurt," she replied.

A hard knock came from the door. The door was pushed but met the equipment that they had put back in place to keep it closed.

"It's Debbie, let me in," came a whisper from under the door.

They looked at each other and Kurt sighed. He stood and pulled the heavy machines out of the way and she stood in the fading light of the dying day.

"I need help, Mike is burning up and won't respond to me," Debbie said shakily, close to tears.

"Let me get my bag," said Christina as she went to pick up her equipment.

"John and I will go with her, the rest of you stay here," Kurt instructed and took his hammer and hatchet in case it was a trap. John gave him a knowing look and did the same.

They hurried after Debbie and she led them to a small ward that was near the children's recovery area. Looking all around as she pushed through the door, they could see Mike laid up and in no position to try any funny stuff. He was red, delirious, and talking nonsense. The sweat was running freely from his body and his uncontrollable shivers had kicked the covers onto the floor.

"What is the matter with him?" cried Debbie, wishing she could help.

"I don't know, stay back," Christina ordered and checked his heart rate and breathing. The look on her face was suddenly filled with concern and she took his temperature with a digital thermometer.

"Do you think he is turning?" John whispered to Kurt while Debbie was distracted. He took out the cleaver in preparation.

"No, it happens much quicker than this." Kurt pushed John's hand down that held the razor sharp weapon before Debbie could see.

"What was he stabbed with?" the doctor asked them.

"A screwdriver," Kurt replied.

"Clean?" she pressed.

191

"As clean as it could be. He fell in the sewer earlier, sat on some filth, poo and such," John added, trying to be diplomatic.

"It's all your fault, you bastard!" Debbie screamed and made to lunge at Kurt who pulled out his hammer. He was fully prepared to use it now on the poisonous bitch and smiled, hoping it would trigger the attack.

"That won't help him, calm down! He has a massive infection, probably colonic bacteria that has caused blood poisoning," Dr Christina shouted at the irate woman. The hammer was more of a deterrent than the harsh words of the doctor and she backed down, scowling.

"He needs antibiotics or he will be dead by morning," Christina added and left them to retrieve the medicine from the locked pharmacy by main reception.

"You need to back off before you get hurt, do you understand me?" Kurt growled.

"Go fuck yourself," she hissed back at him.

"Both of you, stop it now. This won't help Mike get better," John said and they all looked at Mike. His eyes were rolling in the sockets and he was suffering from delirium tremens, his limbs uncontrollably shaking.

"We need to save him, he is all I've got," she wailed and went to him, wiping sweat from his fevered brow with a corner of the blanket.

"And whose fault is that?" whispered Kurt.

"I'm going to kill you," Debbie said, glowering.

"I'd love to see that. You are less than nothing, without us you would already be worm food, you fucking tramp." Kurt laughed in her face, unable to hold back. She ignored him, keeping the hatred inside. For now.

Christina came rushing back in with a clear plastic bag and a handful of medical equipment. She got the others to hold Mike down while she inserted the needle into his arm. The saline bag was mounted on an intravenous drip stand which then started feeding the medicine and much needed fluids into his bloodstream to counteract the infection. Taking another sealed needle, she removed it from the packaging and drew a small dose from a separate bottle.

"Morphine, to let him sleep. His body needs time to heal," she explained to them. "Debbie, would you be able to hold him on his side? Kurt, please keep the arm steady. I want to clean the wound on his bottom."

They took opposing sides and lifted him slightly so that the doctor could clean the stab wound thoroughly. The tension that passed over the shivering body of Mike was so highly charged, John wouldn't have been surprised to see electricity arcing between the pair.

"I think we got it just in time, look." Christina pointed to the neat round hole in the buttock muscle. Threaded veins of angry red spread like cobweb from the wound. "That's the septicaemia infection spreading. I have cleaned it out with antiseptic wash and will stitch it once the infection is under control. We should see an improvement in his heart rate and temperature by the morning."

They lay him back down gently and the morphine was taking effect. The shivers had subsided a little and he breathed slow and rhythmically, fast asleep. The drops of the antibiotic fed down the tube, working their magic on the illness that had nearly claimed Mike's life.

"We really need to move him into x-ray so I can keep an eye on him," said the doctor.

"No!" Debbie said.

"But it would be better…" continued Christina.

"I said *no!*" shrieked Debbie, pushing them out of the room.

"Listen, I will be back every hour during the night. If anything changes come and get me from x-ray immediately," ordered the doctor.

Without saying another word, Debbie slammed the door on the three.

"Now you see what we have had to put up with?" Kurt stated, throwing his hands in the air.

"She is just worried." Dr Christina tried to legitimize the behaviour that she knew could be brought on by stress.

"No, I'm sorry, Christina, she is pure evil. She used to beat Peter when they were an item, she has attacked us repeatedly and nearly got us killed by those things," John informed her.

"Oh, I didn't know,"

"It's ok, we rescued them when we hit the road. Peter fit in straight away but she is like a square peg to our round hole. It just hasn't worked. We will be leaving them somewhere safe and making our way to Arundel Castle," John said, knocking the door to x-ray and waiting for the bulky blockage to be moved.

"Wake me when you go and make your checks, I will come with you just in case she tries anything," warned Kurt.

"There is no need for that, without me he wouldn't have survived," she said.

"I would still be happier if I went," he insisted.

They bedded down for the night and Dr Christina set her small battery alarm clock to go off in sixty minutes. The group was asleep before their heads hit the pillow; exhaustion was an excellent sedative. Even the shrill of the clock and moving the equipment failed to rouse the group. The doctor checked on Mike without incident and was happy to see improvement as the hours passed. The candle died and the room fell into darkness, an extinguished light that could have easily been Mike's life force had they not discovered Dr Christina Hargis.

CHAPTER EIGHTEEN

Dr Hargis woke them with plates of buttered toast and jars of condiments; jams, Marmite, and chocolate spread.

"How do you still have bread?" asked Paige with a huge grin.

"We still have gas for some reason. I just made it yesterday, we have all the ingredients in the kitchen," she replied, handing out the small plates.

"We are fed by gas holders," said Kurt, spreading strawberry jam onto a slice. He looked up and saw that she didn't have a clue what he meant. "They are the huge round cylinders with stairs running around the side to the top. There is one just on the outskirts of the city, near Lavant."

"Is that what that awful looking thing is? Well you learn a new thing every day, don't you?" she smiled at the new knowledge.

They ate with relish, savouring the bread. They had nearly forgotten how good it tasted.

"I'm just going to take this to Debbie and Mike, see how they are getting on." The doctor stood and put four slices on a separate plate. Picking up the medical bag, she pushed out and Kurt jumped up to follow.

"I'm coming too," he said, stuffing the last of the toast in his mouth. She nodded and they checked on the pair.

Mike was looking much better; the fever had broken and the wound was no longer streaked with infected veins. Without even saying thanks, Debbie grabbed the food and started tucking in.

"He is doing much better; the danger is passed. We just need to keep an eye on him now. Excuse me, some of that toast was meant for him when he wakes up," Christina scolded as Debbie finished off the final slice.

"Well you should have said something. You will just have to bring some more," Debbie huffed as she brushed crumbs from her jumper.

"That's all that was left. I'm sorry," said the doctor, feeling bad that she hadn't made more.

"She's not your fucking chambermaid, you rotten cunt. From now on you go hungry. As soon as Mike is fit, you can get your stuff and get the fuck out before I throw you out. If Mike decides to go with you, you're his problem." Kurt picked up the empty plate and threw it against the wall, smashing it into pieces.

"Do you really think you can make me leave if Mike doesn't want to, you pussy?" she sneered.

"Maybe, maybe not. But you will be damned sure that if Mike kills me, you will be shot in the fucking head," he replied. Looking over, he could see Mike was awake. Groggy but still able to glare with malice. "Did you hear that Mike?"

He nodded slowly, refusing to break eye contact and look weak.

"Good. If you didn't hear, she ate your breakfast." Kurt pointed to Debbie who started to bluster her denials. "Enjoy your empty stomach."

They left the room to the inevitable argument and returned to the others.

"I see what you mean, what a bitch," smiled Christina, "I can't believe I offered to make her more."

"She is a vile manipulator. Don't give her any more thought," he said as they entered.

"Ok, I won't. Why can't people just get along?" she complained at the contrary nature of human beings.

"Who wants an ice shower?" Kurt asked, and the response was not as excited as he had expected. Now that he thought about it, the chilled cleaning didn't seem that tempting. Their sour odour convinced him of the need to ignore their comfort for five minutes.

Christina took them through to the operating rooms and the three showers that stood in a row. The water came flowing out in an icy torrent and there was much complaining and gasping as the survivors got clean. Those that waited laughed at the antics of the ones washing, but their mirth was short lived when they realized they would be next. After washing and changing clothes they felt renewed.

"How is it that you still have water?" asked John as he towelled his hair dry.

"I think we have a tank on the roof, it holds a lot of water and with no one else to use it, it just keeps running and running," Cristina explained.

"I think we should take the time to wash our clothes, if you have gas we can heat water and wash them in the kitchen sinks," Kurt said, looking at the filthy garments they had just taken off.

"Why not? We haven't got anything else to do," Sarah responded.

They all worked together to heat the water and scrub the clothing, getting as much grime out as possible. The water turned a grim shade of brown and had to be emptied on more than one occasion. Christina collected more IV drip holders and they hung the items from the hooks, positioning them by open ovens whose convection heat rose and caused the water to evaporate. Steam wafted on the up draughts like a ghostly mist.

Debbie came into the kitchen and her presence was like someone farting at a funeral, the jovial atmosphere disappearing. They all stared and she shuffled awkwardly from foot to foot.

"Mike wants some food, Peter told me you were in here," she said. Her demeanour had changed with the verbal abuse she had taken when left alone.

Kurt stormed over to her. "I don't give a flying fuck what Mike wants, you are the reason he is starving. If he is so hungry he can come and ask himself. The next time you think of making demands after the way you have acted, think of the fun you will have when I lock you outside."

"He still can't get out of bed, whose fault is that?" she answered with a mocking tone.

"I didn't make him attack me twice. It's his own fault that he nearly died and you are responsible too, egging him on. Do you think I wouldn't remember?" Kurt ridiculed her, "Now fuck off!" He pushed her towards the door.

"It's ok, Kurt," Christina took his arm, smiling, "We have plenty to go round."

Kurt softened and left Debbie alone. He realized he was becoming harder which was necessary, but at the same time his humanity was suffering; acts that a month ago would have been abhorrent, would now be considered reasonable. The morality of survival would be a fluid concept in the future. The survivors they had encountered so far had been an even mix of friendly and selfless, and evil and dangerous. Their plan to meet up with other groups who shared common values would be nearly impossible with the wildly divergent personalities of the world.

The doctor handed over some foil sealed cheese portions and crackers.

"Thanks," Debbie muttered and left them.

"I'm sorry if I come across heartless. We have seen what that pair are capable of, and it's not good for anyone," Kurt apologized.

"Please don't apologize. After what you have told me I am not surprised they have been ostracized," replied the doctor.

"I just didn't want you to get the wrong impression. My only concern is the survival of those I love," he tried to justify himself.

"Honestly, I totally understand. It's commendable how you have prevailed through all the horror," she complimented.

"I hope you will join us when we leave for the castle," John asked, hanging the final clothes on the hooks.

"I will have to think about it. I was gathering the nerve to try and reach my parent's home. I warned them when it all started but I haven't been able to reach them since the phone signal died," she said with sorrow. They noticed that Jodi had turned away, trying to hide the tears that flowed at her lost mother and father.

"It would be suicide on your own, where do they live?" Sarah wondered.

"Houghton. It's north of Arundel. I don't suppose we could try and see if they are still alive?" she asked with a pleading look.

"I'm sorry, but no. We need to get inside and lock the castle down. But I promise on my soul, that as soon as I know my family are safe, we will go together and find them," pledged Kurt, clasping her hand tightly to emphasize his promise.

198

"I will go with you too," declared Gloria, placing a supportive arm round her shoulders.

"I know the chances are poor, but I have to know. Thank you all," Christina said, her voice breaking with emotion.

CHAPTER NINETEEN

"Peter, would you mind coming with me somewhere?" Paige asked quietly.

"Of course not, what did you need?" he asked, following her from the kitchen.

She didn't answer his question so he just walked beside her in silence. The look on her face was a mix of sadness and anxiety and Peter felt the emotions transfer to himself in empathy. His mind raced with questions about what she was feeling, was it their burgeoning relationship? Had she changed her mind and no longer had any feelings towards him? Or was it something worse? His mouth had never been as dry as it was during that short walk to a small office that said 'X-ray Administration'. She pulled the sticky tape from the door and pushed it open.

Three small, cluttered desks sat against the walls with paperwork filed and stacked in piles across a shelved area at the back.

"We have already cleared this room," he croaked feebly, the lack of moisture in his mouth confusing the syllables so that it was barely intelligible. It was just a way to break the quiet between them, to try and solicit any kind of response. She seemed fixated on the first desk and stared at it for several minutes while Peter just stood there feeling foolish. He couldn't see anything out of the ordinary with it, nothing that would indicate a need to regard it with such trepidation. Paige took him by surprise and reached for his warm hand, squeezing it tightly.

"Please, don't leave me," she said, not breaking eye contact with the wooden talisman.

"I won't, but what are we doing here?" Peter replied.

She looked at him and it was such a forlorn expression he let go of her hand and pulled her in to his protective arms.

"I am afraid I imagined it, that when I open the drawer it will be empty," she said cryptically.

"Imagined what, Paige? You are scaring me." Peter held her face in his hands.

She glanced around the room nervously, as if uttering the words would legitimise her inner fears. "A picture of my daughter." Her eyes met his as she whispered the incantation, expecting a cosmic intervention that would rob her of the small prize.

"I don't... Oh, that was your desk!" Peter exclaimed as he finally understood the turmoil she was suffering. Through terror she had lost her baby. There was no way to safely reach her old home and if the drawer was empty, she would have nothing to remember her child. In time the memory of her angelic face would disappear and it would be as if she had never existed, except as a figment of her imagination.

"Peter, I can't. Would you please look inside the middle drawer? I am sure I brought one in to show my work friends and left it in there," she asked him and he treated it as if it was the most important mission of his life. "I'm so scared I took it home to frame it."

He walked over and held the drawer handle, feeling as scared as he had at any point facing the Hellspawn legions on the street. His new love would be crushed if she had no focal point to channel her grief. You couldn't apologise and say a fond farewell to a memory, but a picture was a relic of happiness. Her smiling face could act as a balm to her broken heart. Pulling it out on the runners, it revealed a clutter of stationery; post it notes, Tippex, staples, discarded memos, and scribbled notes were crammed within. No picture was immediately visible and he looked at Paige who was biting her knuckles, drawing blood with the intensity of her concentration.

He delved deeper, throwing the contents aside as he checked. He was growing in frustration as each new layer revealed more rubbish and the frenzy as he tossed stuff aside was reaching a point where he would launch the whole thing through a window. The bottom was revealed and no picture sat inside the drawer and Paige burst into tears, wailing in the silence. Peter was heartbroken he had failed her, even though there was nothing he could have done. He ripped the drawer out and smashed it against the side of the desk, splintering the wood into small fragments. He lifted the side and tipped it over and it crashed into the next desk, scattering the computer and other objects all over the office floor.

"I am so sorry." He held her tight, feeling the anguish as her body shook and tears flowed, soaking his chest. "I will go to your home and find you a picture!" he vowed, looking at her. She smiled with gratitude and shook her head.

"No, I won't lose you too. It's my own fault for getting my hopes up," Paige said, stepping back and leaving the office.

Peter was so angry with fate he kicked out at anything in his way; the chairs, the computer monitor whose screen cracked as he stamped down on it. The other two drawers had fallen out and laid amongst the overturned contents was the glossy corner of a picture. Unable to breathe, he stepped forward and took hold of the exposed edge, lifting it with exaggerated reverence. The back was plain white with a date of print and he found he couldn't turn it around. If it turned out to be the wrong one, he would be devastated. The door opened again and Paige walked in, seeing him knelt on the floor and staring.

"Oh my God," she cried, "is it..."

Peter stood and held it out. She took the picture and lifted it to see the coloured image on the reverse of the white side. She collapsed into his arms and dropped the picture and Peter assumed it was a different one, that her disappointment had made her faint. It fluttered to the ground at his feet as he lay her gently down, the photo landing face up. Her beautiful face smiled at him, and cradled in her arms was the most precious little baby girl he had ever laid eyes upon.

CHAPTER TWENTY

Three days passed. Peter was still suffering with his broken ribs, but the period of calm and inactivity had allowed the bones to begin their laborious task of knitting back together. Mike was up on his feet with the aid of a crutch, and the wound had been cleaned and stitched now the infection had gone. His mood had improved and both he and Debbie had joined in some of the normal activities. The restocking of the backpacks with fresh supplies, water, and medicine gave them time to adjust and find their new places within the group. John took Kurt to a quiet corner of the pharmacy as Christina guided their search, ticking off the most important medicines that would save their lives.

"What do you think about Mike and Debbie, they seem to have had a change of heart? Even though they won't stay with us, they are helping out more and more," John whispered, observing the pair.

"I don't buy it. How many people do you know that can switch personalities like that?" Kurt said.

"I see what you mean, but with all that is going on, maybe they can see the benefits of being with a strong group," John tried to convince himself as much as Kurt.

"Look, Dad, I understand we need people. We just don't need people like that, they are too volatile." Kurt had made his mind up. He couldn't argue that they were being totally different but he still caught the occasional look passing between them. Their eyes would narrow with secret knowledge and he was certain it bore nothing good for the rest of them. He would still watch them intently for any signs of subterfuge.

Earlier in the stay, they had taken the time to clear away the rotting meals that littered the dining area so that they could sit and eat properly.

Rows and rows of long life canned goods sat on shelves in the kitchen pantry; beans, meats, ready mixed meals, and various fruits. After finishing the medicine reclamation, they feasted on a dinner of tinned curry. The large containers were designed for commercial purposes and easily fed the whole group in one sitting. The spices left a warm glow in their stomachs and the memory of their local tandoori takeaway gave them a strange yearning. The variety of culinary expertise was one of the great things about living in England. Thai, Indian, Chinese, Middle Eastern and countless other cuisines were available around the clock. Their new diet would be bland and designed for survival only. It seemed the little losses were mounting day by day, chipping away at their resolve.

"We will clean up today," said Mike, putting the dirty plates onto serving trays. Debbie followed and they disappeared into the kitchen. The bemused looks that passed between the remaining diners all spoke of the same confusion.

"Where have the old Debbie and Mike gone?" Gloria asked.

"Maybe they have been taken over by aliens?" Sam joked and they all chuckled. Except Kurt. He knew in the back of his mind that the alien theory was more plausible than their hair trigger, psychotic behaviour being reined in.

"I'll go and see if they need any help," Kurt offered. He wanted to put them in a situation where they were alone with the person they had the biggest score to settle. Their demeanour would be a good indication of their hidden motives. He entered the kitchen and they were busy washing the cutlery with cold water. The plates had been cleared of food and stood to the side of the sink, ready to be cleaned.

"Hey, I was just wondering…" was as far as he got.

A massive, rumbling explosion blew the swing doors of the dining area open. A wave of heat and dust billowed in, covering them in a fine powder.

"What the hell was that?" Kurt screamed at Mike and Debbie. The fear in their eyes was genuine and left him in no doubt that they were not the cause of the latest calamity. He rushed out to check his family. The blast had been diverted down the corridor by the heavy doors and the worst injury was ringing ears and coughing.

"What happened?" he asked as he went to his wife and sons.

"Something exploded, it sounded like the houses that night, Dad," Sam wheezed.

"A gas leak?" Kurt questioned.

"I can't see how, we would have smelled it, surely?" John shrugged as he helped Gloria to her feet.

"It doesn't matter now. Get your weapons ready. That noise will bring them in their thousands," Kurt ordered. He could see it in his mind's eye, the putrid heads turning in unison at the blast. The slow turn and shuffle as they came to investigate the disturbance.

They filed out and the smoke in the foyer was starting to clear. Small patches of fire still burned on a couple of surfaces but the risk of it spreading was minimal. The hospital had been designed to contain the spread with little combustible material, concrete walls, fire resistant ceilings, and fire breaks were at regular intervals. The danger they now faced was the gaping hole where the entrance used to be. The doors had shattered and embedded themselves behind the reception desk, the locked chain still holding the two together. Rubble had collapsed in place of the doors, but only enough to cause a nuisance to the dead who could be seen in the distance, eager to eat.

"Someone blew it open! It must be the same person who attacked us along the way. Who the hell are these people?" Kurt screamed out through the wrecked entrance.

"Jesus Christ, there are hundreds of them," Mike shouted.

"What can we do?" shrieked Debbie, hiding behind him.

"I don't know. We can't block it with enough objects to keep them out, they will just push through it," Kurt said.

"We need an escape route, quickly," John called out to Christina.

"The roof is the only way, the other routes are blocked," she answered as the massed moans of the dead became a crescendo.

"We will be trapped up there though," Kurt said.

Indecision overwhelmed the group. There was no good option, only varying degrees of how painful they would die. Exposed on the roof to the cold and elements, discovered cowering in a room and battling until they succumbed to the never ending swarm of dead, or lastly, making a break for it without supplies and with two injured members.

A rapid succession of *phut phut phut* from close by caught their attention and a gruff voice shouting, "Get in there, you cunt!"

Around the side of the concrete barricade came the bleeding figure of a stranger, who fell to the ground, banging his head on the concrete. Two men followed in full combat fatigues, crouching low and letting off short bursts from their assault rifles. The suppressors swallowed much of the noise and the closest dead fell to the ground as the high calibre bullets shredded their brains. Kurt immediately recognized the friendly soldier from the fence at Thorney Barracks but his friend was a new face. He was big, six foot five, and as black as the night. His clothing screamed at the seams from the layers of muscle that flexed inside. The beaten man was bound with cable ties holding his hands behind his back. The friendly soldier was in full battle mode, his face a scowl of business as he grabbed at the tied hands and pulled the captive up. His arms strained at the shoulder joint and he cried out in pain at the rough treatment.

"Take him, keep watch on him. He's the bastard that blew the entrance," explained the new soldier. Gloria aimed her shotgun at his chest and the man sat down heavily in one of the only undamaged chairs remaining in the foyer. He glared at the group with such hatred they all questioned what they could have possibly done to solicit his anger.

"I'm Jonesy, that's Doughball," said the friendly soldier whose face was streaked with dark camouflage paint. "Can any of you drive a forklift?" He looked around quickly and Braiden held a hand up.

"I stole one of those too." He grinned and blushed at the thoughts of his old life, then reached out and caught the key that Doughball threw.

Jonesy continued speaking. "Good man, now listen. We need to hold those things back and two guns are better than one. While we shoot, you need to pick up those dividers and move them to block the entrance, see the sections at the bottom?" Jonesy pointed and indeed there were two thin wedges missing that the blades of the forklift would slide between.

"Shall I do all three at once?" Braiden asked, moving to climb in the Army green forklift.

"No." Jonesy fired three rounds and Doughball had gone to his knees behind the existing sandbag machine gun nest. "You have to do one at a time or it will tip you over, when you have two in place I will take over and move the third to block it completely."

Braiden stopped moving, "But how will you get inside?"

"Let me worry about that, now get moving!" Jonesy shouted.

"What can we do?" Kurt asked, hovering behind the field of fire.

"Get everything you can carry inside. Guns, ammunition, everything," he answered while sighting a small group of zombies who had been horrifically eaten before they turned. The accuracy was astounding and with each shot, one of the corpses was blown backwards as the head exploded.

"Did you all hear that? Let's move!" Kurt yelled and the able bodied members commenced the task. Mike and Peter started to help but Kurt advised them to save their strength in case they needed to make an escape. They reluctantly agreed and the rest worked like their lives depended on it, which they surely did.

"Doughball, how wet are the LMG's?" Jonesy asked between gunfire.

Doughball tipped the barrel and a few drops of moisture ran from the end of the light machine guns. He put down his personal assault rifle and pulled the stock of the machine gun into his shoulder. Pulling the trigger, he fired a short burst and the belt fed bullets into the firing chamber without jamming.

"We are good, get me a couple of extra boxes of ammo," he called out. Jonesy made safe his weapon and was glad to see the people rising to the task. Boxes of grenades and ammunition were being placed inside the doors. Abandoned guns were reclaimed and placed down with exaggerated care, as if they were liable to discharge and kill someone if they dropped. Braiden had reversed with the top section of concrete and moved it into place by the door, covering the hole completely. It made things difficult for the collection as they had to jump over the three-foot barrier with any items.

"You!" Jonesy shouted to Kurt.

"It's Kurt," he replied, running over to the man.

"Kurt, can you grab the other two machine guns for me?" Jonesy asked, waiting for the pause between his partner's gunfire. Kurt hurried over and hefted the gun onto his shoulder, offering it over the divider to Jodi and Paige.

"Done, what now? Can I help?" Kurt asked, feeling like he should be more involved.

"Watch the young lad's back in case any come from our flank," Doughball answered without breaking his concentration. Jonesy nodded in confirmation and Kurt took out his hammer, jealous of the firepower of their new friends.

Braiden was struggling to get the second section loose and it kept trying to pick the bottom piece up at the same time.

"Try and shake the blades if you can," Kurt shouted over the noise of the engine and bullets flying. Braiden nodded and wiggled one of the levers. The bottom divider dropped and hit the ground with a loud thud.

The car park was filling with walking death. The soldiers chose their targets carefully, aiming for the fastest moving zombies. The machine gun spat normal rounds interspersed with tracer bullets. The brightly blazing shots buried inside skulls and sizzled, the Hellspawn looking like human candles as their heads burned. Bodies were torn asunder without mercy. The bursts of machine gun fire were less accurate than the single shot option on the assault rifle and they ripped through limbs and torsos, throwing shredded body parts across the tarmac ground. The zombies had formed into an unbroken line as they crushed over hedges and fences in ever growing numbers. Braiden pulled up with the third section perched on the forklift blades, ready to drop and block the entrance.

"Go, get inside!" Jonesy shouted and Braiden jumped down before hauling himself up and over the six foot, solid barricade. "You too, now!" he tapped Doughball's helmet and without pause he picked up the smoking gun and ran to the entrance, passing the weapon to those inside.

"What are you going to do?" he asked as Jonesy climbed into the cab of the machine.

"Don't worry about me, get inside," Jonesy said and put the forklift in gear, ready to move forward and complete the blockage.

"Don't be so fucking soft, I ain't leaving you out here." Doughball laughed and ran over to one of the occupied Foxhounds.

"What the fuck are you doing?" Jonesy shouted, leaning out of the vehicle. A raised middle finger told him to mind his own business. Time was running out, they had a minute and a half maximum before they were devoured. Surging forward, he quickly lowered the last section in place and turned off the engine, leaving the several tons of metal forklift as an extra weight to keep the dead out.

Doughball had climbed onto the roof of the locked armoured vehicle and withdrawn his pistol. Crossing himself and apologizing, he shot the reanimated soldiers with regret and sadness.

"We need to get to safety you bloody fool!" Jonesy yelled up at his friend who just laughed down at him. Without pause he dropped through the vacated heavy machine gun position on top of the vehicle. He unlocked the doors and Jonesy jumped inside. Starting the vehicle with the push button control, he gunned the engine and exhaust gasses belched from the high set pipe.

"Get in the seat, give me some cover," Doughball told him and Jonesy climbed over his fallen comrades, stepping up and chambering the 7.62 machine gun.

"Where are we going?" he asked and started firing. The lethal gun chattered, spitting hot lead at the zombies. The shortening distance between the corpses and the vehicle meant each round blasted through several bodies before the velocity dissipated. They were ripped to shreds by the barrage, collapsing into smouldering heaps of unidentifiable flesh and protruding bone. The vehicle trundled forward and turned down the side of the building, aiming for the side entrance and the projecting canopy that covered it.

"We climb up on that and then onto the roof!" Doughball shouted over the racket. He swung it around and backed up, not stopping until he hit the concrete dividers that protected this wing.

"Go, go, go!" Jonesy called and they both climbed onto the roof, "You first!" he interlaced his fingers and held them out, ready to boost the bigger soldier.

"Nah I will boost you first," he argued.

"Get your fat ass up there, I wouldn't be able to pull you up," Jonesy said and Doughball roared with laughter. He stepped in the hands and pushed from the roof of the vehicle, reaching and then pulling himself onto the canopy. He spun round and dropped, offering his hand to Jonesy who grabbed it and leaped. Doughball was as strong as two men and pulled him up as if he weighed nothing.

The crowd of dead surrounded the Foxhound, frustrated at the escape of their prey who just laughed. Doughball went a step further and unzipped. Taking his penis out, he started to urinate on the frenzied zombies, which brought renewed laughter.

"Eww, that's gross," came a disgusted laugh from the roof above them. Sam grinned down at the pair.

"Shit, sorry folks," he apologized and put it away, soaking the inside of his trousers where he hadn't quite finished.

"You get it out as much as you want, we owe you our lives." Kurt smiled and the group lined the roof parapet, desperate to greet their saviours.

"Take hold of this, I've tied it off," John said and threw a length of rope down.

They shimmied up expertly and grabbed the outstretched arms of the family who pulled them over the short wall. Hands were shaken and backs were patted with gratitude.

"Can we get you anything?" Christina asked as they walked toward the roof access door.

"Umm, would you have anywhere I can wash some clothes?" Doughball said with embarrassment, looking at the wet patch on his trousers.

"I'm sure we can get you cleaned up," she answered and they were unable to stifle their chuckles as they descended into the hospital.

CHAPTER TWENTY ONE

athered around the captive stranger, they looked like an inquisition. They stared, not speaking as they appraised the individual who had tried to kill them on several occasions. He glared at them like a cornered animal, ready to launch himself at them even with his hands bound. He was filthy but didn't seem to have suffered any dehydration or malnutrition. He was wiry and strong looking, with a dead stare that gave them the chills.

"We were watching from a flat across the road, deciding on our next move when we saw that piece of shit throw grenades and blow the doors. We would have tried to reach you at some point, your antics with the car alarm was genius," Jonesy complimented them.

"How did you know we were even in here?" Kurt wondered.

"We wanted to reach our friends but it was too late. Then we heard the alarm and we saw you all. You looked like a meerkat, the way your head popped out of that hole and looked around," answered Jonesy.

"We saw that too. I'm really sorry about what happened to them, they were some damned brave soldiers to try and save people in this mess," Kurt commiserated, putting a hand on the soldier's shoulder.

"I appreciate the sentiment. They were good guys, each and every one. That leads us to this mother fucker," Doughball added, scowling at the bloodied figure on the chair.

"Who the hell are you?" Kurt asked, "Why have you been trying to hurt us?"

"You haven't got a clue have you?" he seemed amused by his anonymity.

"I must be missing the joke," said Braiden and pulled out his screwdriver.

"You must be Braiden," smiled the man, knowingly.

"Yep," he answered and stepped out of line to stab the man who had endangered those he loved.

"Hold it. He will get what's coming soon enough," Kurt promised Braiden as he held him back. The smile wavered at the knowledge of his possible death.

"Maybe if you talk we can see what your problem is, if not, we don't have much use for you." Kurt shrugged and took his hand from Braiden, threatening with the young lad who would happily finish him off.

"Are you really telling me you have no idea who I might be?" his amusement had turned to incredulousness. He had hoped they would live in fear of every act he perpetrated against the group. That they didn't know was an insult.

"I'm dying to know, even if you lot don't care," Doughball admitted.

"You killed my friends, you cunts. Remember them, the ones you blew up and fed to those fucking creatures?" the last was shouted and he tried to stand but Doughball threw out a sharp jab into his face and he fell back, blood spilling from a split lip. His eyes swam from the blow but then they focused and he licked at the red liquid that was coating his jumper.

"How can that be, we killed you all?" said Kurt, struggling to see how it was possible.

"I fucked off as soon as I heard the glass breaking, the rubble damn near crushed me but I got away and hid in another house. I heard Eddie's screams as they ate him, you bastards," Phil spat blood at them. It hit Kurt and he just looked at it dismissively.

"You tried to kill us first! Don't act like a fucking victim, you savage," growled Kurt and pulled out his hammer.

"So you're the one who knew Morse code, you were in the Navy…" John said with despair. He had such high regard for those serving in the armed forces, and to think someone like this had ever sullied the uniform was disturbing.

"You're a Matlow? What the fuck are you playing at, why aren't you on your ship? Didn't you get orders to return to dock?" Jonesy took a warning pace forward, he hated deserter's who tried to avoid their duty.

"What's a Matlow, Dad?" Sam whispered.

"It's what our soldiers call sailors," he answered as the interrogation continued.

"Not that it's any of your fucking business, but I was discharged," Phil explained.

"Dishonourably, according to Archie," goaded Kurt. It was a sore spot and Phil tried to attack him again, only Doughball's huge hand held him in place. Unable to move he tried to bite at his flesh like a rabid animal.

"Don't be silly now," chided Doughball as if he was talking to an errant child.

"So you couldn't handle the life? Only a weak man could fall so low," said Jonesy with derision.

"Go fuck yourself, you pathetic piece of shit. If not being able to be told what to do every minute of the day makes me weak, what does that make you?" Phil tried to get a rise out of the soldiers.

Jonesy smiled and leaned in close. "It makes us real men; you weren't even tough enough to fight. You hid on a floating pussy barge with all the other cowards," he said and punched Phil in the stomach. Vomit burst from his mouth at the power of the blow. He doubled over and retched, trying to regain his breath in ragged gasps.

"Wait a minute, none of this makes sense. How the hell did you know where we were?" Sarah asked, frowning.

"I've followed you the whole way. I saw your little rescue on the estate as my friends were still burning. I saw you sail away and I thought I'd lost you. Then you came back so I slashed your tyres to keep you on foot," he said, still struggling to breathe properly.

"You threw the stone!" Kurt proclaimed and Phil nodded.

"I didn't count on you being so bloody slippery and resilient," he complained.

"Happy to have disappointed you." Kurt smiled at him.

"Ok, that explains up to the pub. How did you know that we hadn't died when you crashed into the place and it burned?" added Gloria.

"I thought you were dead," Phil admitted, "I'd heard you inside the farmhouse when you discussed the plan about the soldiers. I figured I could hook up with them for some protection but the car park was swarming with the zombie soldiers. Then fuck me if you didn't pop up like a jack in the box and get yourself safe again. The zombies were meant to flood in and eat you."

"You piece of shit," Jonesy shouted and kicked him full in the face with his heavy boot. The head snapped back and he fell to the floor, unconscious.

While he was incapacitated, the survivors told the story of the child rape and killing of the family in the mystery house by Phil and his goons. Looks of murderous intent settled onto the soldier's faces and Phil's bravado disappeared when he awoke. He knew what was coming.

"Please, listen, I didn't mean it. Don't kill me. Let me go and you will never see me again," he blubbered, sick still dripping from his chin. He was never informed by Archie that they had made the same deal, only to fall victim to the arson attack that nearly killed them all. Fool me once, shame on you, fool me twice, shame on me, Kurt thought of the old proverb.

"It's your call," growled Doughball who was ready to twist his head off. He had a young son that lived off-base with his wife in Crawley, the idea was to be closer to her family when he was on deployment. It was home to a huge population and he had watched the aerial drone footage of the massive waves of walking dead. He had refused to zoom in on the swarm in case the high definition display had shown the torn forms of his kin, irrespective of how unlikely it was among the tens of thousands on the move. Command would have had their asses if they knew the troops were quietly checking the areas that their families lived with the multi-million-pound equipment. After the first eight had been shown nothing but unfolding horror, the others had left and mourned without needing video evidence.

"You can trust me, I will go far away, I promise." He was wailing like a baby, but the pity for this child murderer was non-existent.

"Take him to the roof," Kurt said with a deadpan expression.

"Wait, no, please…" Phil begged.

They were not careful as they frog-marched him up the stairs, dragging him where he fell to try and postpone the inevitable. The group followed, all pity exhausted. Phil pleaded and screamed with fear but it was all fruitless, he had committed atrocities that would have included them if his plans had worked. Jonesy and Doughball held him by the low wall of the roof and Gloria offered the shotgun to Kurt. He looked at it for long moments and Phil's desperate eyes flicked from the gun, to the young man who only needed to take it and pull the trigger. Kurt shook his head and Phil nearly collapsed with relief, until he saw the look on Kurt's face as he marched over. Grabbing him by the shirt, they looked deep into each other's eyes, before Kurt thrust him backwards with all his might. The parapet took out Phil at the knee and he fell from the roof, landing amongst the milling zombies. He had crashed down on his legs and the splintered bones stuck through his trousers, spraying blood from torn arteries. The shock of the impact wore off and the screaming began. Looking down, the dead filled the gap that Phil had caused like water closing over a dropped stone. The tearing and cracking bones accompanied the gradually dying sounds of the doomed murderer's cries as he was eaten. They watched without any satisfaction, only a sense that justice had been served.

CHAPTER TWENTY TWO

The barricade was solid but it left them sealed within the hospital with the roof being the only way out. The locals were restless and had begun to surround the whole, vast building.

"I'm sorry about that folks. The light machine gun was too noisy and it's woken the whole neighbourhood," apologized Doughball.

Kurt walked up and shook his hand, "Don't worry about it, we are in your debt. Doughball?" he smiled.

"You can call me DB. And it was nothing, we saw how you all handled yourselves and you weren't even armed properly," he nodded at the shotgun.

"It serves me well enough, young man," Gloria chuckled.

"I meant no disrespect," he apologized to the small, elderly woman. It amused the group to see the giant contrite and embarrassed.

"I know you didn't," she replied and gave his cheek a playful squeeze, like a favourite grandmother.

Introductions were made in the dining room and the survivors laid on a welcome feast for the new guests. The party atmosphere was a mix of adrenaline at surviving another assault, and the knowledge they had trained soldiers among their number. Jonesy and DB were treated like royalty, the youngsters fascinated by tales of war in Afghanistan. Christina even found a small bottle of brandy that she knew was hidden within the desk of a senior cardiovascular surgeon. It was a well-known fact that he performed surgery while tipsy most of the time, sucking a mouthful of breath mints to try and hide it. The management turned a blind eye because his results didn't seem to be affected by the drinking, but she had been sure he would eventually cause a fatality and then the shit would hit the fan. In the end the drunken genius had joined the ranks of the walking corpses. She had seen him shambling around, still wearing his hospital whites that were no longer white.

Jonesy stood with his plastic beaker and proposed a toast, "To new friends, and to kicking the asses of those dead fucks!"

"New friends!" they all shouted in chorus.

DB was eating like a horse, tucking into plate after plate of tinned sausage and beans. Jonesy took Kurt to one side to talk in greater detail.

"Look, I'm sorry that we turned you away at the base. We apparently had orders from command that we couldn't house civilians, only set up outposts as we saw fit. We made the mistake of choosing the hospitals to try and defend the injured. We wrongly assumed that we could help." Jonesy looked far away as he remembered the screams of pain as they came over the radio from the troops, between gunfire and explosions. "We were wrong."

Kurt put a hand on his shoulder, "Your friends went up against a city full of zombies to save people. They will never be forgotten for that bravery; we won't let it happen."

"Thanks for the sentiment; it may be a bit more difficult than that." Jonesy nodded and shook himself out of the funk. "We are in major shit for going AWOL. Lieutenant Baxter is going to have us locked up, or worse."

"He has to find you first," Kurt vowed. He had his own issues with the lieutenant and the way he had behaved towards his family. John came across and sat down with them.

"I wanted to thank you personally, you showed up just in time." John shook his hand again. DB had excused himself from the rapt, wide eyed teenagers and joined them.

"So what's the plan?" he asked, the chair creaking in protest as he sat down.

"We only have one option left. We were going to try to reach Arundel Castle," explained Kurt.

DB burst out laughing and the room turned to look at him. "I was just thinking that we abandoned castles hundreds of years ago, now we need to rely on them to keep us safe like Kings of old. King Doughball, has a nice ring to it I think."

217

"Don't you expect me to be your handmaiden," joked Jonesy, punching him on the solid shoulder.

"You will do as you are commanded or I will have your head!" DB put as much of a regal tilt on his words but the London accent betrayed him.

"If you get us there, I will be your handmaiden for life," offered Kurt with a grin.

Jonesy finished laughing and got back to business, "What is the plan once you are there?"

"There is fresh water in the well from the local lake. Plenty of fertile ground inside the walls for crops and the best thing? High walls of solid stone that have been standing for a thousand years." Kurt detailed their plan and it met with approval from the soldiers.

Honey sat patiently watching them, wagging her tail. DB fed her pieces of cut up sausage and she daintily took each piece and swallowed without even chewing.

"How do they even taste the food when they gulp it so quickly?" Jonesy pondered.

"God knows, but she likes it," DB stated, offering the last piece.

"The only thing we haven't mentioned yet, and it's a little difficult to explain because you haven't seen what we have seen," Kurt started to speak but couldn't find the words.

"What's up Kurt?" DB asked, stroking Honey under the chin.

"Mike and Debbie." He pointed to them where they sat on their own, avoiding most of the fun and happiness. "They won't be coming with us. They are poison and have nearly gotten us killed more than once with their psychotic behaviour."

"They don't seem so bad." DB wasn't convinced, but he had come to trust the judgement of anyone who could survive this mess on foot and with only the most rudimentary weapons.

"It's your call," Jonesy shrugged. "Do we leave them here? It's safe."

"No. I don't want to leave them trapped, no matter how much trouble they have caused. We can find somewhere quiet and secure on the route," Kurt decided and John and the two soldiers agreed.

"When do you plan on leaving?" DB enquired, all business again.

"Soon. Christina will need to gather medical supplies so we can have a basic health facility there. We would need to raid the local doctors for extra equipment and medicine if we run out," John said.

"We are gonna need that second Foxhound," DB announced and Jonesy did the same headcount, before agreeing. With all the people, spare guns, and medical apparatus, one would never be enough to get them clear.

"The one that is mounted on that shit pile of corpses will be no good, we need the third one. How we get to it is another problem entirely," Jonesy said, thinking of a way to get them out of the mess.

"We can give this some thought over the next couple of days," Kurt said, ending the conversation.

**

The rooftop was alive with movement as the group searched for any side that wasn't ten deep in hungry flesh eaters. Thousands had heard the siren song of the battle and joined the crowd who enveloped the hospital building. Like a perpetual Mexican wave, the dead reached for the unattainable meal, mouths snapping at the air.

"We are in a spot of bother," Paige whispered as they all gathered at the stairs that led to the roof.

"You're not kidding," agreed Debbie, the first words she had spoken to Paige in many days.

"We have searched the building from top to bottom and those three entrances are the only way out. The basement and morgue have no exits. We can't reach the other buildings because they are too far away. In short, we are fucked," Jonesy informed them all.

"Not necessarily, we have herded them before with a distraction. We could try and draw them away from this side of the building," Braiden said.

"It's worth a shot, let's try it," DB agreed.

Braiden and Sam started at the same spot on the roof, overlooking the vehicle they hoped would get them to safety. Whooping and hollering they parted ways and started to skirt the parapet, pulling the interested zombies away, while the rest kept down to minimize their attraction. Kurt took a mirror and used the reflection to check the progress. The others watched with interest but he lowered his head and shook it.

"Sam, Braiden, it's not working!" he called and they came running to look.

The principle was solid, but the weight of numbers meant that the dead couldn't disperse properly. By the time the ones who were following managed to walk off, the rest had lost interest and returned to the task of beating on the walls. As soon as the youngsters ceased the calling, the waves of corpses refilled the line.

"That was a waste of time," Mike commented and Debbie sniggered. Their façades had been slipping during the past day or so. The amount of mental energy it required to keep their anger in check had left them drained. The brief glimpses of sarcasm were enough to convince DB and Jonesy beyond doubt that the stories were all true.

"What about fire?" Jodi proposed after hearing of the fascination the dead had for the cleansing flames.

"What did you have in mind?" John asked, interested in the plan.

"Why don't we set fire to the antenatal wing?" she pointed to the adjoining building, "It could draw them inside and burn them."

"It's a great idea, but I don't think it will burn properly. And I don't like the idea of that thing collapsing on us if it does go up," Sarah pointed out. The six floors could potentially crush a third of their single story building if it fell the wrong way.

"How about those?" DB pointed at a block of flats across the other side of the carpark.

"That could work," admitted John, "But how the hell can we get to them?"

"We don't need to. We can use the tracer rounds in our SA80's." Jonesy ran down the stairs and came back with a box of the ammunition. The sizes meant nothing to the non-service personnel, but the word 'tracer' was painted on the side of the green container. They emptied their magazines and started adding the ammunition before locking and loading. They dropped to a knee at the wall and used the concrete to steady their aim. The suppressors spat their rounds and the fading light was illuminated by brilliant lines of phosphorous. The faint sounds of glass breaking carried on the air as the burning slugs embedded into walls and furniture. After firing two magazines each, the entire ground floor, and two of the first floor flats were an inferno. The dead saw the fire and started to make their way toward the burning building. By nightfall, the whole tower of fourteen floors was raging out of control. The communal gas main has melted and added superheated high pressure jets of fire to the mix, belching from the windows.

"The heat is tremendous, look at them all burn," shouted Gloria. The smoke was rising in huge clouds from the ignited dead, mixed with steaming bodily fluids.

"At this rate, they will all be gone by morning. That was so easy," yelled Braiden over the noise, and the group laughed with excitement.

The fire was loud, but the real horror was the sound of one hundred thousand dead that had been drawn to the building like moths to a flame from the entire city. It drowned out the crackling and popping as windows exploded outwards, cutting into the melting zombies. A series of loud cracks echoed in the night and the tower crumbled in to itself, sending a cloud of sparks into the dark sky like fireworks. The vibration reached them and the gravel on the roof shivered underfoot. The compressed concrete caused the fire to nearly extinguish itself and the heat waves that reached them were cut off instantly.

"Shit. It was going so well," complained Debbie.

"At least it killed thousands. We have a lot less of them around the hospital to worry about now," Kurt said.

"What does everyone feel about moving out at first light?" Jonesy scanned the group and they all nodded.

"We should bring the gear up now so that it is ready to drop in the morning," Jodi suggested. It would be safer while they still had the glow of the dying blaze and they formed a human chain to pass everything up.

Kurt and the soldiers looked over the wall surreptitiously, counting the zombies. Around the two vehicles they would face about eighty, which would be dangerous but manageable, provided they didn't alert the main horde by the collapsed building. The chorus of the dead would penetrate every corner of the hospital, denying them a settled night's sleep for the coming day's trials.

CHAPTER TWENTY THREE

"Does anyone want to hear from the radio? We can see if there is any news?" John asked as they settled in for the night. He pulled out the wind up radio from his backpack and Kurt explained the most up to date news they had received from the husky voiced lady in the centre of London.

"Yeah sure. Some good news would go down well right now," DB said.

"What was the latest that you had from your superiors, if you don't mind me asking?" Kurt inquired of the two soldiers.

"Nothing. We are on total need to know lockdown. Because of the few deserters at the start of this mess, the brass has been treating us like mushrooms," Jonesy said with anger.

"Mushrooms?" Jodi said, confused at the meaning.

"Kept in the dark and fed on shit," DB explained to her and they all laughed at the analogy.

"It was another reason we left. We joined the army to kick ass, not sit behind fences while the world died. We felt we could do more good on the streets." Jonesy laid bare their motives to the group and Jodi reached over, taking his hand and giving it a small kiss.

"You are heroes," she smiled.

John finished winding the charging point and tuned the channel in. The airwaves were dead. Only silence transmitted from the speakers and the group felt like they had lost a close friend. The lady had been a comfort through the first weeks of survival and now she was gone.

"Sorry folks, call of nature," shrieked the radio where John had turned the volume to full, desperate to see if it was just too quiet. The group jumped as one and then burst out laughing.

"This is Gabrielle, calling out to any remaining survivors. We have been through the meat grinder and come out unscathed. If you are safe, stay that way. Keep warm, keep fed and stay out of sight. Our friends outside have mostly left the area completely now. The zombies that remain are thin on the ground so they are moving somewhere. I just pray it's not towards you."

"She sounds sexy," stated DB with a grin.

"After being cooped up for months, you'd probably find my voice sexy," joked Jonesy and they all laughed. DB jumped on top of him, pinned him down and smothered his face with kisses.

"Get off, you bloody lump!" Jonesy said through bouts of raucous laughter.

"Guys, listen." John hushed them and the woman got to the important bit of her broadcast.

"Our power has been steady for over a week now, so whatever the government engineers were working on, it's now fixed. We can only assume it was old power lines requiring attention that interrupted our supply. We have heard a few words on the emergency frequency from the bunker, but at present they have not managed to get their equipment working correctly and we are awaiting a full message of their intended action and response to the catastrophic events of the past months."

"About damn time!" John sighed.

"Ladies and gents, I'm afraid we also received some more bad news the other day. The fortification and armed forces at the Porton Down site were overrun by the dead. We maintained contact until the last moment, but by all accounts, very few had managed to relocate when the zombies breached the outer defences. Without regular supply lines, they did the best they could against impossible odds. There was no time to evacuate the science laboratories and all research has been deemed lost. I don't need to tell you what a blow that is for the fight back against the dead legions. The Daresford Institute has confirmed that breakthroughs were being made in the biological component of the outbreak and they feel without syncing their efforts, a solution is unlikely. I would like anyone listening to be silent for a minute to pay their respects."

"Oh, man." DB was in tears. Seeing the big man crying was symbolic of the band of brother's mentality in the military. They all lowered their heads and said a prayer for the fallen.

"God bless each and every one of you. I am going to sleep for a month and pray this mess sorts itself out. Wake me when we have won." She ended the broadcast with a level of dejection that was well known to the group.

"Well I wish I hadn't bothered," John threw the radio back into his pack and lay down, turning his back to the rest of the group.

"Don't sweat it, Dad, get some rest. We are going to be up against it tomorrow." Kurt leaned over and squeezed John on the shoulder to try and make him feel better. He wasn't responsible for the remorseless nature of their foe. Their definitions of combat strategy would need to adapt if they were ever to beat back enemies that didn't need to eat or sleep and experienced no fear or doubt.

CHAPTER TWENTY FOUR

awn broke and their eyes opened almost in unison. Their dreamlike haze where they were safe and in the old world faded. Looking at the hospital walls, the nerves at the coming undertaking grew until they all had a heavy weight in the pit of their stomach. The soldiers were out of bed and ready to move, checking the moving parts of their guns for functionality. They carried the last of their belongings onto the roof and tied the three sections of rope they had made the previous night around the steel service pipework. At one meter intervals the soldiers had tied knots to give a hand hold.

"Kurt, we will cover you from up here," DB informed him.

"John, Braiden, and Sam will give you close cover from the ground, agreed?" Jonesy asked and they all nodded.

The two soldiers took up positions and laid out their magazines on the wall to give easy access should they run out. In total they had over three hundred rounds ready to fire, more than they needed for the zombies that hovered close by. Their drill sergeant had always instilled the mantra; better to have and not need, than need and not have. This was the difference between life and death on the battlefield.

"Guys, get ready!" Jonesy nodded to DB and they shouldered their rifles and started firing. The muzzle coughed with a flash and the silenced rounds found their targets, drilling through the skulls with an explosive mist of blood vapour. The dead fell to the ground, spilling their brains onto the concrete. The area immediately around the Foxhound was clear and Kurt, John, and Braiden shimmied down the ropes. It was a little awkward with their arm shields and body armour, so they took their time. Reaching the ground, Kurt opened the vehicle doors and dragged the soldier's bodies clear, placing them under the canopy and laying them with as much dignity as time allowed. Sam had joined them and took out his slingshot that had been fitted with fresh banding from the spare roll he carried. They couldn't afford for any mistakes.

"Ok, start lowering the gear," Kurt said quietly. The ropes had been pulled up while they prepared the area and had been tied to packages of medicine, ammunition and the spare guns. Tinned food had been put into laundry bags for the journey and to give them time to carry out the task of securing the castle, without having to worry about foraging for meals.

Gloria kept a close watch on the massive bulk of the dead that had started to lose interest in the pile of rubble that used to house eighty families within the city of Chichester. Thankfully, the gunfire was too quiet to signal their whereabouts and the loading went easily.

"We are all set," Kurt called up. Sarah tied a harness that they had made for Honey and lowered her carefully. She couldn't get used to the feeling and kept trying to run, but only managing to kick her legs in mid-air until she touched down and shook herself.

"Sorry girl, you didn't like that did you?" Sam asked and she sneezed.

"We have you covered," DB called down and moved to the front of the building to cover the retrieval of the second Foxhound.

"Folks, six per vehicle, get mounted and buckle up, we will be down when the coast is clear. Make sure to shut the doors and keep your heads down," ordered Jonesy, picking off two more cadavers that had appeared from the back of their hospital block.

Christina, Peter, Sarah, Sam, Gloria, and John climbed aboard and sat in the bucket seats that would normally hold rough and ready trained professionals. Honey stood guard at the windows, scanning the road. The others filed off to the main entrance of the building, happy to see DB's muzzle flash as it kept them safe. They formed a crescent around the rear door of the vehicle and they prepared to do battle. Kurt took a quick glance inside and three zombies hammered at the windows.

"Three," Kurt whispered as he took hold of the handle, "Ready?" They all nodded, weapons poised. Kurt yanked and the door swung open. The first zombie spilled out and Jodi swung her bat in a downward arc with all the power she could muster. The skull shattered and the bat tore down through the front of the skull, taking the jaw with it.

"Oh shit!" Mike yelled and they turned to see what had scared him. A crowd of nearly one hundred poured from the other side of the building.

"Where the fuck did they come from?" Kurt called up to DB who started picking them off.

"Dunno, but you need to hustle!" he shouted down, changing magazines in the gun.

Jodi had swung again and another zombie fell to the ground, still alive. Paige dropped to her knees and hacked at the head, splitting it into pieces. Braiden reached in and grabbed the uniform of the remaining zombie, pulling it out and throwing it to the tarmac. He stabbed straight through the top of its head and let it fall, circling around to face the growing horde that descended on them.

"Fuck! Jonesy, get your ass over here!" DB cried out, pulling at his gun, trying to release a jam in the chamber.

"I can't, we have company at the first Fox!" came the yelled reply.

"Jodi, get inside and get it started while we hold them off!" shouted Kurt and she stepped over the bodies, climbing aboard.

"Fuck that, why don't we just get inside and shut the doors?" shrieked Debbie.

"If they surround it, we will end up like those poor bastards!" Kurt pointed at the stranded vehicle where the undead still flailed underneath, trapped by the crushing weight.

Jodi pressed the button and the engine just turned over without starting. She pressed the button again and had the same result, "It's not starting!" Jodi shouted from the front seat.

"Keep trying, give it some gas!" Mike called back.

"Everyone get ready!" said Kurt breathlessly. The fresher zombies were only a few paces away and Kurt, Braiden, and Paige dodged forward and backwards, slashing at the heads. The first few fell but the next group was nearly twenty strong. The engine coughed briefly and then died again. They were so focused on the dead; they didn't see Debbie and Mike exchange murderous looks. Mike moved behind Kurt and Debbie behind Braiden. This was the opportunity they had been waiting for. Instead of killing them quickly with the blade of the hand axes, they took them by the steel heads and swung for the back of Kurt and Braiden's skulls. Debbie moved a split second before Mike and the crack of wood on bone warned Kurt, who ducked to the right in the nick of time. The wooden handle caught him on the ear, splitting it and ripping the top section. Braiden had fallen hard to the ground, unconscious. Mike cursed as Kurt screamed his pain and jumped back just in time to miss the swing of Kurt's bloodied hammer.

"You're fucking dead!" roared Kurt with rage, ready to run at the retreating pair. He was torn between revenge and protecting Braiden.

"I've got the mother fuckers!" bellowed DB as he cleared the jam in his gun. Mike and Debbie bolted, clouds of concrete dust puffing up with the bullets that ricocheted on the ground in their wake.

The zombies were nearly on them and Kurt knew that their time was up, this was the end. DB was firing rapidly, and Paige was trying to pull Braiden's weight toward the Foxhound. It would never be enough; they would soon be overrun and devoured. Their eyes met and she smiled; the most loving and genuine look of thanks and trust that he had ever witnessed. Kurt hacked at another, cracking the head open like an egg.

"Tell Peter I love him. Tell Braiden he is the bravest young man I've ever known. Keep them all safe, Kurt." She threw a small photograph at him and ran forwards, arms held wide to embrace the monstrous dead.

"Paige! *No!*" Kurt screamed.

She hit the first zombies and clothes lined them, dropping on top of the writhing mass she had knocked over. They clutched at her, pulling her limbs to their mouths and ripping into her. The rest of the group piled on top, smothering her and tearing into her midriff, pulling intestines and organs out, veins still attached and pumping a scarlet spray over the cadavers. Her face was a mask of pain, but she stared at him and he could almost hear her telepathic cries, *Go! Get to safety!* DB had aimed carefully, pressing the trigger gently while breathing out a cloud of chilled breath. The bullet punched through her forehead, snapping it back, mercifully ending her torment.

"God, *No!* Jesus, dear God, why?" Kurt shouted at the sky as he hefted Braiden onto his shoulder.

"Kurt, move your ass, *now*!" DB yelled, knowing the emotions that would be battering at Kurt's psyche. It was no different when he had lost friends on the battlefields of Afghanistan to the Taliban. The time to mourn would come if they ever made it out of this mess.

Jodi tried the engine one last time after pumping on the gas pedal. It coughed and choked, finally caught, and roared as she held her foot down, giving it full throttle. Kurt flopped into the back with Braiden's unconscious body.

"Get us out of here!" Kurt yelled.

Jodi wrestled with the gears, grinding it into first with no finesse. The tens of thousands of dead had heard the activity and their massed moan flooded over them. Like a plague of locusts, they would wash over the survivors and pick their bones clean. Kurt pulled the rear door shut, after taking one last look at his fallen friend. Paige's sacrifice had worked. The ones who had been close to reaching them were fighting over themselves to reach the last morsels of her meat. Tears flowed as he seated himself, feeling the judder as the vehicle bounced over rotting obstacles. They pulled alongside the first Foxhound and the confused faces of his friends peered out.

Sarah mouthed, *'Where are the others?'* and Kurt's face answered without words. A black well of hatred formed in the pit of his stomach and only the blood of those murderous bastards would suffice to fill it. He prayed with all his soul that they would survive so that he could torture them for hours before he snuffed their life forces. The rest started to console each other and Peter had to be held back to prevent him jumping out to try and help.

Jonesy hopped in the first armoured troop carrier and gunned the engine, moving away down the road. DB had climbed in with Jodi and was happy to leave her driving.

"Kurt, I'm so sorry mate. I couldn't get the jam cleared in time." He held himself responsible for her death. It was only a cruel stroke of fate that caused the weapon malfunction and Kurt patted him on the back, unable to speak through the sobbing.

Braiden was coming round, groaning and feeling the growing bump on the rear of his skull.

"What happened?" he asked, groggy with possible concussion.

Kurt could only shake his head and Braiden looked around frantically, seeing the empty seats.

"Dad, where's Paige?" he asked quizzically, refusing to accept what his eyes were telling him. Instead of answering, Kurt grabbed him and held him in a bear hug until the young boy broke and started to wail. He thrashed and struggled but Kurt just held him tighter, smothering his hatred with love.

"She's with her baby now, mate. She will be happy," Kurt gasped with emotion.

"And those cunts?" Braiden was still bucking, desperate to help their lost friend.

"They ran off; they are probably dead too. If not, we will find them, and we will kill them slow," Kurt promised, reddened eyes meeting reddened eyes in mutual despair. Braiden stopped fighting and hugged his dad close, taking strength from the contact and steely resolve in his eyes.

DB had climbed into the gunnery seat and it rotated to the rear. The heavy gun chattered and the smoking cases fell tinkling like snowbells into the Foxhound, bouncing around on the metal floor.

"Kurt, grab that box! Rip the lid off and pull the first part of the belt out," DB called down as the final rounds were drawn through the firing chamber. He reached down and took it, loading the gun and commenced firing short, controlled bursts.

The roads were blocked and they could only move at walking pace as the heavy vehicles muscled through, compressing metal bodywork. The row of dead stretched back for a mile or more and was gaining by inches each time the lead Foxhound slowed to clear a blockage. The bullets tore into the mass of flesh but were having no effect. DB thought back to his younger years where he would pretend to throw stone grenades at the incoming waves on the beach. Each projectile would be swallowed without slowing the roiling water in the slightest.

"Jodi, flash the headlights and get Jonesy's attention," DB ordered and she complied without hesitation. The forward vehicle stopped and Jonesy opened the driver's door to see what was going on.

"We don't have time to stop, they are on our asses!" he shouted with annoyance.

"No shit, Sherlock!" replied DB. "Brother, we need to make it rain,"

"As soon as we break radio silence, Baxter will be on our asses!" Jonesy protested but the rotting tide was approaching.

"Ideas?" DB shrugged.

"Do it!" Jonesy shouted and climbed back in, revving the engine and pushing the next car out of the way.

DB turned on a small radio and it crackled into life. They had a private frequency that a lot of the troops on Thorney Barracks used to avoid the ears of their superior since the world fell. It would only remain secret for a few minutes before those scanning locked on to the signal. He prayed the guys hadn't lost their nerve and could still be called upon to help.

"Alcatraz this is Eastwood, come in, over," DB said and waited.

"Alcatraz this is Eastwood, come in, over," he repeated, watching the onslaught of the corpses as they funnelled between any available gaps.

"Eastwood this is Alcatraz, its damned good to hear from you, over," came the reply. They had chosen their call signs to reflect one of their favourite movies, *Escape from Alcatraz,* with Clint Eastwood. They increasingly felt like prisoners on the base, no requests to try and reach loved ones were granted. They understood the seriousness of the situation, but human nature was to protect those they loved.

"Thank God you are there. I never thought I'd be glad to hear your voice, over," DB joked with corporal Bennett then got straight to business. "Requesting fire mission." He double checked the laminated map in his hands, "Coordinates fifty, fifty, fifty-nine north, zero, forty-six, forty-seven, three west, over."

The artillery crew recited the digits and asked, "What is the nature of the target, over?"

DB knew they had a clear picture of what they faced, they had asked it so many times in training the question was second nature. It was designed to ensure the right shells were fired, "A hundred thousand biters on our ass, go high explosive and give us some cover, over," he shouted into the handset.

"Shot over," warned Bennett, seconds later. It meant a howitzer shell was arcing over them, soon to impact the area that DB had cited.

231

"Shot out," he replied.

"Splash over," stated Bennett, meaning the projectile was five seconds from target.

"Splash out," answered DB, taking cover.

The whistling noise of the projectile reached his ears a second before the ground erupted like a volcano, spewing fire and blazing flesh high into the sky. The explosive fire caused a heat wave to wash over DB and he shielded his face as much as possible. The smoking craters filled with the advancing horde which rolled on undeterred once they were full of crushed, struggling monsters. It had slowed their advance by seconds, though, which could mean the difference between escape and death.

"Fire for effect, over," DB shouted, ordering them to blanket the area with everything they had.

"Fire for effect, out," Bennett confirmed and DB watched in awe. The shells dropped into the tightly packed dead and blew them apart with righteous hellfire. Round after round whined as they fell from the sky, bringing a thunderous shockwave of force with each detonation. The zombies showed no concern as they entered the kill zone to be destroyed, the parts that were left continued to try and reach the survivors with whatever limbs remained. Houses that were directly hit scattered disintegrated rubble into the swarm, smashing bones and skulls

"Ceasefire. Immediately," came the order from Lieutenant Baxter over the radio. Their hidden communication was at an end.

"Ceasefire confirmed, over," murmured the artillery gunner with fear in his voice.

"Mr. Abentu. Mr. Jones. It seems your infection has spread deep within your fellow soldiers. Like all infections, it must be excised to prevent the transmission to others," said Baxter without emotion, refusing to give them their assigned rank.

"Sir, we just wanted to help. They were going to see if the hospital was operational," pleaded Bennett.

"*Silence!*" Baxter screamed at the soldier and even DB, as big as he was, felt his stomach clench in fear.

"Sir, it's not their fault. I accept full responsibility," DB said with as much conviction as he could muster.

"Oh, forgive me. I wasn't aware that you were here, firing expensive ordinance at unassigned targets," he replied sarcastically.

"Sir, I-" DB continued.

"Tell me where you are so that we can come and get you. I promise your court martial will be fair and any punishment carried out quickly," Baxter offered.

"I'm afraid I can't do that, sir. We are in the middle of a rescue mission," DB growled back. He knew they would be shot as deserters for what they had done.

"In that case, Corporal Bennett, resume fire. North of previous fire mission by two clicks, over" Baxter ordered, which would mean the shells would land right on top of them.

"Sir, I cannot follow that order, over," Bennett replied, barely a whisper.

"Soldier, you either begin firing, or face the same consequences as Abentu and Jones!" Baxter screamed over the radio.

"As you wish, sir. Over and out," Bennett replied with resignation. He would not hurt his friends, no matter what he was commanded to do by that psychopath.

"There is nowhere that we will not find you, do you understand me?" asked Baxter now that Bennett had gone radio silent.

"With all due respect. Go fuck yourself, sir." DB smashed his fist onto the top of the Foxhound and turned the radio off.

They had reached a section of clear road and pulled over. DB jumped down and started pacing like a raging bull, wanting to hurt something. Jonesy climbed out and came to see what had him so steamed. The family went to Kurt for news of what had transpired in the hospital car park.

"What's up, big man?" he enquired.

"Baxter is going to shoot Bennett for helping us," he said quietly, although he seethed inside.

"Fuck!" shouted Jonesy, "What can we do?"

DB thought long and hard. "Nothing. We just have to hope the others rise up and kill his ass!"

A lone zombie came through the undergrowth and DB ran over, raising a heavy boot and kicking it in the chest. The zombie fell and he

233

jumped on its stomach, crushing the internal organs. He held its head and wrenched, twisting it free from the neck. It came away still trying to bite, until he threw it like a ball to split on the trunk of a nearby tree.

"Feel better?" Jonesy asked. DB just grunted and climbed back into the vehicle.

"Folks, we have to go, now!" Jonesy apologized, hating to break up the mutual support they were giving each other as they broke their hearts over the loss of Paige. They reluctantly parted and the convoy continued with the Chichester swarm in hot pursuit.

They passed the fenced off area that housed the huge gas holder. It towered over them, one hundred and twenty feet high. In the distance, the road was blocked with more cars. The artillery strikes had bought them time, just not enough. He called for Jodi to alert Jonesy again and they pulled over.

"We need to use that bomb," said DB pointing at the vessel that contained millions of cubic feet of natural gas.

"Do we still have tracers?" Jonesy questioned, loving the plan.

"Yeah. What is safe distance do you think?" DB looked at the cylinder thoughtfully.

"Fuck knows, as far as possible. I think if we reach those vehicles we should be ok," Jonesy pointed at the blockade over half a mile away on the straight road.

"Let's do it," DB cried out with excitement and they sped for the end of the road.

Pulling up with a screech of protesting rubber, the soldiers jumped out and loaded the remaining tracer magazines that had not been used while igniting the flats the previous night.

"What the hell are you doing?" demanded John. He was bereft and was taking it out on the men that had saved their lives. They ignored the aggressive tone and explained their idea to the gathered survivors. Peter remained with the Foxhound after passing out with the grief of losing his soul mate in such dire, unnecessary circumstances. That she had died to save Braiden was cold comfort to the group.

"What are you waiting for, blow the damn thing and let's get out of here!" John said with frustration.

"Wait for it, wait for it," Jonesy was watching the head of the column of zombies as it skirted the container that would be their demise. When enough had passed to ensure as many casualties as possible, he shouted, "NOW!"

The rifles belched out streamers of fire which drilled holes in the thick metal of the holder. The gas ignited as the oxygen mixed and the whole thing erupted, laying the high metal sides open like they were no more than a soda can. The mushroom cloud climbed into the air, lifting the huge roof and the ground was vaporized for nearly a quarter mile radius. Trees were uprooted and thrown aside like matchsticks from the concussive wave that threw the group to the ground. The heat singed their hair and they scurried into the armoured cars for protection. Nearly half of the zombies had ceased to exist, their dust carried away on the wind. The ones that remained walked through the cataclysmic fire that raged, burning themselves to a crisp.

"Bloody hell," gasped Sarah, seeing what looked like the bowels of hell from the window. Heat waves distorted the scene and she had no difficulty imagining demonic entities running to and fro, inflicting more misery on the trapped souls that burned within. She waved her hand at herself, trying to cool the stinging skin.

They spoke through the windows, reining in their frayed emotions for now. The grieving would begin properly when they were secure and had time to reflect.

"What route do you suggest?" Jonesy asked, relying on the locals' knowledge of the area.

"We go through Westhampnett, then Boxgrove. If we can reach the station, we could always try taking the train tracks all the way through to Arundel. Would these beasts handle it?" Kurt posed the question, eyes still wet from withheld tears.

"These fuckers are designed to withstand explosions, the metal tracks would be nothing." DB was confident of their chances.

"Let's go," Kurt sat back down, pulling the harness and latching it.

The sound of metal on metal shrieked in the afternoon air, competing with the crackle and roar of the fire. They sat in their seats, silent and lost. The loss of Paige would affect them all deeply, not least the growing capacity for violence in defence of their loved ones. Or, in this case, vengeance for sins committed against the group. Jodi sat in her seat and refused to meet the gaze of the others, they had spoken no words of malice towards the actions of her ex-lover, but the guilt ate at her core.

Kurt stared at nothing, deep in reflection.

Peter slumped, still refusing to come back.

Gloria questioned God in her mind, unsatisfactorily.

Sarah and Sam held each other tight, ignoring the smell of burnt hair.

The others thought of better times, better places.

Only Braiden was smiling. He had gone deep into his own mind, planning the depravity he would inflict on Mike and Debbie when he got them in his grasp. He had nursed Paige back from catatonia, fed her, helped her to drink until she was capable of carrying out the simple task on her own. His thoughts flashed to the memories of her smiling face, the kindness of her soul, how she always had a way of brightening the lives of those around her. The darkness returned and their agonized screams echoed within the walls of his mind. It was a comforting sound. A good sound.

A NOTE FROM THE AUTHOR

I hope that you enjoyed the second instalment of the Hellspawn journey as much as I enjoyed writing it. The worry for me as a father, is how on earth would I manage to move my family safely in an environment so unforgivably hostile. Every inch of the planet could contain danger for me and mine. I tried to capture the terrifying indecision as the survivors made their way towards their destination.

For those that want to see who makes it, fear not, book three is currently over halfway done and will be published before the end of the year.

Another project I have embarked upon is a demon series that came to me in a nightmare a few months ago. The first portion of terror is written and I will be aiming to release the, as yet untitled, first novel by early 2017.

For upcoming news about future books, info about contests and prizes, or if you just want to chat, please follow me on my Facebook page (www.facebook.com/Author-Ricky-Fleet) and on my publisher's page (www.facebook.com/OptimusMaximusPublishing) and on Twitter (@AuthorRickyFleet and @Optimaxpublish)

THANK YOU

ABOUT THE AUTHOR

Ricky Fleet has been a lifelong horror fan ever since he was (almost) old enough to watch the original Romero trilogy. Those shambling horrors gave birth to an insatiable appetite that has yet to be sated.

After spending years working in the plumbing trade, he then decided to start teaching, passing on his knowledge to the next generation of engineers.

Born and raised in the UK, cups of tea are a non-negotiable staple of the English life and serve as brain fuel for his first love, writing.

With book one in the Hellspawn series receiving love from across the world, the second in the saga takes the action to a whole new level.

Today he shares his time between his real life students, and the students of the zombie apocalypse in his first series: Hellspawn. At least the fictional students do as they're told. Most of the time anyway.

ALSO FROM OPTIMUS MAXIMUS PUBLISHING

10.35 AM, September 14th 2015. Portsmouth, England.

A global particle physics experiment releases a pulse of unknown energy with catastrophic results. The sanctity of the grave has been sundered and a million graveyards expel their tenants from eternal slumber.

The world is unaware of the impending apocalypse, Governments crumble and armies are scattered to the wind under the onslaught of the dead.

Kurt Taylor, a self-employed plumber, witnesses the start of the horrifying outbreak. Desperate to reach his family before they fall victim to the ever growing horde of shambling corruption, he flees the scene.

In a society with few guns, how can people hope to survive the endless waves of zombies that seek to consume every living thing? With ingenuity, planning and everyday materials, the group forge their way and strike back at the Hellspawn legions.

Rescues are mounted, but not all survivors are benevolent, the evil that is in all men has been given free rein in this new, dead world. With both the living and dead to contend with, the Taylor family's battle for survival is just beginning.

Book 1 in the Hellspawn series.

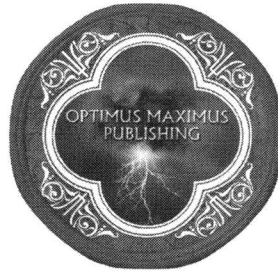

BALLYMOOR, IRELAND, 1891

Patrick Conroy, a young American student of medicine in Dublin, decides to take a break from the hustle and bustle of the big city and spend a month in the quietude of the wild and beautiful Glencree valley, County Wicklow. However, surrounded by local legends and myths, he is soon dragged into an ancient mystery that has haunted the village of Ballymoor for centuries. Set on the background of the tumultuous years preceding the War of Independence, and colored by Irish folklore, the Haunter of the Moor is a ghost story written in the style of Victorian Gothic novels.

OPTIMUS MAXIMUS
PUBLISHING

55930347R00137

Made in the USA
Charleston, SC
09 May 2016